For Davis,
With all best wishes,
Walt Brown

# The Mickey Mantle Murder

by Walt Brown, Ph.D.

Published by:
Trine Day LLC
PO Box 577
Walterville, OR 97489
1-800-556-2012
www.TrineDay.com
publisher@TrineDay.net

Library of Congress Control Number: 2015937478

Brown, Walt PhD.
The Mickey Mantle Murder—1st ed.
p. cm.
Epud (ISBN-13) 978-1-63424-032-1
Mobi (ISBN-13) 978-1-63424-033-8
Print (ISBN-13) 978-1-63424-031-4
1.. 2.. 3.. 4.. 5.. I. Brown, Walt PhD., II. Title

FIRST EDITION
10 9 8 7 6 5 4 3 2 1

Printed in the USA
Distribution to the Trade by:
Independent Publishers Group (IPG)
814 North Franklin Street
Chicago, Illinois 60610
312.337.0747
www.ipgbook.com

*This work is lovingly dedicated to Mickey #7 Mantle, and to all those who met him, watched him play, or saved his cards.*

Secondary thanks go to Mike Gordon, Richie Klein, Alan Rosen, Kit Young, George Kruk, Stephen Hart, Dave Medema, "Murf" Denny, Lou Lampson, as well as Greg, Danny, "Skip," Ray, Jonathan, Patty, Dee, and dozens of other good and decent folks who made collecting a joyous hobby.

# Prologue
## The Carefree Days

# The Initial Discovery

I remember it like it was yesterday, and considering that you need a good memory to study the lengthy and often-challenging history of police science *and* keep a near-perfect mental accounting of your baseball card collection, I *do* remember that last full day of summer like it was yesterday, even if, to my horror, the calendar reminds me it was forty years ago. The sun was bright and the skies were blue with barely a breeze, but the air was brisk, and I had the strong hunch the ol' swimming hole was done for that season.

It was Saturday, September 20, 1952, ten days after my fifth birthday. I had raked in a full $5 on that occasion, but my "five-packs of baseball cards" limit, parentally-imposed, meant that I only needed twenty-five cents of that largesse on this day to buy my limit. Still, the fiver had given me the potential to make twenty trips over the coming weeks, each with my five-pack per day limit.

The concept of 'limit' gave me a taste of what fishermen felt in those days, but then again, how many of them ever hauled in a valuable baseball card on a ten-pound test line?

I was walking into town with Bobby, a neighbor who was three years older than me and basically only came near me when friends his own age were not around. He was wearing his trademark dungarees, and a t-shirt that reflected attendance at a local day camp. He was, or seemed, a foot taller than me, and probably at least twenty pounds heavier, but his occasional bullying made him seem bigger; or made me seem smaller, and I was of a size that guaranteed that pro football scouts would not be following me to sign me to a contract. Put another way, my future in athletics would have been as a jockey.

Bobby only got away with his behind-the-scenes bullying because he had a freckled, puckish face that always looked like he'd been sucking on ice cubes. Naturally, like me, his hair was short, but that was a dozen years before the Beatles, so short hair shouldn't come as huge news.

It seems odd to go back to the way things were then, but in those days, children did walk into town, even at five years of age, on their own, or they rode their bicycles and were not helmet-mandated. At age five, I could buy cigarettes for my father, as he had cleared the purchase of Lucky Strikes (only) with the local management. "Oh, Luckies? Yeah, it's okay, Morty, as long as it's the little toe-headed blonde kid."

Who's 'toe-headed'? And who is 'little'?

Little did I know that I was investing in my inheritance every time I bought a pack of butts for either Mom or Dad, as those cigarettes would leave me orphaned at a relatively young age. But that was in the future, and baseball cards were in the present, so Bobby and I turned the corner and I went to the candy store right there at the corner, but he kept walking, as he'd been caught shop-lifting at the place I was going, so he had been banished and could only traipse down the block to the candy store at the far end of a 500-foot 'main drag.'

It didn't trouble Bobby. The candy was the same at both ends of the street. As it turned out, though, the baseball cards would not be.

It happened that my five packs were the last ones in the display box, comfortably situated between a stack of Chuckles and countless bars of Bonomo's Turkish Taffy—all vanilla. Having emptied the box and been told I could keep it, I suggested to management (and considered it a threat to take away my cigarette business) that they had better restock. They let me know that those were the last 1952 baseball cards, and since the next day was the first day of autumn, it would be several months before they would be selling any more cards.

However, I was assured that the 1952 *football* cards would be available soon; in fact, a stock boy yelled, "Beginning Monday." Big deal.

As I left, crestfallen, I saw Bobby at the other end of the block and he jerked his head to indicate "across the street," which meant the town park. It was almost a certainty that baseball cards would be opened by local youths sitting on "the rock," a sizable survivor from glacier days that just happened to fall off a flatcar on the railroad siding 75 feet away. It required a team of thirty-two horses and a dozen men to pull it away from the railroad siding to its present location. Whatever its original intended destination, it would most likely remain in the town park in the bucolic village of Hamlet until the next Ice Age.

It only took one or two kids to light that rock up with new baseball card finds, usually several times a day all summer. For me, however, it was not to be. I opened the first pack—several beautiful slices of the great American pastime, and repeated the traditional mantra, "Got it, got it, got it…." In the second pack, I was overjoyed to find a Pete Runnels, a journeyman infielder, and Bobby Hogue, a pitcher on the Yankee roster but rarely on the Yankee mound. Packs three and four were all "dupes," meaning duplicates, not simpletons, but pack five treated me to a Hank Thompson and a Leo Kiely. Four new cards out of over two-dozen. My average was worse than the Cubs.

For his part, Bobby was whooping it up with the unveiling of each new pack, but that was his traditional game. If he had opened a pack filled with worn-out, dog-eared cards, he would have made a big deal out of it, for no reason greater than to get attention. He could make a big event out of a Hopalong Cassidy sticker on the end of a loaf of Wonder Bread.

Looking at the value of them nowadays, I probably should have done likewise.

In the baseball card milieu, however, today was different. When he got done whooping it up, I told him, "I got four." When he looked me in the eye, it was like the feeling you get when someone walks on your grave, but at age five, I didn't know that feeling, so it was just, "Well?"

"These are all new!" he whispered, as if they were those large items of currency, $20 bills, that we never saw.

"Lemme see," I demanded.

"I'll show you," he said, making sure I did not touch or deface his precious treasures. And they *were* precious. There was not a card in his stack that I recognized; he started out to get five but since there were only six packs where he went, they gave him the extra one, so he had somewhere between two and three dozen cards. Some of them, admittedly, I had never heard of: Bill Posedel, Clyde Sukeforth, Jack Merson- who were these guys?

Then the treasures: Bill Dickey, Roy Campanella, Eddie Matthews, Alvin Dark, Jackie Robinson, and two—not one, but TWO—Mickey Mantles. Two 1952 Topps Mickey Mantles! They were damn sure a treasure that day, and they would only gain in stature over the next forty years.

I was absolutely in awe and had no explanation for the disparity between the slabs of ancient news that I'd bought and these Dead Sea Scroll icons that he'd discovered. It just made no sense. If they did not look 100% genuine, I would have thought he was trying to pull a fast one.

But he wasn't. He had what I would later learn was called a 'tell'; and it was that his narrow face turned almost weasel-like when he was up to something. But there was none of that amidst his absolute joy. To prove the authenticity, he showed me the backs of the cards, and the numbers of those cards were also totally different from mine. My Runnels and Hogue were numbers 2 and 9 respectively, but his Mantle was 311, Robinson 312, and Matthews, 407! We definitely were not in the same league with those cards. Of course, I had Hank Sauer and Bobby Shantz, who would be the league MVPs that year, but still, he had the marquee names.

We mulled it over on the way back home, or perhaps I should say I mulled it over, because Bobby was so overjoyed that he was telling strangers, out working in their yards, "I got Mickey Mantle!" Geez, I mean he had two of them, and if pushed, I'd have given up both Runnels and Hogue for his Mantle dupe.

Nothing doing. I followed him home, and his always well-dressed father, who could immerse himself in logic, which he undoubtedly put to good use as a high school musical instrument teacher, was on hand to attempt to rationalize the disparity.

He took both stacks of cards, careful to keep his son's pile as far away from mine as black people got to white people in Mississippi back in those days. Having a penetrating grasp of the obvious, he noted that there was not even one card that appeared in both piles. I offered to take one of the Mantles to fix that problem, but it did not take a degree in higher education to figure the answer to that one. Besides, I'd only had eleven days of Kindergarten under my tiny belt, so higher education to me was third grade.

Then Robert Sr., a heavy set yet always distinguished-looking man who would, a few years later, be institutionalized for mental illness, turned them over and noted the numerical disparity. He spread out my cards and quickly noted that the numbers ran from 2 to 77. His son's cards, on the other hand, ran from the 311 Mantle to the 407 Matthews. He used his hands to indicate, "Let's walk away from this and sit down," as if we were going to find out what happened to Judge Crater.

"You went to different stores," he stated, making sure it didn't sound like a question, because as a question it would have demanded the answer that his wonderful, sticky-fingered son was *persona non grata* at one of the two establishments.

"There are at least 407 cards in this set," he mused aloud, "yet Decker bought very low numbers and cleaned the place out, and you," turning to his son, "got only the higher numbers and you cleaned the second place out."

He pondered his reckoning of the obvious. I sat there, pondering only the absence of Robinson, Campanella, Mathews and Mantle in my pile and I still didn't know who Posedel, Sukeforth, and Merson were, and at that specific moment, I didn't much care. What I did care about was where they were: in Bobby's pile.

"I have an idea," said Bob Sr., breaking the silence again. "These cards that somehow fascinate you seem to be printed in numerical groupings," offering another painful grasp of the obvious. So vendor A has low-numbered cards and vendor B has high-numbered cards."

"But nobody else has talked about or shown off any of the high numbered cards," Bobby told his father.

"Strange. It seems like there had to be packs in the same box that you bought from," again looking at his only child, "and that some of the kids at school would have had to have gotten them. Unless there was water in the basement from that last hurricane, or some total stranger from Sticksville Notch (a mythical town he often referenced) came through and bought an arm-load of cards for his kids. Why don't you go back to where Bobby got the cards and see if they can order some more, and we'll see what happens."

We ran out of there like the place was in the midst of an electrical fire, sped all three blocks into town, and braced the store owner with an entreaty for more cards.

We were reminded that the next day would see the beginning of autumn, and they had to spend their card budget on the new set of football cards that were in production from the Bowman Company, the counter-point to Topps, the publisher of today's new-found treasures.

We begged, pleaded, and cried. The owner reminded us that there were two "New York Giant" teams and we should get ready to embrace the ones with huge numbers on their shirts, and not some newcomer named Willie Mays in the outfield.

Maybe the next town still had some cards left.

Nobody, it seemed at that moment, had any, and the existence of cards 311—407 seemed to become a mystery that would go unsolved forever.

As things happened, although nobody could possibly have known it then, the eventual owner of thousands of those cards numbered 311—407 would also become a mystery that would go on forever. More specifically, the Mickey Mantle card, which would, in the future, become the collector's dream, almost instantly took on a life of its own.

At age five, I didn't even know what Tarot was, and I haven't learned much about it in the intervening forty years.

But I came to learn one thing: that beautiful blue Mickey Mantle card, with the featured player holding what looked like an old yellow bat on his shoulder, would become the Death Card.

That, however, was in the distant future and no five-year-old with a pocketful of baseball cards could have had that kind of foresight.

# Time Between

Nobody in the Decker household made any sense out of that day's collectible anomaly, but then again, Mrs. Decker was too busy taking care of too many things, and my father was, as always, in his cups. It was such a typical occurrence that when he died, I expected his mail to be sent to "Decker, in care of 'Cups.'" Or simply forwarded to his local watering hole, where he spent more time than at home.

It would wind up in the dead letter office, of course, but that is where he would have been also.

The following day, Sunday morning, before the 'church-key' opened the first Rheingold of the day, I explained what had happened, and my father was so upset that "Bobby Babe," his pejorative nickname for the lad across the street, had something I didn't, that he set out to do what he could to make up the deficit. I should have told him that "Bobby Babe" had a sober father, but when Mr. Decker got his keys to take his son Chris to find baseball cards, sobriety was an issue that could wait for another day.

Luckily, on what had portended to be a rainy day, my father drove me to at least ten or twelve candy stores in the general vicinity of Hamlet, the town we lived in, situated cozily in northeastern New Jersey. I had what was left of my $5 birthday money, and in my father's zeal to outdo the Mantle-card owner, he gave me a glorious Silver Certificate and such change as he had in his pocket.

But there were rules: In each store I could buy only one pack. While there, I was to open it and ascertain the numbers contained within. If they were 311 or above, I could buy as many packs as they had, at least until my funds ran dry. If they were the same old slabs that I had stacks of, I could buy candy—or save for other card shops or, with regret, look forward to football cards and we'd move on.

Two outlets were already out of cards, and I struck out swinging at almost all the others, batting three for sixty: Joe Ostrowski, a Yankee hurler of the Bobby Hogue type,who bore an odd resemblance to our school custodian, Dale Coogan (He was a short-time first baseman for the Pirates, but a potential future employer—totally by accident, years later); Boston Brave hurler Johnny Antonelli; and St. Louis Brown catcher Les Moss. Looking at his stats, I realized no moss would ever gather on him.

Not exactly the beginning of a dynasty, but those were the exceptions from the usual litany of "Got it, got it, got it." I think the candy store owners probably had had their fill of hearing that depressing recitation, because not only did it have the same distinctive melody as "It's a Small World After All," it also meant that they were not selling the cards that the kids wanted.

So, after a brief three-hour stop at the local tavern, I made it home alive with my sixty new cards, fifty-six dupes and three additions, dreams of Mickey Mantle shattered, and an assortment of candy that ranged from enough white paper for a roll of adding machine tape, covered with candy "dots," several Clark bars, made famous by the camel that advertised them, candy cigarettes, and those wonderful if too-small wax bottles that contained a dollop of colored liquid.

The most troubling thing about the three-hour pit stop at the local tavern was not that I had to while away the hours playing a bagatelle game, but rather that I kept hearing that I was a spitting image of Decker, Sr., and if I were lucky, I'd grow up to be just like him. *Please...*

The baseball card mystery would remain unsolved for years, but over that fall and winter, once school got going, I talked to some of the older kids on the playground and a few of the higher numbered cards had shown up. One perfect-attendance Sunday school acquaintance had the Bill Dickey card, but oddly, he didn't recall any others above 311. Must have been a bad summer for Sukeforth, Posedel, and Merson, but it gave me the idea that the Topps company had put out a "last gasp" collection, which included some relative unknowns at the outset of 1952—which would account for Matthews and Mantle, as well as some throw-in players (Merson), and some coaches and managers, which would cover Posedel and Sukeforth, and, as I later learned, Frank Crosetti, Leo Durocher, Jake Pitler, and Billy Meyer, to name just a few too many.

Suffice to say I did not have any of them, and I would not own even one of them for 25 years, but I had no idea of that at the time. Back then, the focus was on learning to work with color, to finger paint, and, to keep the ol' man happy, I was required to play some manner of baseball at every possible occasion, regardless of weather. If I broke a window with a home run, *who cared?* If I broke a window with a foul ball, I got to hear Decker, Sr. using his sailor's vocabulary for hours. Not about the window, mind you; I had committed a mortal sin by hitting a foul ball.

Nineteen fifty-three arrived, and with it, people named Eisenhower and Nixon. My father explained Eisenhower to me, pronouncing "Republican" with the inflection subsequently given to words like "terrorist." When I asked about the guy named Nixon, my father dismissed him as a greasy mechanic who got lucky.

My card collection continued to grow, as I bowed to the inevitable and bought a cigar box full of 1952 football cards, although they were manufactured by Bowman, not the same company as the 1952 #311 Mantle, and I also branched out into non-sports cards.

"The Red Menace" was one of the sets, although they were hold-overs from 1951, but it really didn't matter as long as Joe McCarthy—the Senator, not the baseball manager of the same name—was alive, as his act was being held over as well. At one point, I got the bright idea that I should collect photos of members of Congress, or maybe the Supreme Court, and publish my own "Red Menace" set. At least I'd have the complete set. I'd have even mailed a set to the Russian guy, Stalin, in '53, but he died, so that pipe-dream got ruled out.

There were cards of show business personalities, some of whom would be wholly unknown to today's readers, as well as cards with drawings of aircraft, photos of aircraft, automobiles from around the world, and the American presidents as well. There was also a set of "World Flags," but it was only an 80-card set, so maybe the world was smaller then. The 80-card set made us believe that the universe was expanding when our teachers pronounced that maxim.

There were also "Look 'N See" cards, with drawings of people that someone out there thought were famous; one ballplayer—Babe Ruth, along with such notables as Joan of Arc, Nero, Annie Oakley, and some American presidents. Even at that age, I found errors of fact on the back of some of the cards, but I kept that to myself. The 135 people pictured were from all over the world, some perhaps from places that didn't have a flag card.

I knew that the world was small to me, because as I was halfway between my fifth and sixth birthday, I had only been more than ten miles from home once, and the thought of ever traveling anywhere did not even enter my mind. With my father's expensive habits, bus fare to the YMCA was a challenge.

Finally, baseball season rolled around, and I was in good financial shape when it came to investing in the summer's main event. Although it was still cool and brisk when the first cards came out, I was always able to swipe a jacket off the back door of our modest home and skip the three blocks to Cardboard Heaven.

To my initial shock, Topps, which had published players' photos in 1952, now reverted to drawings, and in some cases, the drawings were nothing more than a sketch of the 1952 photograph. The Bowman cards featured full-color photos on the front, with no team names, personal names, or replica autographs to break the majesty. Just color photos that spoke for themselves and challenged the collector to name the player. With Mantle, of course, it was easy. With Don Johnson it was another matter, and he was such a confusion that the Topps set of drawings included a # 219, labeled Pete Runnels, but the sketch was of the lesser-known Don Johnson.

The Bowman set was a joy, with glorious photos, especially the Pee Wee Reese card with Reese in mid-air after having turned a double play. And there was not only a Mickey Mantle, but also a card that featured Mickey, Yogi Berra, and Hank Bauer on the steps of the Yankee dugout. It took about twenty packs to lay my hands on that gem. But just as the higher-numbered cards were unknown to most of us the previous year, Bowman also issued photo cards later on in the season, with an additional 64 cards featuring black and white photos.

Never saw them. Never heard of them. I would discover them at roughly the same time as I acquired my first "high-number" 1952 Topps cards, many years after the candy stores had shuffled them into the hands of the sugar-crazy young populace. That was also the time of the belated realization that Don Johnson was not Pete Runnels.

The color photos, while they were not universally spectacular, were certainly an improvement over the earlier sets that had featured drawings or some oddly shaded photos that would have shouted, had I been better educated, "Fellini meets Bob Feller."

In the Topps sketches, Jackie Robinson was card number one, and as soon as I saw it, I knew it was sketched directly from his 1952 card. Naturally, I looked for New York team players, and there were more Yankees than Dodgers or Giants. Hey, one of those three had to have more cards and it might as well have been the Yankees.

The Mickey Mantle reminded me of the 1952, if you held it up to a mirror and got the reverse image. Still, it was number 82, not 311, and they were plentiful, even as Mantle's reputation (and my collection of his likeness) was growing. But mindful of the previous year's perfidy, I was cautious in noting the numbers of the cards. From Robinson at number 1, I quickly got to Satchell Paige at number 220, and that was that.

Or was it? 220 seemed like a good point to end one series and begin printing another, just as number 310 had been the previous year. Sure enough, by early July the stores were filled with cards from 221, a smiling Bob Milliken, to 280, a smiling Milt Bolling. I wonder how much those fellows would have smiled if they knew that their yearly baseball salaries, somewhere between five and eight thousand dollars, would someday be one game's salary for a cheesy utility infielder, soon to be "designated for assignment" in the free-agency years.

Those last 60 cards were the good news and the bad news. There was only one real star, and that was Willie Mays at number 244. But the artist's rendering, even to an almost-six-year-old, was insulting, because it depicted Mays with hands that would have been monstrously huge on an orang-outang. With those hands, the "say hey" kid could have palmed a garbage can. Or maybe a Volkswagen.

Maybe the artist knew what an absolute creepy s.o.b. Mays would be once he was out of baseball: he'd insult you up one side and down the other while charging $50 for his autograph. I sometimes thought his ugliness might have been a cover for his difficulties in spelling "Willie" and "Mays," but it would be a while before I spent $50 to find out, and by then, he'd gotten it right.

Back to the numbers. 280 did not seem like the end-all, particularly since they were all we could get from July onward. I had so many cards of Dixie Howell, Roy Face, Harvey Haddix, and Bill Norman, coach of the St. Louis

Browns, that those were always my first choice when I needed cards to put in the spokes of my bicycle to turn it into a quad-stereo putt-putt-putt mobile. If Milliken and Bolling shouldn't have been smiling, I should not either, as those cards, 221—280, would command the most money in the distant future, as they were the 1953 version of the 1952 Mantle to Matthews run. On a much lesser economic grid, of course, since they were almost but not quite as common as numbers 1 to 220.

And they were in the spokes of my bicycle, being turned into mulch.

And the crazy thing was, because the high numbered cards were in the stores as early as they were, we kept buying new packs, expecting a card series beginning with number 281. It didn't happen in 1953, but we kept buying, but sure enough, numbers 281—337 would arrive somewhat belatedly, many years after Bobby Babe's huge discovery that fascinated a five-year-old. For anyone who knew me in the days of the 1990s re-issue, they'd assure you that when it came to opening packs of cards, I could remain a five or six-year-old forever.

But the eventual 1991 releases of numbers 281--337 weren't sketches; they were photos—not a good fit with the earlier sketches, but as nostalgia, who cared, really? The last three, 335, 336, and 337 were check lists, and those were always just slightly more popular than school detention. They would have been "bicycle spoke" cards if they had existed in 1953, and, accordingly, worth a fortune by the early '90s, because nobody kept them.

I would learn, many years later, that one of the keys to an active and busy mind for an adult was an active and busy mind when he or she was a child. In that regard, I was good to go, as I always knew which cards I needed, and I got pretty good at remembering the numbers that went with the cards. Bobby Shantz, you ask? Number 219 in 1952, but one of the last-series cards in 1953, at number 225.

The cards were becoming a household glut, as there were usually more piles of cards than there were empty Rheingold cans. Well, at least the cards only smelled of gum. But our house had two unfinished rooms at the top of a straight-up, fifteen step stairway that was pitch dark on the 4th of July. My card rooms....

That year also saw more non-sports stuff, and on days when the baseball card sales area was vacant, I managed to garner enough of each variety to eventually fill a cigar box that accordingly went upstairs to the card rooms. *One for baseball, one for 'the other stuff.'*

The next year, the two card companies swapped styles again. Topps, which had published sketches in 1953 went to a color-photo pose format, plus a smaller black and white "action shot," with name and data on top. These were set against backgrounds of red, green, yellow, blue, white, and orange, and I remain convinced to this day that someone researched the lousiest ball players out there and made them all orange. Except Shantz, of course, who had been MVP in 1952, and Ted Williams on card number 1. Once again, there was a mixture of coaches sprinkled in, along with some truly inglorious nobodies. I once tried to research their stats, only to find that they had never played in the bigs, and they had only played "professional baseball" in cities I was barely familiar with: Keokuk, which sounded like something an Eskimo would sleep in, or Boise, which at least rhymed with "Joizy," where I lived.

By contrast—literally, Bowman created and published what looked like photographs cum sketches, with the name at the bottom. Suffice to say it was always easy to tell the two brand names apart.

But when I compared the players, I began to note that very few players were in both sets. Mantle and Campanella were on Bowman cards, which featured no coaches or managers, but did enshrine "Memo Luna," and I'm sure not many teams ever got the "Memo" in his case.

Topps still led "in market shares" with Thornton Kipper, Mike Blyzka, Gair Allie, Jehosie Heard, and Leroy Wheat with their two-picture format, along with Warren Spahn, Eddie Matthews, Duke Snider, Willie Mays, and Jackie Robinson—along with at least 23 coaches and managers who got their 15 minutes of fame by being bracketed with gum and a wrapper. They also threw in some players new to the game, and collectors did not give the proverbial tinker's damn for such unknowns as Al Kaline, Hank Aaron, and Ernie Banks. They weren't fooling us six year olds....

On the other hand, they also had an unknown named Bill "Moose" Skowron, a chunky first-baseman set to take over first base for the Yankees from Joe Collins, the brief incumbent. He may have been widely unknown, but he lived on "the rich side" of Hamlet, and one of the ultimate thrills I'll ever recall was sitting on the curb, opening packs, and having Moose walk out of one of the stores behind me. "Got your card, Moose."

"Way to go, kid..." Fan-tastic.

There were number anomalies, of sorts, in both companies. Topps, when not busy familiarizing us with third-base coaches, had one small group, maybe 25 players, that were hard to come by, and since they were in extreme numerical proximity, it was the old "scarce number" scenario revisited. You could get the cards, but you had to have deep pockets.

Today, that would be called creative marketing. And believe me, today, the numerous companies do it all the time.

The Bowman set had one anomaly, but it, like the number sequences, took some time to discern. When I got a dupe of Jimmy Piersall, I checked the number and thought I'd found a rarity, because Piersall's card was number 210, and the one I'd unearthed was number 66. Identical front images, but different numbers. Huh.

It turned out that number 66 had originally been Ted Williams' card, but he was injured very early in the season and they pulled his card from the presses. However, for reasons never to be learned, Bowman put in a second Piersall. And it was really Ted Williams' year, because I'd never had his card before (he was in the Armed Forces for '52 and '53). Topps had put him on card number 1, one of the rare, impressive orange slabs, and then when they ran out of coaches to acknowledge, they added a second Ted Williams as the last card in the set, number 250. Maybe it was to remind the other company that Teddy Baseball should never be left out.

But still, only Williams, Whitey Ford, Yogi Berra, Duke Snider, Willie Mays, and Phil Rizzuto—among big names---appeared in both sets. So, I credit myself, Chris Decker (for trademark purposes) with inventing "Fantasy Baseball Card Ball," a game that pitted the best stars from one company against the best stars of the other company. I'd pick starting lineups from both companies, spread them out and then create some moronic fantasy that rarely lasted past the second inning. Still, it was an improvement over watching "Bobby Babe" and his peers take up the fine art of cigarette smoking when the adults were not around.

Because Hamlet was the home of a gentleman from the New York Yankee front office, one of my friends saw him in the "shopping district" one day and asked him—out of the clear blue—why the sets of cards were so different. He answered that it was his belief that the card companies were really mercenary and fought to sign players to "exclusive" contracts, meaning that if you were on one company's cards, you could not catch a few bucks for appearing on the other company's product. And both products, we were later shocked to learn, were nothing but shills to sell gum (oh, the innocence of youth).

So we weren't really collecting baseball cards, but rather gum advertisements. And the advertisers wanted exclusive rights to a player's features, be they photographed or sketched. In theory—but only in theory, it meant that two sets of 250 cards each, if there were no instances of the same player in both, would mean rounding up 500 ballplayers. But in those days, there were only 16 teams, all no further west than St. Louis, each with 25 players; so that only added up to 400 cards. The managers, coaches, and "nobodies" filled in where the greed of some players to be in both sets did not quite fill the void.

That never stopped Yogi and Phil, who were on both sets for every year there were two companies, which is to say 1951—1955.

The fall and winter of 1954 really did keep the momentum of cards going, because the World Series—absent the Yankees—had been a wild and crazy four-game sweep for the New York Giants, with Dusty Rhodes as the unlikely hero. Ten years later, long out of baseball, he was driving the parking lot busses at the New York World's Fair.

But while Topps had stayed out of the football card market, Bowman put out some truly magnificent football cards, with excellent action photos, statistics on the back, and a decent number of well-known players. Of course, football was never to be confused with baseball, as football rarely even made television and the one local game—the New York football Giants, was on the radio. The announcers could make Gifford sound fast, or make Chuck Bednarik (who later broke Gifford's leg) sound like a real hitter, but you needed the newspaper to know who the real stars were. For the record, Bednarik was a better tackler than Gifford was a speedster—check Gifford's leg X-ray for details.

Gifford carried the ball, so, notwithstanding talent differentials, his card was more sought after than Bednarik.

In the meantime, you were stuck with the realities of traditional bland, non-football television on Sunday, Monday, and Thursday night. Luckily, they had enough bland rubbish, Uncle Miltie, Red Skelton, and sitcoms that featured near-perfect families, to fill six local New York networks from breakfast until midnight, after which you got to listen to patriotic music and then static.

But the cards of Otto Graham, Bobby Layne, George Blanda, Leo Nomellini, and Leon Hart got us through the winter, along with a collection of no-names that even a trivia expert today could not cite. My favorite, for reasons I can't really discern, was Bert Rechichar, a Baltimore Colts receiver and kicker. He couldn't kick worth a damn, making well under 50% of his field-goal tries, but he set the NFL record for the longest kick, at 56 yards. In those days when players lived with concussions, the goal posts were on the goal line, so Rechichar's kick did come from beyond mid-field. And his record stood for a dozen years until broken by a kicker with a partial foot and partial arm.

At least the cards confined themselves to statistics of the past and limited hopes for the season that the cards represented. Perhaps sanity was announcing its presence in the cardboard slabs as advertisement market.

# My Mother Threw Them Out

Hamlet and the surrounding towns and counties were heavily blanketed with three feet of snow in late March 1955. It was hellish for my parents, as we had a long driveway and it took hours to get the car out so they could get to work by about three in the afternoon.

The schools were closed for two days, giving us time to build a magnificently architectural snow tunnel that ended in an igloo-like cave. Nowadays, the cops would instantly ban any such construction and the town ploughs would turn such an edifice into suburban renewal, but in those days, nobody quite understood safety the way they do today.

Despite our glee, equal no doubt to that of Pharaoh's pyramid builders, we were ready for spring, and spring of course meant the return of baseball season, and, far more importantly, baseball cards. The bottom line in all of that rationalizing was that the young kids—I was only approaching my eighth birthday in my fourth year of card collecting—really believed that we would never get to attend a real Major League Baseball game. So, the cards were our vicarious means of approaching the great American pastime. I proudly note that having shared my innovative "fantasy" game with others, it was becoming widely adopted.

As long as I could hold Mickey Mantle, Hank Bauer, Bob Feller, or Satchell Paige in my hands, that was Major League Baseball. They came alive, animated cardboard that lived and breathed.

And occasionally struck out or pitched no-hitters. But when you have something that is essentially ersatz, but is as close as you'll ever get to the real item, it takes on a very genuine quality. Going to a real game would almost demean the precious cardboard, we told ourselves. Particularly because if, by some miracle of modern science, we could somehow get to a game, we'd be sitting so far away we'd have to listen to the broadcast to know what was happening.

But anything beyond Hamlet and a couple of neighboring towns was just mythology to us. In 1955, I actually got to cross the Hudson River on a ferry boat—a major excursion of sorts, but it was also the year that Disneyland opened in California, and every one of us knew that was a place we would see from time to time on Sunday night television, but never in person. California, for all it mattered to us, might as well have been a province of Australia, wherever that was.

But we had our cards, and subsequently, the expectations of heading for third grade, because there, our teachers told us, was where the work really got hard. To me, that meant we had to use popsicle sticks instead of tongue depressors to work with that lugubrious white paste that came in mayonnaise jars.

Yuck.

The 1955 cards hit with a splash, and it had to be that way, because 1954 had been the first year in my memory that the Yankees were not in the World Series, and the collecting world would be turned, literally, sideways.

Both companies' cards left the vertical mode and became horizontal. Topps simply turned the previous year's cards sideways, with a color mug shot, a black-and-white action pose, a stamped-on signature, and the team logo. Like the previous year, the cards appeared against yellow, green, white, red, and blue backgrounds. I guess they had to virtually eliminate orange—except for a couple of late-season cards, as almost none of the previous year's orange players made it back for a second look.

What did make it back were the previous year's mug shots. That meant that many of the 1954 players, now turned sideways, featured the identical pose, with perhaps only the background color changing for their 1955 cards. And 1956 would be a repeat of 1955—same mug shots, but with color backgrounds. Willie Mays, Hank Aaron, Hank Bauer—identical for all three years.

Card number #1 was, not surprisingly, Dusty Rhodes, following his World Series heroics, and it turned out that he hit .305 that year. But he only played in 94 games with 187 at-bats, one less than two per game; so it's courteous to say he saw "limited action." There was also by now the familiar "number groupings," with the higher numbers appearing later in the year and being a challenge to find.

The Bowman Company went out on a limb and sawed it off behind them. Their cards were full-color photos of the players, well centered within the framework of a television set, giving the appearance of "color TV." Some of the photos had striking color—Milwaukee Braves like Johnny Logan still come to mind, with the rich, red and blue "Tomahawk" uniforms. Logan stands out in memory because his pose showed him reaching across his body to snare a liner or a grounder. A number of cards, however, included photos with the same light towers in the background, and the cards didn't quite shine like Johnny Logan. Mickey Mantle's card, among others, suffered from that weakness. He looked like a batboy posing for a test photo, but still, the name on the card simply said "Mantle," and that was all it needed to say.

And once again, there were numerical sequences in the Bowman set as there had been in the Topps set, and the higher numbers were once again the challenge, but they came with a built-in pitfall. Instead of picturing only unknown coaches and managers, they completed their print run with about fifteen or twenty umpires—I can't give the exact count because I never kept one of them. They were, quite simply, horrible. Generic faces of men wearing blue suits, bow ties, and hats that would have been ridiculed in the Easter Parade. I'd have sooner kept and cherished a set of photos of prison wardens.

Of course, by that time, I was playing organized ball, although at age seven, I had to be sneaked into games when my father was nearby—and hopefully sober. That meant that umpires had also become, for a time at least, the enemy.

My father was in the process of creating a dry well in our back yard. My contribution to the effort was all of the umpire cards I pulled out of packs. And they were plentiful, as it took me at least thirty packs to get the Bowman high number Hank Bauer and Jim Konstanty cards I needed to complete the Yankees.

Because of the competition to sign players and the tentative prohibition against a player signing with both companies—a concern bypassed by Willie Mays, Eddie Matthews, Gil Hodges, Hank Aaron, and Phil and Yogi, of course, the Topps mug-shot cards got by on Eddie Lopat, Ted Williams and newcomers like Tommy Carroll; and a good number of those included the same shot that was used in 1954 and would be used again in 1956. To fill out the mug shot grouping, they threw in the usual cast of nobodies, including a hideous teenager named Sandy Koufax, (who would, as it happened, be elected to the Hall of Fame at age 36), plus two other unknowns named Roberto Clemente and Bob Grim. They also printed cards of three players on the Phillies who never appeared in a major league game.

Some of us chuckled as we wondered if *any* of the 1955 Phillies ever appeared in a major league game.

As the summer wore on, my father made his usual pretense of caring about my collection, and asked to see what I had in terms of Yankees, as the other 15 teams were simply pretenders. He waded through the limited Topps group, Yogi, Phil, Turley, Bauer, Bob Grim, Joe Collins, Frank Leja (who?), Andy Carey, Charlie Silvera, Tommy Carroll, Moose, and Eddie Lopat (a resident of Hamlet and commonplace in the town, as was Bill "Moose" Skowron, another mug shot who also wound up on color TV).

The Bowman color TV Yankees included Yogi and Phil as a matter of course, plus Bauer, Grim, Whitey Ford, Mantle, McDougal, Billy Hunter, Jerry Coleman, Irv Noren, Allie Reynolds, Bob Cerv, Eddie Robinson, rookie Elston Howard, and veteran Jim Konstanty. For my dime, it was a better fantasy team, but it was always debatable, even if they had failed to sign Leja and Lopat.

The TVs troubled my father; he seemed to take it almost as a personal insult that cards had color televisions when our house did not have one (and would not, until 1968, when I bought one), but the insult should have been mitigated by the fact that nobody in the neighborhood—lower middle class, but well above a housing project—had a color television. In those days, there were only about five programs in "living color" and a color television cost about a month's pay in a good-salaried job.

But the dislike was there. "Keep these, and don't flip them or put them in your bike spokes," Decker-in-Chief told me. "Get as many as you can, especially the good players, and take good care of them."

"Why?"

"Because those will be the last baseball cards from Bowman," he said, presciently. And, of course, he turned out to be right, although his reasoning—the color TV deprivation syndrome, was probably not the reason. Still, when it became obvious the following spring that there would only be one set of baseball cards, there was a near-perfect bifurcation of opinion. Some kids clung to the color TVs "because some day, they'll be worth something." Others tossed out the Bowman cards simply because they were an abject failure, or so it seemed.

The big fish,Topps, simply ate the little fish, Bowman. The Topps Company was aided by a 1955 summer release of football cards. But they weren't, for the most part, the current crop of knuckle-draggers, but rather 100 "All-Americans." Looking back on those cards, their intended market seemed to be the adults who would have remembered Tom Harmon, Red Grange, Johnny Lujack, Jim Thorpe (who had died two years before, forty-one years after his retracted Olympic triumph in 1912), the Four Horsemen of Notre Dame—all on one card—plus Don Hutson, Sammy Baugh, Ernie Nevers, Doc Blanchard and a host of West Point players when Army was a powerhouse and a team the bookies noticed.

The cards were mostly horizontal, but with a few verticals, and had a color depiction of the All-American, set against an action photo of most likely total strangers playing college football. The backgrounds were the traditional red, green (all the West Pointers were green), yellow, blue, and even orange made a comeback. Their advertising might as well have been "Back in the days when men were men...." but they went over with their intended audience, because several fathers explained the exploits of Thorpe, Grange, et al, to a group of us, with fond nostalgic recall.

A few of us also had the chance to speak to the Yankee executive that lived nearby, and while he did not espouse my father's "TV" conspiracy, he did say that those would be the last cards from that company. But we were shocked to learn that the issue was about gum, not cards. All along, we learned as our hopes were dashed, the concept had been to sell gum. The cards were a bonus. And one company sold so much more gum, both with cards and in individual cubes, that they were able to buy out the other company. The purchaser would again issue the other company's cards a few years hence—in 1989. Topps and Bowman had been marketing Double-Bubble and Bazooka, and one brand cannibalized the other.

But we were warned, so when the 1955 football season rolled around, (and before 1956 arrived with only one company selling baseball cards) the company on the verge of disappearing put out its final football card run—current teams, not past heroes, and their 160 card offering had some very talented players and some nice art work we had "insider information" that it was the end, so we grabbed up as many of them as we could, particularly what had come to be known as "the high numbers," which arrived about the time of the spring thaw. And long after the championship game, in the pre-Super Bowl era, had been played.

I had never imagined I'd keep my cards as anything more than a nostalgic collection of cardboard, but could people have been right in saying they'd be valuable some day? Only time would tell on that one, but now, fully eight years old, I could consider myself not just a collector; I was an investor. I was buying stock in cardboard futures, which were bedecked with low-salaried heroes and goats, but they were athletes and that was all that mattered. The seasons came and went with their predictable humid and snowy events and card collecting went on and on.

The years 1956 through 1960 were largely anti-climactic after the cessation of two competing companies. With a monopoly, Topps could put out whatever they wanted and we the consumers could take it or leave it. I was slightly miffed because I preferred the gum from Bowman's cards. I could still get that gum, but without any cards. *Why bother?*

Not only was I an investor, I had become a sugar-confection aficionado.

In baseball, the 56's were sharp cards, except for the addition of the two league presidents (almost as lackluster as the previous year's umpires), and team cards, featuring team photos taken before mid-season, so there were frequently 35 players, and they were named in tiny captions at the bottom of the cards.

This, no doubt, increased sales of microscopes.

Since cards were now to have a value, we were always on the lookout for the star-cards. The '56 Mantle was a beauty, and it seemed the perfect match for his Triple-Crown winning year, which earned him a raise to $100,000 a season.

That was, believe it or not, unheard-of money, and I know that prior to the 1954 season, pitcher Vic Raschi had asked for a $500 raise, to something like $8,500, and despite his excellent record, he was traded to the Cardinals while standing in the Yankee front office with his hat in his hand. His 1954 card still showed him as a Yankee, but at some point in the season, an extra line was added on the reverse side saying "Traded to the Cardinals." Thereafter, he became an asterisk for serving up Hank Aaron's first career home run in 1954.

Aaron had the unique distinction of being confused with another super-star, as the '56 Hank Aaron showed an action shot of someone sliding into home behind the now-familiar Aaron pose. But it was not Hank Aaron. It was Willie Mays. I have to believe that, if this was pointed out before that card was distributed, someone gave the then-traditional answer, "Well, they all look alike."

Hank Aaron, slender to the point of wiry, looked nothing like Willie Mays.

Aaron, like Mays, Ford, Snider, Spahn, Hodges, Williams, Matthews, Campanella, and assorted others were becoming stars in their own right, but it was surprising that Don Newcombe was the National League MVP that year. He had an incredible year on the mound and also batted .305. I guess the touts considered that atonement for 1951, when "Newk" ran out of gas in the one-game playoff with the Giants and gave way to Ralph Branca.

Who, in turn, gave way to Bobby Thomson. End of story.

But now, collecting was more about getting the stars and not all the numbers, even though the numbers were somewhat easier because they were issued in clearly defined series, with accompanying "check lists." I was told, before the cards were issued, that if my final report for grade three was exemplary, I'd be allowed to buy not a pack of 56s, but *one box. Twenty-four packs. A buck twenty.*

*Heaven.* As it happened, that box contained the Mickey Mantle series, and it was redemption because the only other thing I remembered about that prize was a stack of Jerry Schumacher cards, and I figured they'd have some value since he wouldn't be around long.

Football cards and "craze items" also consumed my personal budget, but since I wasn't driving yet, and buying gas at seventeen cents a gallon—well, do the math. Two gallons of gas was seven packs of cards...

And if memory serves, that was the summer of the Davy Crockett card craze, which also came out in two series—orange backs, and green backs. I had both sets and Fess Parker went on to found a private entertainment empire that once lured in someone named Jack Ruby. Whoever he was.

But "doing the math," as noted above, became the challenge, because I'd gotten so good with the ability to recall the numbers of cards and how many packs could be bought instead of two gallons of gas or a house in Florida, when I went back to school, I had "mathematics" with the eighth graders while my classmates were bogged down in fourth grade. I can't say it was fun, but it kept Mr. and Mrs. Decker from *ever* complaining about the grades I got, because thanks to the location of one tavern in downtown Hamlet, everyone for a three mile radius knew that "the Decker kid" was doing math with the big kids. Long division with remainders. What a concept.

I continued to fill my upstairs room with cards, always grouped by year and type—baseball in one stack, football in another, non-sports stuff elsewhere, but foolishly wrapped in rubber bands, which destroyed the "condition" of the card on top and bottom, so if cards were grouped numerically, it meant that from 1952 to 1956, the top cards—Andy Pafko, Jackie Robinson, Ted Williams, Dusty Rhodes, and executive William Harridge were always kind of mottled and were not worth much as trade bait or, years later, on the baseball card market.

At one point, I think I had several stacks of 30 cigar boxes in each stack, with nine years of baseball cards (some years, two companies), seven or eight years of football, and some of the non-sports stuff which was the first thing which tired me out in card collecting.

The second thing would have been my ability, beginning in about 1959 or 1960, to notice that there were girls in my class and in the neighborhood, and some of them were pretty sweet. "Hey, Geraldine, want to sneak over and see my Minnie Minoso?"

I had to graduate from pick-up lines like that, and in doing so, I left the world of cards behind, or perhaps it would be better to say that I left them upstairs.

When the family, without my input, decided to move away, there was no thought whatsoever given to allowing me to crate up almost 200 cigar boxes full of cards, so some very painful decisions had to be made. Regrettably, I was not consulted on the decisions. They were handed down to me on cuneiform, undoubtedly etched by one of Pharaoh's scribes, so Mom and Dad could remain blameless in my card collection being annihilated.

So, like so many others, I sadly joined the fraternity whose slogan became, "My mother threw them out...."

# Book One
## The Magic of Mantle

# Where Have You Gone, Joe DiMaggio?

In retrospect, it would seem that the end of my first card-collecting era overlapped with the emergence of baseball "superstars" who had simply been multi-colored cardboard abstractions to a young child.

Looking back to my disappointment with cards from 1954, I noted the arrival of several new "nobodies" in the card market, and in those days, the cards of Ernie Banks, Al Kaline, Hank Aaron, like those of Roberto Clemente and Sandy Koufax the following year had as much interest as the '55 Mayo Smith, the manager of the Phillies. His card showed a nice profile with an "action shot" in the background of him appearing to be trying to stop a runner.

Wait a minute. Managers don't coach on the baselines, and that was especially true for the Phillies, if one recalled the Connie Mack era. Years later, I happened to see that beautiful blue 1955 Mayo Smith card fetching—or attempting to fetch—a high price, and when questioned by me, the dealer indicated it was Smith's "rookie card."

"Rookie card?" I exploded. "He's the manager. He only played 73 games in the major leagues, and that was in 1945 with the Philadelphia Athletics, where he hit a magnificent .212. You're taking this rookie card stuff to extremes, pal."

The dealer moved the card out of his prime display space but I had no doubt that he quickly put it back there after I moved on to ridicule the retail methods of other greedy dealers.

But that would be in the future. As the 1960s began, the baseball superstar was Mickey Mantle, and he only trailed slightly behind Ruth, Gehrig, and DiMaggio and they were legends of the past. If any further punctuation was necessary, two of them were already deceased. Gehrig died in his late 30s, and the Babe in his early 50s.

New York, it seemed, had a solid monopoly on talent. And a modern star—Mantle for instance—whose photograph and generic autograph could be purchased in a candy store, easily surpassed deceased superstars or those who'd had unsuccessful marriages to buxom Hollywood blondes.

The 1960 Yankees were to baseball what terrorists would become to unprotected sports venues in the distant future. Most major league teams by 1960 had well-established farm teams, where nascent talent either bloomed vividly or wound up riding buses to games until advanced age caused skill deterioration.

The Yankees, always possessed of a good farm team in the Newark Bears, had two even better talent pools: the St. Louis Browns/Baltimore Orioles and the Athletics, by then in Kansas City, a rest stop on the way to Oakland from Philadelphia.

The front office of the Bronx bombers had a unique knack for dumping tired talent onto the Oriole and Athletic rosters and plucking superstars for Bronx fame in return.

In a famous 17-player deal in late 1954, the Yankees got Don Larsen, Bob Turley, and Billy Hunter (along with players to be named later) in return for Gus Triandos, a journeyman catcher who would never supplant Yogi Berra, and Gene Woodling, a veteran outfielder who was competing on a daily basis with Mantle, Irv Noren, Hank Bauer, and Bob Cerv. Turley went on to with the Cy Young Award, and the 3-21 Larsen would pitch the first and only World Series perfect game in 1956.

When Larsen's arm got tired, the Yanks shipped him to Kansas City along with the now-aging Bauer, plus Norm

Siebern and "Marvelous" Marv Throneberry. In return, the Yanks got utility infielder Joe DeMaestri, and a future janitor named Kent Hadley.

Oh. Yeah. They also got Roger Maris.

But the team was always built around solid pitching plus the offensive power of Mantle and Berra, both 3-time MVPs, as well as Maris and Elston Howard, who combined for three MVP honors. That crew cleared the bases that were frequently crowded by singles hitters like Bobby Richardson and Tony Kubek. If the big names were not enough, the Yanks also got their money's worth out of Moose Skowron, still a Hamlet resident who would undergo a scandalous divorce from an adulterous wife, Johnny Blanchard, Hector Lopez, and defensive gems like Clete Boyer and Elmer Valo, who became Mantle's defensive caddy in late innings.

The year 1961, my first year without cards, was simply too exciting on the field to worry about gum and cardboard. Mantle and Maris chased the Babe all season, although in truth, Mantle chased the babes his whole career. Sizable four-baggers were added by Skowron, Blanchard, Berra and Howard; with Yogi and Elston alternating at catcher and left field. Whitey Ford won eight games in June and 25 in the season, and Turley, Terry, Coates, and Stafford collected enough "W's" to have serious talks with the money-men at the end of the season.

Mantle fell ill and "only" belted 54 homers. Maris, amidst serious flak from fans who hated the very idea of the Babe's record being erased, nevertheless jacked homer number 61 on the last day of the season (also earning an asterisk for doing in 162 games what Babe Ruth did in 154). The 19 year old who caught that hallowed ball sold it to a man named Sam Gordon, an occasional friend of Jack Ruby.

Whoever they were.

But Mantle would always be the focus, and his cards would always be the ones to get (to invest in) and to protect. Yogi eventually went to the Mets, a status drop that registered on the Richter scale, Howard went to the Red Sox, and Maris went to the Cardinals for a nobody and several nobodies to be named later. Skowron went to the Dodgers when the Yanks suspected that Joe Pepitone could replace him, while Richardson, Kubek, and Clete Boyer hung around till they had to be replaced.

By 1966, the Yanks had gone from "Murderers' Row" to the "Ugly" part of "the Good, the Bad, and the Ugly," and that fall from grace may have even exceeded that of gravitational pull. On a September night in 1966, I sat in an otherwise empty left field area of Yankee Stadium, the House that Ruth Built, and when Clete Boyer hit a home run that landed ten rows in front of me, I didn't even get up to get the ball. Some little kid ran about 200 feet from somewhere along the left field foul line to claim it.

When I got home that night, I thought I heard my surviving collection of baseball cards crying.

My wallet sobbed a bit also, because the Kaline, Aaron, Banks, Koufax and Clemente cards that I had left unprotected were spiraling upward in value.

But in 1954 or 1955, much less 1966, who knew?

It would be fifteen years between ventures into the card-collecting world, and obviously, much had changed. My last purchase, a 1960 pack that was re-wrapped in cellophane in a "5 & 10" and showed Whitey Ford on top, happened when I was twelve years old.

My next card purchase would be at age 27, following what could reasonably be defined as an intense education, which, at one point, even forced me to decide between continuing my education or taking a shot at professional baseball.

Admittedly, a long shot. Accordingly, I stayed in academia, and after discovering that employment for a history major was as rare as that 1952 Topps Mickey Mantle card, I went back to school for a Master's Degree in Police Science, and that eventually led to employment in 1974.

I thought back to all the work I had done to earn that Master's Degree every time I wrote a ticket for an expired parking meter or had to clean someone else's stomach contents off my uniform when I was required to haul some inebriate to the drunk tank. But it was a job, and my parents were beginning to fail in health, so any reasonable-paying job in 1974 (read: $13,000) was a good job. Actually, the salary wasn't bad because the local cops all had strong professional associations—sometimes referred to as "unions," and it was an article of faith that with ten years on the job, we'd be making fifty thou, and would have outstanding benefit and retirement packages.

Fifty thousand dollars? It was hard for someone my age, particularly someone who never had any money, to conjure that sum, and to put it in 1974 perspective, that kind of money would have bought seven Corvettes (six, if convertibles), or it would have been a hefty down payment, or perhaps the whole nut, on a decent house in or around Hamlet. Of course, I was thinking about the money I would theoretically be getting in 1984 and comparing it to 1974 prices.

Obviously, I'd slept through Economics 101 as an undergraduate, and I would certainly prove that all too frequently as my card-collecting addiction returned.

In early 1975, we had had a truly horrific auto accident in Hamlet, and I had the misfortune of being the first officer on the scene. A car carrying a family of five had crossed the midline and hit, head-on, a car with an adult and four young children.

Six of those ten people were dead by the time I reached the vehicles, which, I humbly add for the record, could have burst into flames at any minute. I got the survivors out as other police vehicles from different towns began arriving, with ambulances not far behind. The corpses were laid out on a nearby lawn, to the chagrin of the owner and his roses, and the media got a picture of me, as I lifted the blanket covering an incredibly beautiful young child, un-bloodied and peaceful in the repose of death.

I figured that would make the papers the next day, and I was not disappointed. It appeared on the very top of the front page, as a tease for the complete story and details on page one of the B section—local news.

Luckily, though, they got it backwards. The caption had me covering up the child, not uncovering him, for a last look before the county medical examiner turned him into giblets.

Below the fold, as they say in the newspaper business, was news as startling as the item about me that I had been dreading. Apparently, collecting old baseball cards was now fast becoming a major nostalgia item, and a business had opened nearby that specialized in old cards and sports collectibles. It has been years since I read that piece, but I can still see the illustrations—a 1954 green-colored Dick Schofield, a Cardinal utility infielder as a rookie, and a 1953 Wayne Terwilliger, the poster boy for hard-working but underachieving athletes.

I remember the article, but more so the photos, as they suddenly brought to the surface so many memories of a childhood that had been all about baseball and the collecting of its historical artifacts. I cut the article out and then committed my article to the fireplace. I would no more forget the look on that child's face than I'd forget Dick Schofield or Wayne Terwilliger. And the irony surged through my memory: the night in September, 1966 that I ignored the Clete Boyer home run, the Yankees' public address announcer made it known that the Yanks had acquired Dick Schofield.

Could Wayne Terwilliger be far behind? In fact, he was, as he was much older than Schofield. If the Yankees signed him, it would have been to tear up ticket stubs. Or sell Grape Ne-Hi to Radar O'Reilly.

The difference suggested to me by one page of newsprint was that I could now recapture Schofield and Terwilliger. That poor, beautiful child would be dead forever. And I knew that no diversion—even one as immense as returning to card collecting—could ever help me forget his almost angelic visage in death.

In the immediate aftermath, I could not get baseball card fever out of my head, and as I write these words years later, the nostalgia thermometer tells me that the fever is still there. But as I thought about the article, I realized that what had been a hobby for me had now been transformed into a business for others, and with the passage of time, there would be fewer and fewer hobbyists and more and more people carrying price guides and calculators.

And the overlap of timing was just as critical as the Yanks' acquisition of Dick Schofield in 1966, because in 1975, "free agency" burst onto the baseball scene, meaning that a super-star could command a fee of $1 million from any team that had that much money.

Eventually, it became commonplace for the unknown utility infielder—you know, the guy who hit .233 in 67 games last season, to sign on with some team for $7 million over three years.

Ticket prices skyrocketed, so while I had been easily able to afford the luxury of avoiding that home run by Clete Boyer in 1966, now a pair of ducats, plus parking, food and potables could easily run into hundreds of dollars. Warm up the television, Decker.

That took me back to the days when we knew we wouldn't see the games, so we held tight to the cards, in lieu of actually being at the games.

Now the prices of the cards skyrocketed also.

Where have you gone, Tinkers-to-Evers-to-Chance?

# All The News That Was Fit To Print

There can be no underestimating the impact that small news clipping had on 'me' in general, and on my psychological makeup in the ever-so-*chic* clinical sense.

Before that day, it had been as if all the cards that Mom threw out had disappeared from planet Earth and had been put in a permanent orbit around the sun. Never again would I see, much less possess, a 1952 Topps Howie Pollett, the stark, aged and gaunt Topps sketch of Satchell Paige in 1953, or the beauty of the 1955 Bowman Johnny Logan, crossing his body with his glove hand to snare a grounder or a low liner, and all on color TV.

But now, anything was possible—well, anything within budgetary constraints, as I had to remind myself that no nostalgia business was going to be a going concern for very long if they tried to market the "old stuff" at the original prices of the old stuff.

And since it was now ten years since I turned in my wooden bat for an aluminum knock-off for softball, I convinced myself that getting the old cards, "pre-owned" as it were, was well worth the effort, just as softball had come as close as anything could to replacing my first love, baseball.

I decided to pay a visit to the place that was written up alongside the photos of Ducky Schofield and Wayne Terwilliger, and found it in an enclosed mini-mall, meaning each store (perhaps "booth" would be more accurate) was not much larger than 150 square feet, if that.

But as any treasure hunter knows, the size of the treasure chest is never as important as the contents, and as I walked in, I was transported back to a point in time when I was in touch with training wheels, electric trains, roller skates that needed "skate keys," whiffle ball, hula hoops, girls in poodle skirts, and good ol' Speedy Alka Seltzer.

It was a cloudless, mild-for-November Friday night and the two proprietors, both casually but not "sport" dressed, were both on hand. There were, somewhat to my surprise, several customers, most of whom were trying to prove they were knowledgeable, as if that would get them a baseball card merit badge, or a trip to "Jeopardy!" as a contestant well-versed in sport.

It took less than five minutes to discover that in virtually every instance, "Mom" had tossed their original collection of cards out. Apparently, fathers never committed such acts of perversion.

I just minded my own business and looked at the antique prizes. One showcase was loaded with stacks of cards, some as far back as 1910, but continuing upward to about 1972. My '52s through '60s were in there as well, and I recognized most, but not all of the cards on display. I knew I'd missed a few early number '53s, as the later numbers appeared early, and the 572 card set in 1960 had later-number cards that never made it to the candy stores in Hamlet.

Still, it was hypnotic. There, right in front of me, sat my childhood, and it could be recaptured. Literally, a cardboard fountain of youth.

Sadly, that thought included "for a price," and I quickly discovered that the cards that meant the most to me in order to recapture the lost childhood ranged in price from a quarter to half a buck—for the ordinary players. "Stars" were another matter, and I quickly discovered that those cost factors could best be determined by the Federal Reserve Board, in terms of the national debt.

"Rookie cards," something I was educated in that evening, were also another matter, no matter how trivial the player's career was, his "rookie card" still commanded additional revenue.

I was also reminded of my father's injunction to take good care of the 1955 Bowman color TV cards, as "condition" was to baseball cards what "location" was to real estate. Put another way, a dog-chewed Mantle or Mays commanded a lot more money than a "perfect" Lou Limmer or Ebba St. Claire. That made sense after all, since anyone who went to a local game involving the three New York teams (when there were three) never came home and bragged to the other kids that they'd seen Lou Limmer or Ebba St. Claire play.

Mantle, Berra, Ford, Mays, Irwin, Robinson, Reese, Snider, Campanella and Hodges were different matters altogether. If a kid went to a game and even saw Whitey Ford tossing a ball but not pitching, it was a more important moment than to be chosen for astronaut training.

Except for the statistics on the back of the cards, I can't even prove that either of those two giants of the game—Limmer and St. Claire—ever did play. But we did know that Hodges, Snider, Reese, Robinson, Campanella, Mays, Irvin, Mantle, Ford, and Berra had played as New York players, as well as Kluszewski, Matthews, Ashburn, Kiner, Williams, Rosen, or Fox, when they were in town against the New York teams. In Ashburn's case, as an aged has-been with the early Mets.

Strange how there were more "local" stars—just New York players—than all the out-of-towners combined. Of course, the New York teams won the World Series from '47 to '59, with only one loss to Milwaukee to break the skein.

In the face of my quick lesson on the economics of collecting, I had flipped through stacks of "New York teams" (which also cost extra) and found a 1952 Johnny Sain, a 1953 Tom Morgan, and a 1954 Gene Woodling that had escaped my Yankee magnet in childhood. Because the Sain card was an error, with Joe Page's information on the back, and because they were New York teams, that was a quick five bucks, and I made a point of asking for them to keep an eye out for the Joe Page, as I needed that one too. I tried very hard *not* to let on that I did not know of the existence of either Sain or Page in 1952. Sain still had his good stuff. Page was retired, but they needed a face on a card.

I flipped through a couple additional stacks and took some St. Louis Browns that I didn't recognize as well as the ones that I did, but not Satchel Paige, as he was going for four bucks, and I could get eight "commons" as they were known, for the same money.

Mistake number one: Now that cards are both a hobby and an investment, always put your money into "stars," as they will eventually be "super-stars" and beyond, while "commons" do not have the ability to become "super commons."

Bottom feeders will always be bottom feeders. With apologies to Lou Limmer and Ebba St. Claire, unless you saw them play, they would be forgotten by the legions of collectors eager to re-connect with Mantle and his unique stratosphere of talent.

Having left behind $15, I knew I would not be going out for dinner the following Saturday night, and while not admitting it to myself, I knew that I had to get back to that booth regularly and get beyond a couple of shoe boxes of long-preserved but poor condition Yankees that had survived Mom's trips to the trash can years earlier.

The money was the challenge, but the fever burning inside was so intense that I started considering a part-time job to pay for my hobby/ addiction. It was to remain a hobby, not a business, although as time would pass, I'd pile up doubles and beyond and try to swap or sell them to get cards of which I still did not have a copy.

It truly was a magical re-connection. It was as if as a boy, my puppy had run away, and now, despite the many years, the full-grown hound-dog had come home to stay.

As I got in the car to go home, I had to re-visit my purchases before I could even put the key in the ignition. Sain, Morgan, Woodling—how was it that I'd never seen these in their respective years? And then the St. Louis Browns, 1953: Clint Courtney (once knocked cold by Billy Martin for threatening Rizzuto), Cliff Fannin, Gordon Goldsberry, Virgil Trucks—future Yankee, but a Brown then, and with two no-hitters to his credit—plus Hank Edwards; Phillies Granny Hamner, Karl Drews, and Johnny Wyrostek.

And, of course, the '55 Johnny Logan. If I'd had the resources, I think I would have bought five of those. Those combined twelve cards, even at $15, were priceless treasures, and their intrinsic value aside, their treasure value was enhanced by the realization that additional treasures would always be available.

Grudgingly, I started the car to leave the land of cards, for now. On the way home, I played the numbers in my head. With respect to Topps, 1952 had meant 407 cards, *or at least 407 cards,* of which I had about 15, all Yankees; 1953 was 280 cards, of which I had about 19; 1954 had 250, and I barely had 10 of those, although each cited number was exclusive of doubles and triples. The 1955 set was.... was it 210? I wasn't sure, and I was lost with respect to the numbers in the later sets, because my focus had always been on the earlier ones.

I had a lot of work, both physical and mental, to do if I was going to make the decision to go back into card collecting full-tilt.

If?

# With All Entrees, You Get Egg Roll

Before I could even imagine an area of the house well-stacked with cigar boxes full of cards, I had to put economic realities into focus. Both of my parents were aging slowly but ailing accordingly, and I certainly needed a rainy day fund for their needs, as in both cases, they were not old enough for Medicaid, and "health insurance" in the workplace was not commonplace except for very lucky folks like teachers.

And cops. *Hello.* And for spouses, but not for parents.

Secondly, I had a serious fund going in order to put a down payment on my own house, so what was left after parental concern and real estate savings amounted to the traditional "egg money."

I didn't have to concern myself with a social life, as my beautiful girlfriend, who was truly beautiful as well as truly ignorant, had found yet another tiny college in the Midwest to attend, so that devolved to phone calls and they became more and more distant as she did. I was thus alone, but hoping she'd come to her senses as well as to her SAT tutor from years earlier, before she spent a few years working to pay off the Nebraska state debt.

So Friday nights were usually visits to "the booth," where I gathered in Yankee cards first, finding perhaps another dozen between the two companies, from 1952 to 1955. It was on my third visit that my eyes became riveted upon "the card," the 1952 Topps Mickey Mantle that Bobby Babe, so long ago, had uncovered. The booth owner could not help but notice my hypnotic trance, so he came over and announced, "That's a beauty, ain't it?"

And it was, but it wasn't priced, and when I asked how much, I got the feeling that there was no set price and I was being gauged for what I could possibly afford. The answer, $100, was not a possibility unless they were willing to go on the installment plan, and they claimed to have a waiting list for that card. I did part with $10 for a Bill Dickey card from the same "high number series" (a phrase I came to detest) as the Mantle, and while the Mick was always the headliner, I knew Bill Dickey was no slouch and I'd even written to him once or twice in Little Rock, Arkansas, as a kid and he was a truly elegant man.

My collection of '52s through '56s continued, but I was trying to get the most bang for the limited buck, so I was frequently settling for lesser condition cards—a serious mistake, but at the time unavoidable. Well, I'm rationalizing that it was unavoidable, because I made it so. If I had it to do over, I would have only purchased top condition cards and then been very careful with them.

But "be careful with them"? That didn't get entered into my mindset because baseball cards were always items that you constantly went through, put into teams, created fantasy teams, or wrapped with rubber bands. I learned to avoid some of those mistakes, but considering the condition of some of the cards I bought, rubber bands could only have improved them.

But to me, they were priceless; to anyone else, they were probably worthless. Schofield and Terwilliger were not memories to some; they were marketing items and nothing more. To me, they were childhood revisited, and "childhood" that could be somehow mentally maintained into the distant future.

I then got a somewhat accidental look inside the business of baseball card buying and selling, and it was not pretty. We had had a home burglary in Hamlet on a snowy Friday at dinnertime, when I'd normally make my card purchases, and the homeowner had been beaten badly. It meant working all night, but I'd get comp time, which I took the following Monday.

I was virtually alone in "the booth" at mid-day on that Monday, and I'd been there enough times that I felt like I was part of the displays, when in walked a total stranger with a very large box—the kind of thing that would hold two dozen packages of paper towels, or about 9 cubic feet at the very least. And it gave every indication of being heavy.

It was filled with old cards—my kind of old cards. There had to be 8,000 to 10,000 cards in there—with a weight approaching fifty or sixty pounds, and from the brief look I got, they seemed like they'd just fallen out of the packs. I gave the guy credit for carrying what had to be a lot of precious cardboard.

Gently fallen out of the packs. "Mint" as the saying went.

One owner kept me preoccupied with baseball trivia—and it was truly trivial—while the other one took a fast look through the box, stopping occasionally to note that he'd found a card that wasn't perfect—like the car dealers who kick YOUR tires when you want to trade in your car for one of theirs. Eventually, he wrote down some hieroglyphs and offered the walk-in a total of $91.

Ninety-one bucks? Even at 8,000 cards, the low estimate, and they were mint and there certainly would have been stars, so a low-end average of $8,000 would not have been unreasonable, retail. Wholesale, $91. I'll never forget it. Not $90 or $92. Just in-between as if Stephen Hawking had discovered a new planet and had accordingly done the ever-so-perfect math calculations.

The walk-in happily but foolishly took the proffered money and left, after which the two co-owners had an incredible laugh, high-fived each other for their larceny, and did it right in front of me. The partner who had looked through the cards noted that there were several of the rare 1954 Ted Williams' card—the one that had been replaced by the curious Jimmy Piersall at number 66. One of those cards by itself was worth a good $50 (THEN), and there were multiples. I know they did not know my occupation, and I could not have arrested them, as it was not the town of my jurisdiction and there was no real law against making a walk-in customer look stupid.

But it told me they were nothing but investment capitalists who were preying on the unknowing. I had seen people come in with handfuls of cards knowing what they wanted for them. Sometimes they won and cashed in, and sometimes they got bupkis. Somewhere along the line I'd mentioned that all I had left was a big box of Yankees, and they made me aware they would gladly take all my doubles off my hands.

Not for $91, and I didn't have 1% of what that poor schlep had. I can only remind myself that if he had those cards to sell ten years later, when things were more contentious in the buying market, he could easily have gotten between ten and fifteen thousand dollars.

But now it was Scylla and Charybdis, the dueling mythological rocks and monsters, because I did not want to have anything more to do with those vultures, but it seemed like they were the only show in town. Hoping to find out otherwise, I tried the old cop trick of pretending to know something I did not know. When they asked about the Yankee doubles for perhaps the third time, I said that the demand for that stuff was amazing, and that "the other guy wanted them also." That brought the response, "Oh, do you mean Harry, up on the highway, or Ray on the other side of town?"

"Yeah, the guy who is up on...."

"Route 17 in Rynbrook," I was told.

*Thank you and adios.* I knew where Harry was and Ray was put on the waiting list.

I got in the car and drove the approximate ten miles north to Rt. 17 in Rynbrook, but there were no neon signs advertising baseball cards for sale. I had to ask around quite a bit, and then I was directed to the shop of an electrician who was a collector and seller..

I walked in amidst all manner of electrical stuff—about which I knew less than I knew about the career of Lou Limmer—and one lonesome table covered with cards. It was a little disappointing, as the stock was not as plentiful as at the capitalists' booth, but the prices were considerably lower. I pointedly stated that and was told by Harry that he shared my opinion of the dreadful duo but only shared it when questioned.

I took out the cash I had with me, about seventeen bucks, counted it out, and started looking. Harry walked out from the electrical workshop, and, to my amazement, told me, "Whatever you want, take it, and if you can't cover the cost today, come back and pay it off when you can." Harry was a slightly overweight workaholic, thinning hair, and dressed for his electrical work, not attired in sports memorabilia to get noticed.

Whoa. As it happened, I stayed within my budget, but I gave Harry my phone number—the phone on the wall, with a dial way back recently—and asked him to call me if he came into any serious inventory.

He was as good as his word, and always had items I needed. He had a complete set of the 1953 Topps drawings—Satchel Paige and the deformed Willie Mays. By that time I only needed 17 cards to fill my set, but I figured since they were "stars" they would cost approximately $50, so I drove the ten miles. There sat the entire 1953 set, for $98.00. I had to write a check, but I was not going to pass that one up.

That was in 1976, and by then, you no longer needed to pick up a newspaper article to discover that baseball cards were back in vogue. Other outlets had come into existence, some of which were, like Harry's place, an extension of another business—stamps and coins come to mind, or antique toys or places that had survived on paper, be it old magazines, post cards, or other ephemera.

Now it was cards. And not only were there other outlets, but there were also “card shows.” A good number of people ran ads that said, “Buying Old Baseball Cards,” and cashed in—well, initially they cashed out, but then they sold their wares at collectors' shows.

In the early years, you paid something like two bucks to get in the door, and they would have some local ex-ballplayers at the show, and you could take their cards with you and get them autographed for free. Or you could buy their cards and photos at the show—at inflated prices, of course, and get them signed. The only thing that limited the number of autographs you could get was the size of the line, if applicable.

The autographs were *free.* Suffice to say, that has changed, but this was back then, and it was during the height of back then that I met, for reasons cited above, Larry Doby, Monte Irvin, Joe Pepitone, Gene Hermanski, Alvin Dark, Cal Abrams, the previously-noted Dusty Rhodes, all of whom were gracious and generous with their time. The all-time champ in that department, at least in my experience, was Johnny Mize. What a joy. Runner-up, but in the days when you paid for autographs, was Duke Snider. True gentleman, and it must have been something to be part of that Dodger team.

A generous footnote is necessary for Johnny Kucks, who hurled a three-hitter in Game Seven of the first Subway Series, which ended with him striking out Jackie Robinson, in his last major league at-bat. When Kucks' pitching arm failed him, he played in the Hamlet softball league, and it was a strange feeling for me to be in left field, playing next to a center fielder who'd won twenty games one season *and* pitched a shutout in the final game of the 1956 World Series.

At the other end of the scale you find Phil Rizzuto, who would sign one article, and after that, you paid, but only after you kissed his ring. Hoyt Wilhelm and Enos Slaughter were together once, and I thought they were going to come to blows because the latter was in the Hall of Fame and the former believed he should be there. Both of them were unlettered and obnoxious to the point of being rude and demeaning.

When the pay-for-autographs days rolled around, Hank Aaron, Ernie Banks, Whitey Ford, and Hank Bauer were always friendly and cordial. Pete Rose was positively vegetative. If he ever fell from a height of ten feet and landed in soft dirt, he would have sprouted buds. I have literally had better conversations with house-plants.

Of course, the men of my youth were the heroes, and Mickey Mantle was usually jolly and talkative and kept the autograph line moving—admittedly for a price. He was also usually gassed to the gills, which was sad, but it was in keeping with the way he occasionally showed up at the ballpark. I once saw a pitcher easily fan the Mick in the first, third and fifth innings, but by the eighth inning, Mickey was sober and hit a ball that came down somewhere in Connecticut after being tracked by NASA radar.

The hero who was unhesitatingly the most disappointing (by unanimous consent) was Willie Mays. You had to pay, of course, but that only guaranteed a signature, not necessarily exactly where you might have wanted it. He was known to sign baseballs on the seams, or when he signed a photo that had other signatures, he made a point of signing in such a way that his signature was not unique but rather obnoxious. He was even known to sign the backs of cards, so when my one turn in line came, I put the card down, face up, moved it closer with my finger on it, and did not remove the digit until the signature was done; all of ten letters.

Pete Rose only had eight letters to think about. Joe Dimaggio and Ted Kluszewski must have gotten bored spelling their names out. But Mays— a lot of folks wanted to reach across the table and strangle the bastard–– of course, nobody did, but the idea certainly had merit.

In addition to card shows, there were collectors' conventions, where an indoor mall would have certain hallways filled with dealers. No admission, and most likely, no ex-jock to scribble on your cards. At work, we got a couple of county-wide police notices saying that at these kinds of events—both the $2 shows and the mall events, it was not uncommon for "Smith" and "Jones" to get in a serious fight, and when everyone was watching the two pugilistic knuckleheads, "Miller" and "Brown," both in league with the combatants, made off with binders full of cards.

It was almost the perfect crime, because everyone was walking around with binders or something resembling a brief case—even the kids. Mostly, the kids. And some reminded me of myself at their age, as they could tell you the name of the player, the year, and the number of the card they wanted.

Unlike me when I was just an itty-bitty Chris Decker, these kids also had the price-guide quotations memorized. And if you were standing at a table with cards to sell, the kids would make an offer; usually low, and then pretend you'd hurt their feelings when you declined. At least such antics convinced me that. as a cop, I'd always have work when that generation aged a bit.

So at one mall venue, I was observing from a distance, about 80 feet away, when a fight broke out. Ten feet in front of me, a guy decided it was time to swipe a couple of binders. The first thing he saw was a collection of cards. His next sighted object was my service revolver stuck in his chest. "Going somewhere?"

He actually was sentenced to something like two to five years, because the stuff he grabbed would have retailed for well over ten grand. He probably spent his time in stir writing a memoir, "How cardboard got me an orange jump suit."

Still, it was another reminder of the down side of what had once simply been a very special, bucolic joy that punctuated my early summers, and was repeating the process now, but with more cost, more pain, and not quite as much joy. It was one thing to open a pack in 1954 and await the findings. It was something altogether different to show up with a list of which 1954 cards you hoped to buy at a decent price.

Now the punctuation was different. Harry called me and simply asked me to come up to his shop—without specifics. He knew I was a cop, but I had no real jurisdiction in his town.

Harry was beside himself. Someone had broken into his house and stolen 370 complete sets that he had put together. The monetary value in 1977 was incalculable, and as these words are typed, Republicans and Democrats are calling each other names over lesser amounts; the personal loss was just beneath that of of a relative or pet. Harry was devastated, but after walking me through it and convincing me that the local cops had done everything they could, he told me he still had about 20 premium football sets, involving the early years that I had collected, and on up to about 1963

Harry was giving me the right of first refusal on them. They were probably worth four thousand dollars then, but he told me he'd sell them to me for one thousand, because it was worth the difference in cash to know that someone had them who was not likely to be a robbery victim. I understood, but told him I'd give him $250 a month for four months, if that was okay, and then I'd take the cards.

He insisted I take them that day. I made the payments, and not long after the last payment—perhaps six months, Harry died, literally, of a broken heart. He had his electrical business and his cards, but it was not enough. He couldn't sustain.

Having suddenly became a football card collector but no longer able to deal with Harry, I ventured into another new shop—Ray's place—sloppy and unorganized just like Ray was, but well-stocked, and found a few gems to add to what I had.

On either my second or third visit there, my browsing was interrupted by a grubby-looking character who would have fit right in on Skid Row. He introduced himself as Bart. I checked to see if he was wearing matching shoes.

He was, and he was bragging to the youthful Ray that he had just completed putting together a set of "black-backs." By that time, I knew what those were, and for the uninitiated, they were cards numbered 1 through 80 from the 1952 Topps set that made Mantle famous. Those first eighty cards were issued initially with black backs, containing statistics, but the details receded into the dull background and got lost. The black also bled through onto the colors on the front, which to me made them more attractive.

But they were not attractive to the producing company, for reasons best known to them. Not long after, the production line changed to "red-backs", more readable and also more commonplace. So cards numbered 1 to 80 could be either red or black on the back. *But who the hell turned them over?*

Hmm... a set of black backs. Alert the media....

Little did I know at the time, Bowery Bart would become the *bete noir* of the hobby right up until the day his name appeared on the police blotter as a missing person.

By then, he was on the top of the "A List" of baseball card dealers; though on that day, I could easily have mistaken him for a wino.

And despite economic theories, some things never change.

# Be Careful What You Wish For

As 1977 turned into 1978, events began to overtake me and I was, temporarily at least, no longer the master of my own vessel.

I had made a couple of decent arrests, and was tabbed as the local liaison to the county and state police, and there were about fifteen men (no women yet) in the work place who felt they should have gotten those plums ahead of the "college boy."

It was discomforting to know of their jealousy and remind myself that they all carried loaded guns. Naturally, it was about money and perks, that, more than job satisfaction, drove most folks in the workplace, and police stations were no different. The situation was multiplied when, because of the state police liaison position, I was gradually moved into a newly created local FBI connection. To the other cops, this was almost payback, because the FBI agent, who would drop by every couple of weeks to remind us that he was God's anointed and appointed, was never awkward in his willingness to put down the local contact cop: Me.

He was so obvious about it on one occasion that I took off my shoes, had a good look at both feet and announced, "Nope. They're not flat..."

While that was happening, I discovered that my mother was far more ill than my father had let on. She had been dealing with internal bleeding, and the root cause of it, which had gone ignored for over three years, was cancer.

I came home from the day shift to find a note that Mom had been hospitalized, and the visiting hours were listed. Before that note hit the ground, I was in my car, siren blasting, for a three-mile ride that should have taken ten minutes but was accomplished in five.

Just as we all have certain events we'll never forget, certainly one of mine was the moment when I heard the word "cancer" introduced into the diagnosis. I buttonholed her doctor, a somewhat flighty middle-aged woman, and with the leather gun belt squeaking, I told her I wanted the truth.

I was told it was only 'Stage Two'. and Mom could be cured without question with the right treatment and care. Somewhere in the background, the violins that one hears in special moments were replaced by a quartet of cash registers repeatedly sounding off.

Mom would get all the right treatment and care and be dead in seven months, but that was still in the future. Dad would fall deeper into the bottle, to the point where it would cost him his job.

So it all eventually fell to me to cover the expenses of both lost incomes, plus such necessities as were not covered in my mother's only-recently-secured Medicare coverage.

I could have begged for overtime or security work at the station, but as the "college boy" liaison officer, I had about as much chance of getting additional income as I had to become elected president for life in Paraguay.

With a diploma from correspondence school.

The other officers passed the hat, and I don't think they did so grudgingly, because regardless of who the cop is that's on the spot, the other cops will stand tall when needed. They came through with about $1500, and it did plug a few holes. They also did me a massive favor in alerting the local innkeepers *not* to grant my father a line of credit to feed his habit, and to send him home sober at all times.

Out of sheer desperation, I even took the Sergeant's exam, but the results would not be known for several months, as most of the local chiefs had nephews on the payroll, and nepotism (which soon was renamed "nephewism") was a year-round spectator sport. The officers who deserved promotion but watched the nephews get it were the spectators.

Unbeknownst to me for several years, my mother had sold her coin collection. Knowing what I did about the buying and pricing habits of card dealers, years afterward, I would sit down and go through her checkbook register and note unusual or unaccounted for deposits. The results of my investigation, as we would say in police parlance, were that she could not have gotten much for them.

I knew I had to carry the ball. After Mom's first two-week stay at the hospital, my next pay check, when divided into necessary components, allowed me to hit $20,000 in my "down payment for house account," which I was quite proud of, but equally aware that it was going to go to health-care providers and not to a realtor.

Beyond that, what? I had no 401k, and I was only 30, so I had my clothes, my guitars, a low-end Firebird, and my cards. Again relying on what I knew about card dealers, I knew that the cards had value—but value that I would not see from them.

By that times, "values" were available through "price guides," which were self-serving, greedy economic engines invented by the card dealers union, or something similar. And the prices in the price guides were accepted as Holy Writ with no less swiftness than that of Adolf Hitler's word becoming law after 1933 in Germany.

It had become impossible to get reasonable prices because of "the book." If "the book" said a card was worth three bucks, that was the price, period. Condition was taken into account, so that the three-buck figure would have been for a "mint" card, and any imperfection would cut the price in half. If you tried to sell to a dealer, your cards *naturally* had imperfections, so you got half of the value of the imperfect sale price, or seventy-five cents.

I knew that would not pay for any major surgery....

I made a mental inventory of what I had, perhaps imagining that it was in better condition than it really was, and estimated that between the cards—recalling the 1953 set with a truly perfect Mantle, unlike my own dog-eared Mantles, plus Harry's football cards, I could sell them at "shows" for about $9,000. Still, that involved selling all of them at one time, not over a period of months, and keeping myself fully reminded that $9,000, even in 1978, only covered "minor surgery."

Something which rarely cured cancer.

So I swallowed hard and tried to become a spare-time card dealer, to buy what I could and sell them at shows, at least until Mom was back on her feet and Dad was off the sauce, if either of those events were to come to pass. I put fliers in local supermarkets, and ran cheap ads in print media that reached the older folks who, with luck, would still have cards from earlier times. For all I knew, they flipped through their shoe-boxes while watching the Metamucil and mattress commercials on late night television.

In order to acquire inventory, I had advertised as a collector looking to add to my collection and not as a dealer, as their stock was sinking quickly in the public perception. Amazingly enough, I did get a good number of responses, albeit mixed.

One phone caller told me he had one million baseball cards and he wanted to sell them. Unfortunately, he was located just on the cutting edge of Newark, New Jersey, and it was not a place I looked forward to visiting with a pocketful of cash. I told the fellow (who sounded 18-ish) that I'd be happy to buy his cards if they were not items just dug out of the compost heap, but that I always paid by check. He was afraid he'd get beaten on the deal, but I reminded him that a bad check was jail time, adding that I had no fondness for jail.

I drove the thirty miles to discover that his "million" was closer to 400. He had one plastic milk carton, with the cards just thrown in—there could have been maybe 5,000 if they were stacked, but thrown in—next to nothing. I asked him to come out to my car—the Firebird, to see if there would be room for the collection if he sold it to me. He took one look and said, "Yeah, probably, I think."

Then I blasted him for dragging me sixty miles round trip for what was promised as a million cards but was really about 400. "There's a million in that box," he insisted.

"I tell you what. Let's count them, and for every card over 400—I'll give you $1, and I won't even take the cards. But for every card under a million, you give me a penny, okay?"

Suddenly his powers of estimation returned somewhat closer to reality, and I had a few parting comments for him, probably overdoing it, because if I had called him a mentally-deficient imbecile, I might have been closer to the truth than I knew.

And I would have been insulting the genuine imbeciles, who deserve better than this mathematically challenged clown. And some of them could probably count.

Not all of my ventures were that bad. On one call, a person actually did have a lot of cards from about 1954 to 1965, with that "11 year span" being the typical life of the collector who bought cards in the candy stores in packs, or perhaps inherited the initial five years from an older sibling.

It was a hot, humid day, and everyone, it seemed was belting out contemporary music on boom boxes. I didn't want to appear sweaty when I arrived, and luckily, the Firebird actually did have air conditioning.

This one-time collector was a good and decent fellow, and he had a lot of cards, with stars, a couple of umpires, and even checklists. He also had, in many instances, multiples of some cards—five Warren Spahns from one year, a half dozen Ernie Banks from another, and on it went.

When he met me at the door, he smiled, told me I must be Chris Decker, and that he'd be glad to show me his cards as long as I promised not to nit-pick the condition of each card. I swore an oath.

As I looked through the cards, they seemed very clean, although perhaps not "gem mint," as such things as centering, gloss of the original color, or a gum stain—as in from the slice of bubble gum—could devalue the card. I said to him that he needn't have made me promise not to nit-pick condition, but he quickly made me aware of *why* he had said that.

I sat back, put down the stack of cards in my hands, and pushed them safely out of harm's way as I took a couple of swigs on a can of Coke he'd provided.

"You weren't the first person I called," he began. "I saw an ad from a guy named Pete. Pete Rossi or Pete Russo—I don't remember and won't lose any time trying to remember. He marched in here like he was storming the beach at Anzio, but no sooner did he see the cards on the top of the piles than he started complaining about the condition. I knew they were not just like the day they came out of the packs, but they had not been unearthed by the dog, either. Yeah, I can't remember his last name—and I suspect he had shortened it from either an Italian or a Slavic last name that had been a lot longer. I mean this guy wanted to be important."

"I don't know that I've met him," I said, breaking into a grin.

"You'd remember if you did," he continued. "Guy looked like a wino, but claimed he bought cards every day with 'flash cash' as he called it. But he didn't even want to look through what I had—his time was too valuable, and he only bought 'gem mint' cards. He told me he was proud of the nickname he'd been given—Pete Perfect—and he was going to use it in all of his subsequent marketing ventures.

*Marketing ventures?* I thought to myself. "Well, the guy looked like a derelict and I was glad he left in haste."

I then interrupted to describe the person I had, for want of a better word, 'observed' months earlier at Ray's boutique, bragging he'd put together a complete set of black-backs.

"That's the guy," he said. "Yeah, Pete Perfect. I doubt the guy knows what a library is."

I told him I was a collector and not a purist, as some besides Pete Perfect were, and that I'd be glad to take some of his cards, but I wasn't sure I needed five Warren Spahns, et al.

He was just glad, I guess, to find a buyer who didn't stink up the house, so he told me he was hoping to get $300 for all of what was there, and would I be able to do that? I told him I could, and I did, knowing there was certainly much more than that in card-show value.

Assuming I could find someone with a serious letch for Warren Spahn. I'd have to pitch Spahn's ability—no pun intended, as after all, he won twenty games after he turned 40 and pitched over 300 complete games. I seemed to remember an extra-inning duel between Spahn and a far more youthful Juan Marichal in about 1962, and the Giants were going to hook their starter in about the 13th inning, but Marichal complained that if a forty-year-old could still be out there, so could he, in his early 20s.

Great story, kid. *Buy the Spahn.*

Once again, the asking price was somewhere near $300, but I gave him $500, in the hope that he'd feel better served, and who knew if he had friends with cards in their attics?

Subsequently, a dichotomy involving what could have been brothers, not friends, was the last memorable trip, at least for a while. I drove about 15 miles on a cold, rainy night in December, and had plastic garbage bags with me, on the assumption I'd be buying the cards that I'd been called about. The site was a high-rise close enough to the Hudson River to get a good view of Manhattan, and although I don't like heights, I went up to the eighth floor, because after all, this was about baseball cards. I also knew from the weather that we would not be looking at them on the balcony. Even in summer, I would still not have been on that balcony.

After perfunctory greetings, the potential seller excused himself from the kitchen table and returned with three large shopping bags, and bless his heart, they were filled with cigar boxes. I would have paid good money just for those treasured old humidors.

The cards themselves were magnificent, and were a virtual subset of my childhood 1952—1960 cards; they were in good shape and there was a wealth of duplicates. There had to be six to eight thousand cards, and as I was flipping through them, I came upon a 1952 Topps Billy Hoeft. Hmmm. Don't remember that one. So I made some comment to the effect that I thought he was born on the same day as an uncle of mine, which allowed me to turn the card over. I didn't want to mention that Hoeft had served up a home run to Mantle in Briggs Stadium that was the first ever to reach the upper deck, a feat Mantle accomplished twice in 1952.

What I really wanted was to see the number, and my curiosity was rewarded, because the card was number 370. Anything above 310 was high value, and I had to scream silently that if I came upon the Mantle card, it would be a good thing if I did not scream out loud at that kitchen table.

I did come upon it, after a handful of commons, and somehow—perhaps cop training had something to do with my non-chalance—I sloughed it off. "Huh, another Mantle. Scratch common but I never got all of them."

I was really hypnotized by what he had put in front of me, and I knew that I did not have nearly enough money with me—or in my checking account—to make him a decent offer. Sadly, it never came to that, because just as I was becoming hypnotized in the process, he came to his senses, and before I even got to the second or third shopping bag, he told me, and somewhat bluntly, that seeing the cards again had made him realize that he wanted to keep them.

Period.

So I made a point of noting that I had trekked down to meet him *at his invitation*, to buy the cards, and here I was, miles from home on a lousy, cold, rainy night with nothing to show for my efforts.

Gallantly, he told me I could take one card for my troubles, if there was something in there I needed for my collection. I thought, he obviously does not know about cards, and I was obviously not going to educate him, although I did give him a tutorial. I spread out about five cards—the '53 Topps Satchel Paige, which was the only real card of that ego-centric wizard of the mound except for a couple of short-print issues from the late 40's; a shiny '54 Topps Mays, knowing full well that my host had confessed to being a National League fan and would not want to part with that card. The Billy Hoeft card, as I'd shown an interest in it, plus the high-number 1952 Mantle and Bill Dickey, whose card I already had. I mused over them briefly, and sort of pushed the Dickey away, saying it was too valuable to ask for, and I did the same with all but Mantle.

He wanted to know why Mantle was not so valuable. So I told him the truth, which, as things happened, had nothing to do with the value. Baseball cards are now, and were back then, printed in sheets of anywhere from 32, 64, 100, or 132 cards. In 1952, numbers 311 to 407 amounted to only 97 cards, but they were printed on sheets containing 100 cards, so three of the cards were double printed—Mantle, Jackie Robinson, and Bobby Thomson. I wanted to be vague on the third card, so I suggested it might have been Roy Campanella or Alvin Dark—both national leaguers along with Robinson and Thomson. So the Mantle was hardly as scarce as the Dickey or the Hoeft, and Willie and Satch were in leagues alone and not in the 1952 array.

I succeeded in driving down the value of the Mantle, although in doing so, I know I drove up my own blood pressure.

So, after a few starts and stalls, he gave me the Mantle, and as he did so, there was a serious crack of thunder and he told me I'd better beat it to my car before the storm got ugly—and before he changed his mind.

I got home safely with the treasure, but I was heavily disappointed that I had not had a chance to make an offer on all of them. It would have cost big money, but they were the best single collection I'd ever had a chance to purchase.

As it happened, he kept my phone number and called me years later to bitch me out for the Mantle card. He'd again given thought to selling his cards, and accordingly, he'd bought a price guide, and by then, Mickey was worth about $1500—to the person selling it to a hungry customer, not to someone selling it to a dealer. Que sera, sera.

But he was furious and he let me know it. I told him that the value was less than $100 when I took possession of the card, which he wanted back (fat chance), and I reminded him that he'd wanted to sell the cards and I drove through the rain, blah blah. He remained unimpressed.

And furious.

"Okay, then," I told him. "I'll come down and give you half of $1,500 for that card, which is what a retailer would pay, if you'll sell me the rest of the lot at half of the book value, which is what dealers pay for it, or I'll match any legitimate offer that you've had for the cards."

He wasn't interested; so I told him if he changed his mind, I'd still be around.

Backing up a bit: A week after I first got the Mantle card, a second person with the same last name as Mr. Furious called me with the same story—old cards, wanted to sell them. I had to allow for the possibility that someone wanted either his Mickey Mantle back or a slice of my hide, so I made the appointment, but took my service revolver along just in case.

It turned out not to be a set-up. This second guy, who truly could have been the brother of the first, though I was damn sure not about to ask, had virtually the same cards as the first group—1952 to 1959, excellent condition, and lots of stars and doubles. More to the point, I took mental inventory, and there were 74 of the 97 1952 Topps "high numbers," although there was no Mantle there. I figured the first guy—if he actually was a sibling—cheated his little brother out of it.

I had goose flesh as I went through those 74 beauties, which, by scarcity, dwarfed the "star" cards that were plentiful. Finally, I said, "Great stuff—how much?"

He told me he needed four new tires and wanted to take his wife to dinner, so it would cost me the sum of $355. I had some big bills and gave him $350 and he was good with that. I would have forked over $400, but he might have thought that he was asking way too little; which he was.

I don't think I slept that night. I read the back of every one of those 74 high number cards, and then catalogued my purchase against the book value, which totaled something between five and six thousand dollars *then*, and close to or above a hundred grand if I decided to keep them for a decade or two.

But Mom needed help, although she refused every offer, and I did not feel particularly good about taking advantage of the uninitiated; so I sold the stuff off as quickly as I could, making far less profit than patience would have provided, but time was short and funds were needed.

And I damn sure did not want to feel like Pete Perfect when I looked at myself in the mirror. That was the instant worst-case scenario, and I stopped advertising after that and tended to my "liaison" cop job and other family necessities.

If nothing else, I'd learned that the cards would always be there.

My mother and father, essentially the entire remainder of my family, were another matter altogether.

# And The Beat Goes On

In retrospect, there came a time when everyone would say that Mr. Pete Perfect had ruined the "hobby" of card collecting. His repeated brusque dismissals of any card that had any imperfection—slightly off center, a "soft corner," whatever *that* is—those curt dismissals meant that only perfect cards had any value and that only he had the perfect cards.

That translated into a nightmare for hobbyists, because many were, by the mid 1980s, the same people who had owned the runs of post World War II cards, which began in 1948 but really went into high gear when the larger sets of 1950 and after were produced. So a ten-year-old in 1948, having perhaps seen Dad or Uncle Roy serve in World War II, could have collected the 48-card black-and-white Bowman set of that year with ease. But by 1985, that one-time lad was now 47 years old, desperately hungry for the nostalgia of youth, but hopelessly shackled to a mortgage, car payments, dental debts for children's braces, paying for or saving for college costs, or possibly all of the above.

I don't know how many times I was at a baseball card event and watched as hobbyists (admittedly now a dwindling breed) would approach a dealer to sell their cards to pay the kinds of debts cited above, only to walk away without a penny.

That came about because of several factors: the cards, in most cases, were not perfect. After all, who among us treated our childhood cardboard as if it were the Shroud of Turin?

A second factor was a very poor example of the law of supply and demand. No matter what card you had to sell (unless it was truly scarce and always *in* demand—the '52 Mantle, the '54 sketch of Ted Williams, or rookie cards from the era—Mantle, Mays, Banks, Kaline, Aaron, Koufax, or Clemente), you were told there was no demand for it. And logic had nothing to do with it. If you had, for instance, the full run of Willie Mays, 1951—1955, which included four years of Topps and Bowman, the now vanished competition, you would be told either that, well, the condition was okay but not perfect, but more likely that Willie Mays just wasn't selling right now.

That was because the dealer much preferred to get the cards from some octogenarian who would unknowingly part with them for peanuts. So when you learned that Mays was not selling well, you would point out to the dealer that he had all seven of those cards in his display cases, and the sale prices totaled well over $1,000.

"Yeah, but I can't give the damn things away."

At that point, in any other business, there would have occurred what was known in the world of retail as a "markdown," a marketing technique which dictated that when you could not sell an item for a certain price, you had to lower the price or keep the item expensively priced and hope it came back in vogue in the distant future.

Baseball card dealers did not believe in mark-downs until the competition became so cut-throat that they had no choice. Either way, however, they would find a way to either discourage you from trying to sell to them, or else they'd offer you chump change and try to convince you that they were doing you a favor.

And that scenario was all too regular when you were in the star-card category. If you tried to sell a stack of cards that included Jim Delsing, Don Bollweg, Dick Kokos, Hank Majeski, and Mickey Grasso, to name a few individuals that ultimately went to their graves knowing that they had played for years in "the bigs," at salaries of $6,000 per year (if that), but they did so partly because it beat delivering mail or being a lumberjack, and then, of course, there was also the love of the game. Add to that the job they worked between the end of the season and Spring Training.

But they weren't super-stars.

They were "commons," and unless they were better centered or still had more of the original gloss than cards bought and sold by Peter Perfect, they had no value at all.

None whatsoever. Well, they had had value when you bought them, but if you tried to unload them, you had to spice up the deck with some future Hall of Fame luminaries or you were out of luck.

Peter Perfect had left his impress on what had been a hobby, and other dealers, jealous of P.P.'s success, tried to emulate him. But they could not simply be PP knockoffs; they had to have a similar but somehow unique angle of their own: they only traded in one year's cards by one of the two companies; they only dealt in cards from one or more specific teams (allowing for the very real possibility that some dealers hit skid row after attempting to make a living marketing only the cards of, for instance, the Philadelphia/Kansas City Athletics).

Try as I might, I can't run through a lot of years when that team did not feature any stars beyond the abilities of the former Yankees they dumped, and that was not going to keep the bill collectors at bay for very long.

Other dealers went out of the mainstream and only bought and sold cards from an era that my father could not have remembered, as baseball cards and stickers had existed from 1887, and were reborn once after the turn of the century and again in the mid-1930s.

Others simply abandoned the dead area of baseball cards and went into either football, basketball, golf, et al, or "non-sports," which featured movie hits that became fads (Davy Crockett cards), or the patriotic runs ("the Red Menace"), or just foibles of the emerging modern era. Eventually, every movie that got noticed, and even some television shows—*Gunsmoke*, for example, had their own card items. *How could they have missed Lawrence Welk and the lovely Lennon sisters?*

While I was troubled by what the hobby had turned into, there were a few dealers who simply took their lifelong accumulation of cards to shows and priced them to sell. Their cards, in the retail sense, had cost nothing, as they'd been acquired long ago, and now were marketable. I always found those dealers to be the most generous as well as the most friendly to talk sports with.

The majority—not those cited immediately above—only wanted to talk about my money and how it could become their money. Pete Perfect, having struck gold, only wanted to talk about *his money*, and he became such a totally obnoxious parvenu that a joke circulated that you could purchase "Pete Perfect insurance." What the gag boiled down to was that if you "bought the insurance," and were in proximity to him when he was throwing *his* money around, and you accidentally got hit by wads of cash, you would collect on the policy.

I'm certain he heard about this and it only fed his money-driven ego. After all, there were some among us, Chris Decker included, who could remember when "Pete" was a derelict trying to piece together fragments of something in order to go onto something bigger. To say that money went to Pete Perfect's head would be correct phraseology, because his portrait—easily confused with the stereotyped future Arab terrorist—would soon begin to appear in all the hobby magazines, and it was always his mug and large letters announcing "Cash for your treasures," and promises that he would make *you wealthy*. If, of course, your card is 'perfect.'

Business only became more and more cut-throat, and it took its toll. The "booth" where I first went to see the old cards became a large retail area in a mall, but the two entrepreneurs running that outfit realized that the word had gotten out and people were not giving cards away any more, so they went into selling sports t-shirts, floor mats, thematic clocks, notebooks, garbage cans—anything that could carry a sports logo. They were soon out of the card business.

Harry, who'd sold me his football cards, died, as noted earlier, of a broken heart. Roy, who had always run a sloppy collectible boutique, had some success, but he translated it into drug abuse and he went downhill.

The turnover was not a thing of joy to behold from a distance, and it made me glad I'd stayed in cop work and hadn't jumped into collectibles with both feet.

Eventually, "peripherals" caught on, because some dealers/marketing experts realized they could not compete in the card market, and so they began selling plastic pages and binders in which collections would be kept, or individual card-holders for prized cardboard. Those dealers would also carry the latest "hobby magazines," although the hobby was no longer truly a hobby. When you start printing competing price guides, "hobby" quickly becomes business. T-shirts, mugs, and key chains appeared, featuring images of the more famous cards, no doubt to the copyright chagrin of the companies that had marketed the cards. And once again, the 1952 "iconic" Mickey Mantle card graced the most mugs and key chains.

By the early- to mid-1980s, new companies had entered the card fray, although not without a fight from Topps, the original, early '50s monster company. Because they signed players for their photos, they sued the newly founded companies for contract infringement, or any number of other phrases that lawyers use to say, "It's mine and you can't have it."

Eventually, a federal court ruled that since the mega-company had sold cards in order to market gum, the other, emerging card companies could sell cards, but could not sell them to market gum. Collectors didn't much care, because the gum stained the cards it touched, decreasing the value. And if you bought an old box of cards, with gum, and opened the packs, you experienced a sensation you could not have predicted: the precious pink slab dissolved to nothing on your tongue almost instantly.

Your hopes also probably vanished just as quickly, because it soon became very expensive to purchase an unopened pack from earlier days. If you paid serious money and got a Mantle, you won the lottery. If you paid serious money and got a handful of commons, you were the proud owner of the most expensive nobodies in the collecting hobby. But, at least they were in good condition, even if your bank account was not.

The final change that came about in the mid-80s was the marketing of autographs. In the late 1970s, as I've mentioned, card-show organizers would get a couple of local ball players, and for your $2 admission, you got free autographs. Additional signatures if the player was friendly and you treated them with respect, as opposed to providing them with reminders of their worst days.

Now, the price at the door went up, sometimes to as much as $15, if it was a large collection of dealers, and the promoters paid players to show up from beyond local neighborhoods, and charged according to the players' ability to command respect. I can still recall seeing Cal Abrams and Dusty Rhodes, side by side, getting $2 for their signatures. $1 went to the promoter, and the other $1 went into their respective pockets—literally. Here were two boyhood idols, Abrams with the Dodgers and Dusty Rhodes, 1954 Giants hero, putting dollar bills in their coat pockets. My cardboard wept...

Down the hall, in a private room sequestered from public view, Joe DiMaggio was signing for $6, and tickets were sold for those signatures, as there was not going to be any pocketing of small bills by the ever-gracious Joltin' Joe.

That was a day in collecting I'll never forget. I arrived at the venue to get my DiMaggio "tickets" at 8 a.m., and the tickets I bought were redeemable at between 2:00 and 2:30 p.m. *Six hours later.* So, I wandered around, took notice of Pete Perfect and almost lost my breakfast, and added a few cards to my collection.

But there were no real bargains to be had that day, because the dealers quickly realized that Joe D. was the main attraction, and he'd sell more autograph tickets than they would sell cards, so they had to keep the prices high to pay for their table space.

That marketing strategy would become an ongoing nightmare as "the hobby" continued to develop. On rare occasion, however, dealers would dump their products to make a killing. *Luck, be a lady...*

For my $18 investment—three tickets at $6 each, I was hoping to get a signed photo, a signed card from 1941, and, as an oddity, a signed record label of the 45 r.p.m. record, "Mrs. Robinson," by Paul Simon and Art Garfunkel. I thought the "Where have you gone, Joe DiMaggio?" signed record would be a nice oddity for a collection.

As things happened, the man two spaces in front of me at 2:20 p.m. spread out the *Playboy* centerfold photo of Marilyn Monroe, hoping Joe D. would sign it, but it was not to be. Joe D. turned red as a rose and the offending autograph seeker was thrown through the door by the goons who guarded the superstar. I put Simon and Garfunkel away and settled for three more ordinary signatures.

DiMaggio quickly regained his composure, and when I got to him, I told him I had had the privilege of watching him play.

"That is not possible, young man."

I told him that my parents had gone to a Yankee game and took their three year-old son—me—and that with the Yanks ahead by one run in the top of the ninth with one out and a man on third, an opposing player lofted a routine fly to center. DiMaggio thought his catch was the last out of the game and relaxed. But it was only the second out; and the runner scored easily, tying the game, while Joe trotted toward the dugout with his head down. Joe D. then led off the bottom of the ninth and calmly put one in the seats to end it. When I finished my recollection (which I only knew from my father telling me about it often), DiMag said, "Yes, young man, you did see me play. Thank you for sharing that memory."

And $18.

And if that seemed like a lot, it was only the beginning. It would not be long before Mickey Mantle would be charging $90, and prices for an in-person autograph eventually went into the hundreds of dollars.

The same signature, affixed to a ball, bat, or jersey, would be $10 or $15 more, and an inscription ("To Chris, an obnoxious cop who doesn't want to pay for his name") cost an additional $25. *And up.*

If there was a way to milk pocket change out of collectors, the dealers would find it—if the promoters, the real villains of the piece, had not found it first.

But that would come to pass only after Pete Perfect had retired and gone to his maker.

# Pete Perfect: Who Says Crime Doesn't Pay?

By the mid-to-late 1980s and the early 1990s, virtually everything had changed in the sports memorabilia world, and the change was not always for the good—at least not for the basic collector of childhood memories such as myself.

It was no longer just a paradise of nostalgic old baseball cards. Now, it was anything old, or anything that could pass for old, as long as one understood that dealers considered "old" to mean the day before yesterday if they were selling it. If you were selling it to them, it needed to be autographed by Tutankhamen.

New companies were coming on the market to sell cards, and while the greed factor, sell, sell, sell, remained constant, the laws of supply and demand were in play also. With several major companies producing cards, the company that produced the lowest output would have the most valuable cards, simply because there were fewer of them. So the 1984 Donruss Don Mattingly rookie card was more valuable than the 1984 Fleer or 1984 Topps Don Mattingly "rookie," even though Mattingly was, for baseball card purposes, a rookie in all three seasons—1984, 1984, and, of course, 1984.

"Book price" continued to be a nightmare, as the dealers created the book price. I didn't know offhand of any other industry where the insiders themselves created the value coefficients. I know damn well that local cops such as I was at that time did not set "our price" and then demand it from the local towns and municipalities because, after all, it was the "book price."

I long ago lost count as to how many times I asked about a particular card on display—not priced, of course, but when I asked the price, the dealer pulled out the price guide. "If you even open that magazine," I'd say, "I'm leaving. You know what you paid for it, and you know what it is worth; please just quote a price and either I'll take it or leave it."

Another equally unpleasant exchange would begin when the dealer would say, "The book says…" I would ask to see the book, and hold it to my ear, and comment, "I don't hear it saying anything, actually."

Or: "It's fifteen bucks in the book." I'd take out my discretionary cash and note that there was a lot more than fifteen in my hand, but if he was willing to settle for the money that was in the book, meaning, of course, that the only cash was mine and the only "book" was his.

Or: "I paid full book for it, so…" That meant I was supposed to believe that he bought it for the dealer/selling price instead of the dealer/I'm doing you a favor price, and that I should prepare myself for a price higher than the book suggested.

A classic example, but one that is typical, presented itself in 1991, toward the end of Don Mattingly's career. A dealer had a plastic box with about twenty Topps "Mattingly rookies" as noted above, meaning it was not the really valuable but less produced Donruss Mattingly rookie. I always loved that Topps card, #8, and had a few of them. He was asking $6 each, so I asked how much for the whole box.

The dealer took out a calculator and multiplied 20 times $6, which an infant could do, and announced $120. I shrugged my shoulders and started to walk away. "It's $15 in the book," he noted.

"Then sell it to the friggin' book," I suggested, perhaps not using those exact words. Before I walked fifty feet, however, I stopped at a table that had been slightly sheltered by a sizable column that held up the hall. That dealer had about 250 cardboard boxes for sale, loaded with cards, at $4 per box. Five of the boxes were the complete set of 1984 cards that had the "$15" Mattingly rookie. I wound up buying about 100 of his boxes, and I needed a flat rolling dolly to move my purchase, and as I wheeled it past the "book" Mattingly dealer, I told him it was amazing how much business a person could do if they didn't bother with trifles like artificially-inflated "book prices."

I knew I didn't make friends that way, but I didn't care, because my ultimate gripe was that the dealers were brainwashing every kid that the book price was the gospel according to people like Pete Perfect; and because an entire generation that didn't know better had gotten hooked, my generation suffered too. I should add that dealers had no problem whatsoever robbing kids blind with horse manure stories about cards or "possible finds." A dealer would have a number of open boxes on display, containing packs still sealed. The unopened pack could cost anywhere from $1 to maybe $10, and if you did the math, with 36 packs per box, the separate pack yield would always have been far greater than if you just bought the box. But the dealers would tell the young kids, "Yeah, just put that box out today and there have already been two [name of player on best card] taken out of there."

The traditional card boxes then held 36 packs, with 15 cards per pack, for a total of 540 cards per box. But the sets of those cards, depending on the manufacturer, ran from 660 to 792, so there was the very real possibility of not getting any star cards, or maybe one. Two would be a stretch and the prospect of three... well, study up on probability.

And they were shameless about it. A dealer would say to a kid, "You could find a star in there, and it's worth $25." When I heard that, I'd look right at the dealer, as I took out some cash, and ask him, "If that kid or I find that card, I take it to mean you'll give us $25."

Things tended to get quiet that way. But it had become a dog-eat-dog competition, and one dealer would be selling a certain year's packs for $8, while the dealer right next to him would be selling the whole box—all 36 packs, for $30. And when it came to the expensive packs, don't think for a minute that there were not dealers who would open the packs carefully, examine the contents for the good cards, and carefully re-seal the packs.

Happened all the time.

So, while the card companies dueled with each other for the market share, there also developed a market for autographs, jerseys or anything similar, like boxing gloves belonging to well-known fighters, posters relating to past sporting events, seats from stadiums torn down, pieces of dirt or bricks from past stadiums—anything that related to sports (and occasional non-sports) was now on the market.

And the ball, so to speak, was always in the dealers' court. Whatever a collector had to sell, unless it could truly fetch a good price, was not worth the trouble to even look at, but dealers' recently acquired "stuff" was always of the highest value.

The worst manner of fraud occurred in the "high value" department because dealers literally conspired to drive prices up once they had items whose value they would want to enhance.

The two benchmark cards at that time—1990—and they would pretty much remain that way, were the 1910 Honus Wagner tobacco card—scarce because Wagner allegedly had it pulled because he did not smoke, and the 1952 Topps Mantle. Runner-ups were a card of Napoleon Lajoie and Eddie Plank, arguably more valuable if only supply and demand were at stake, but popularity was always a concern.

So as dealers "A" and "B," and Pete Perfect would be a natural in this category (although I could never absolutely prove he was a party to such a thing), had a stack of high value cards, dealer "A" would hold an auction of one each of his valued holdings, and dealer "B" would buy the offering at an outrageously high price. That would drive all prices on all such cards up, and the two dealers, who never exchanged either cards or cash, would reap the inflationary whirlwind.

In that way, the Honus Wagner card suddenly commanded a whopping $200,000, and Mantle sold for anywhere between $40,000 or $80,000, depending on who was telling the story, second-hand, about the price at the bogus auction cited above.

And foolish card collectors loved the swindle, because they figured all of a sudden their 1954 Vic Power cards would pay off the mortgages on their houses.

All it really meant was that the really hot cards were suddenly inflated, and if you saw a '52 Topps Mantle looking like a dog had chewed it, the price was still $2,000 or perhaps more "because a really nice one sells for $80,000."

Greed, thy name is sports memorabilia...

A market even developed for unopened packs of "old" cards, which caused people to buy a candy-store box of 1984 cards, for example, which might have Don Mattingly and Darryl Strawberry's rookie cards, at $.30 a pack, or $10.80 for the box, and put them away, with other boxes, and hope they would have value at some point in the future.

In most cases, they would and did have value in the future, but usually only if the buyer left them unopened and hoped that they would gain in value with the passage of time—while praying that inflation did not totally deflate the increase in price. But if the unopened box did gain serious value, it could never be opened. The 540-card box might sell for $150, but a complete, 792 card set of the same items would go for $60. *Hah?*

Unvisited cardboard was becoming a generational thing, and I admit that I bought my share of "unopened stuff" and kept them and made a few dimes down the road.

But the real treasures were genuinely *old* unopened stuff, and if you could get your hands on that, you could be looking at a king's ransom. Of course, they had to be marketed as still unopened (and, as noted, some dealers knew how to open them, search them, and re-seal them), and it also became a study in "might have a 'so-and-so' rookie card"), although the odds were vastly against that.

And the older the unopened packs, the greater the value. By the late 1980's, the $100 Mickey Mantle from 1952 that I'd first seen in 1952 but not again until 1975 was now commanding thousands of dollars—many thousands *if mint,* so an unopened pack of 1952's would routinely be offered for sale at somewhere between $1,000 and $1,500, with the advertising hook of "Possible Mantle Rookie."

Of course, there were five or six cards in that pack and that 1952 set had 407 cards, so the odds began at 6 out of 407, but were magnified by the fact that cards numbered 311 through 407 were scarce to begin with.

So, $1,200 might get you a Mantle rookie, although I personally never heard of it happening, although I feel confident that some pedestrian got his picture in a sports magazine for "pulling" a mint '52 Mantle, while the truth was that he was paid to be photographed. But it drove up the price on unopened packs, and it became a mania as bad—and as costly—as Las Vegas.

The greater likelihood was that the $1,500 pack might get you Connie Ryan, Freddie Marsh, Sam Mele, Mickey Vernon, Fred Hutchinson, and Billie Pierce, which, because they should have been mint, would be worth about $25 per card—still a long way from your initial outlay. And it is equally true that any dealer who came into a skid of unopened packs made certain that they contained cards below number 311. An unopened pack, if known to contain numbers 311 through 407 would easily have commanded ten grand, and even at that price, there would have been a feeding frenzy.

I should note for the reader's benefit that those 1952 Topps high numbers became scarce because of the basic economics of 1952. Baseball cards were sold in candy stores, which I doubt even exist any more, or convenience stores. But the proprietors did not know the contents of the packs any more than they knew how many dead fleas were in cheap hot dogs. So, the candy store owner would check his baseball card inventory in late July, 1952, and tell the vendor he didn't need any more baseball cards for that year. As a result, Topps did not get many of the later-in-the-year 1952s to the market, and they lingered in a warehouse. Lingered, that is, until the space was needed and someone put tens of thousands of those rare cards on a barge and dumped them somewhere usually referred to as New York Harbor.

Notwithstanding that tragic loss, it was in the unopened pack market that Pete Perfect made his first big "find" as he called it, and because he made a small fortune on it, the competition in that regard became intense, although Mr. Perfect had crossed the line of honest ethics and made a lot of enemies.

Pete was at a card show that I attended, so it had to be on the East Coast somewhere, most likely Atlantic City. His booth adjoined another well-known dealer who had an ahead-of-its-time portable phone --an item that Pete coveted, and his subsequent ownership of it would be a huge factor in his eventual demise.

On the final day of the weekend show, a call came in to the owner of the high-tech phone, which, with all his cash, Pete Perfect would quickly emulate. But on this day, all Pete could do was listen to one side of the conversation.

I'm using police instincts to attempt to re-create half of the conversation, but I think my estimate is reasonably accurate.

"Yes, this is so-and-so, and yes, I do buy and sell old baseball cards. Are you looking to buy or sell?"

"Uh huh. Can you give me an idea of what you have?"

"Oh. Are any of them opened?"

"Uh huh. Wow! That must have been great, with your parents operating a candy store back in the early 1950s.

Yeah, a Yogi Berra, a Willie Mays....what color is the Mays? Oh, purple. Okay. What else?

I think I know what the Mickey Mantle looks like. Do you have one of those? Yes, I'll hold while you look. ... You do? Uh huh, blue with him holding a bat over his shoulder. *My God, it's a '52.* And you say there are unopened packs? Oh, you only opened a few to see what was in them. How many packs are there? Thirty-seven full boxes of packs? *Holy shit.* And you have a lot of unopened boxes from other years? Well, yeah, I'd be interested. Okay, give me the address. Uh huh, 228 Fulton Street, Mishawaka, Indiana, oh, okay, next to Notre Dame in South Bend. Okay. Well, I'll get there as soon as I can because I'd like to make you a decent offer for your cards, because let's face it, I can only sell cards like that if I can buy them from good folks like you, as they don't make those cards after the year they were in your parents' store. Uh huh. Yes. Thank you so much. Yes, see you soon."

The dealer did his very best to contain himself, as just with the 1952s that were cited, thirty-seven boxes meant hundreds of unopened packs, which meant over 5,000 cards, and if there was one Mantle, there could be ten. And logic dictated that what had been left behind in his parents' candy store were the end-of-the-year cards: The high numbers.

A calculator was exploding in his head.

In the adjacent booth, Pete Perfect was much more in control. He had heard the address and walked to the far end of his retail space and wrote it down. A few minutes later, he told his sales assistant, "Listen, this show is all but over. I'm going to get a few sandwiches. Why don't you close up and we'll eat before going home."

Then, as an added touch, Pete asked the dealer with the hot prospect, "Can I get you a sandwich—the usual tuna melt? I've made about as much as I could here and I want to get home a little early."

The tuna melt was duly agreed upon, but it never arrived.

Pete Perfect went out the door, grabbed a taxi to Atlantic City Airport and paid a then-unheard-of price of $850 to charter a plane to Mishawaka, Indiana.

Upon arriving, he cooled his heels for a couple of hours, but reached the address near 10 p.m. It was a typical middle-class bungalow for the 1980s in Indiana, complete with a swing on the porch and children's toys in the side yard. Pete pegged it to be worth in the neighborhood of forty grand, and calculated his anticipated offer accordingly—but based on the original overhearing of half a conversation.

"Hi. You called me today about baseball cards?"

"Yes, but I didn't think you would...."

"Get here quickly? Why not? You sounded like you wanted to

sell your cards and I made a little money at the show I was at, so I thought we could both make some money today."

The Indiana resident bought the charade and had no reason to suspect anything, so he did not call the original number a second time. He led Pete Perfect into a high and dry storage room, where over 3,000 boxes of unopened cards held over 72,000 *gem mint* packs (450,000 cards) from 1950 to 1959. The previous estimate had been a tad understated...

Pete Perfect took out what he pretended was all the money from his wallet, his pockets, and his briefcase, counting it out as he went. It came to $24,276, and he said, "It's all I've got, but it's yours if you want to sell the cards. I'm keeping a hundred bucks to get home on."

The seller looked at him with a very questioning visage, and Mr. Perfect was not sure if the offer was way too high or way too low. Then the seller said, "You must love them old cards."

"Yeah," Pete said. "My wife has to work because I love them so much, but she understands, and it is better to be collecting cards than gambling debts, so...."

For $24,276, which was a fraction of what Pete had with him, he bought about $7,000,000 worth of inventory, including a stack of the 1952 Mantles, already opened. He sold those alone for much more than his investment, cab ride and plane costs included. He would later boast that he sold the already-opened Mantles for almost half a million.

And he earned the hatred, distrust, and loathing of not only the dealer who should have had the chance to buy the cards, but of everyone who learned of the dirty deal.

From that point onward, Pete Perfect had to change his routine; he didn't rent booths as such, but rather served as the "official greeter" at the larger shows, so that the sponsors would have to put up with him, as his greetings included a plastic bag with cheap junk in it, but with the obligatory reminder that he was Pete Perfect and he would pay top dollar for mint cards.

A year or two later, with the cash from his "find" growing, he took more ads in sports publications and became a household name—at least for collectors who did not know about his Mishawaka perfidy. He laid out wads of cash and got mint cards in return.

He even got a couple of phone calls not unlike the one that made him super-wealthy at a time when $3 million was super wealth. Eventually, he was written up in top sports magazines with the man with the cash for cards.

Pete Perfect had made the ultimate investment deal; he could not have known that it would turn into a pact with the Devil.

And not one that favored *him.* The Devil was the odds-on favorite.

# Book Two
## The Mickey Mantle Murder

# Murder Will Out

*Murder will out, certain, it will not fail.*
– Geoffrey Chaucer

It may seem incongruous, even for a police officer, to mix baseball cards with murder, as the former is the safe haven of the fantasies of youth and the latter is the all-too-real terror of one's adult years.

In the course of what follows, I would point out that incongruity as if I had hit upon a law of physics that Sir Isaac Newton had overlooked, until my syllogism fell apart. A close friend, discussing the events that will follow, found nothing incongruous about the simplicity of baseball cards, memorabilia and nostalgia and the point-counterpoint complexity of murder.

"When we were kids, who taught us everything that was evil and to be avoided?"

I pondered briefly.

"Nuns," he said, as if uttering a toilet-worthy oath.

Point taken.

But that was all in the future, as I was otherwise busy on Monday, March 9, 1992. For those who do not believe in coincidences, please recall that my re-introduction to baseball cards in 1975 happened following a violently fatal traffic accident when I was viewing a very peaceful yet very dead child.

There was another accident on March 9, 1992, almost seventeen years after the noted photo, but this one did not get me into the newspaper.

Not immediately, at least.

Late that evening, a bright yellow Camaro, heavy with horsepower, had hit a utility pole near the high school located in Hamlet, but luckily, the youthful, drunken occupants of the vehicle were swerving slowly enough to survive. Still, it was messy, because the oldest of the five occupants in the car was fifteen years old—way too young to be driving legally, and he was drunk on his ass.

The crash caused enough liquor bottles to break that the interior of the vehicle reeked of Johnny Walker—and I confess to never being able to recognize the difference in smell between Johnny Walker Red or Johnny Walker Black. Maybe I'm color-smell blind....

That, however, would be the least of the problems when the legal system kicked in. The two under-age males in the front seat had been protected by air bags, and suffered only slight burns when the bags deployed.

The three in the back seat, two thoroughly naked young girls and one almost-naked boy—remember, this is March 9th in New Jersey with the temperature hovering in the forties as it was a cloudless night—had all apparently pitched forward and hit the front seat on impact, but being drunk, they didn't have the reactive ability to stiffen and suffer. The boy, I suspected, was already stiffened, but that was his problem.

The first officer on the scene, just before midnight, immediately made the decision that county officers should be called in, because of the age of the individuals in the car, and because one of them, despite being shouted his Miranda warnings, kept insisting that "the adults at the party" had given them the liquor and the car keys.

I was off duty, doing what best could be described as "nothing special," but because I was liaison to the various other law enforcement offices, I was immediately called in to translate Hamlet-speak for the big boys who had red stripes on their uniform trousers.

The good news was that none of the injuries were in any way serious, but for precautionary reasons, all five adolescents (allowing for the fact that they may have entered adulthood as the car hit the pole) were taken to a local hospital and a local or a county officer escorted each one. Two of the youths went in each of two EMT wagons—the two young ladies in one, to be segregated and covered in blankets, and two boys in the second EMT wagon, and the Camaro's driver in an ambulance. By 1992, ambulances had been considered anachronisms in some geographical locations, but a neighboring town had kept its ambulance, just in case.

That night was the "case."

Isolating the young driver was a form of "punctuation" to let him know that in the scenario in front of us, he was, well, different, unique, stand-outish, and in deep feces for being the driver.

I had the good fortune to go with him, and we were the first to leave the scene, as it was feared that locals would arrive and mistreat the miscreant. He was largely incoherent, and if it had not been tragic, it would have been almost funny, as he was lying on a gurney, closely attended by an EMT technician, but insisting that he should be driving.

Whoever said that youth is wasted on the young had the wisdom of Confucius.

Because I was the first to leave, I was not on the scene to prevent the remaining officers from calling in the license plate. It was hardly necessary at that moment, as there were no next-of-kin to be notified because of a fatal crash, and it's always dangerous to put information on the air, because a police radio can be overheard by anyone owning a very legal "scanner." Beyond that, the car was about to be towed to the police impound garage and the ownership could easily have been determined by looking for documents in the glove compartment.

Apparently, nobody wanted to do that without a search warrant, even though the glove compartment had popped open with the passenger side air bag deployment, and the officers cleaning up the air bag mess probably had to move the vehicle's documents, as papers were as widely scattered as the alcoholic detritus.

The chief of the county officers, after consultation with the state police captain *and* the governor of New Jersey, alerted us to the decision that the adolescents, assuming there were no serious injuries, were nevertheless to be confined in the hospital "for observation."

That was a polite euphemism for "they all have wealthy parents and we do not want to be putting them in jail cells, at least not until they are sober and perhaps because Mommy and Daddy are big-time political contributors." Or so it was initially feared. If they'd thought a moment about who owned the yellow street machine, things might have immediately taken a different turn. But it was a mild crisis, and thought briefly left the scene of the crime.

Accordingly, once they were pronounced "fit" at the hospital, although not yet dried out, they were handcuffed to the gurneys and officers stood watch at the door.

I had liaising to do, so I avoided that nightmare, which is a slight malapropism, because the sun was just coming up when I walked out of the hospital, giving occasional thought to how many times I could have been in a car full of teen-age drunks, but preferred to be in the car with my frequently drunken father. At least he had more practice at driving under the influence.

I did make one quick stop based on my previous knowledge of the yellow car, and pieces were exponentially added to the puzzle.

By the time I got back to headquarters, our local chief had come on duty—officially at least—and was sitting across from me in the detectives' squad room as I briefed him on events. The boredom of that routine was interrupted by our Dispatch officer, who cut-in to say that Pete Rizzoli's wife, a resident of Melrose, three miles away, was hysterical in their police station because her husband was AWOL.

"So, I should care about that because....?" the chief asked Dispatch.

"Her husband is that millionaire that buys and sells baseball cards," Dispatch told him.

"So, I should...."

"Decker would know a lot about him, and that is why Melrose called us."

The chief, a pointy-nosed little geek with florid cheeks and a swatch of prematurely white hair (cropped short, of course, as if he deeply admired Spencer Tracy) who could easily have been confused with a failed ambulance chasing lawyer, eyed me somewhat suspiciously, almost as if I was responsible for Mrs. Rizzoli's hysterics. I wasn't, of course, but at least now I knew Pete Perfect's real last name.

I also knew that the drunken kids were but the first inning of what was going to turn out to be a very long, drawn-out, doubleheader, and those suspicions were only compounded when I took a minute to reflect on the identity of the owner of the bright yellow muscle car in question.

# A Long Night's Journey into Day

As I stood in front of my locker at headquarters, the eyes that looked back at me from the mirror seemed clear enough, as the issues, at that moment, at least *seemed* clear enough.

Five kids had gotten smashed with adult permission, and an obnoxious memorabilia dealer had gone missing. It took about five seconds to hypothesize that the kids' issue would be a political football for a few hours and the other pompous clown would eventually show up with a blonde hottie on his arm. Page five today, well behind the weather report for tomorrow.

Still, it immediately suggested to me that I should put a call into the guys at the Melrose P.D. and ask them to give me a description of Mrs. Rizzoli. If he'd married her in his younger days, before he was "Pete Perfect", it clearly allowed for the possibility that her better years were behind her and that he'd gone out and just enjoyed the pleasures of the flesh for a bit longer than he should have, with someone whose best years were in front of her. And then it would be back to the ever-too-familiar lady waiting at home.

The adolescents were the immediate concern, as they were the responsibility of our department, plus such help as we would get from county officers or the New Jersey State Police. I'm not bragging when I say we did not need them in the least to deal with the mess, but their name recognition would come in handy when it came time to cleaning up the event legally.

After all, they weren't local flatfoots who wrote parking tickets or handcuffed jay-walkers. These were the guys... well, for the most part, guys, who dealt with pedophile priests, corporate murders in the even-more-affluent towns, and things like the Lindbergh baby kidnapping.

I had to remind myself that nobody who was going to deal with the five drunken kids was going to be mindful of Charles Lindbergh or Bruno Hauptmann, who was either slam-dunk guilty or a poor innocent slob who had been framed because *somebody* had to be rounded up.

For the briefest of moments, the thought coursed through my head that of all the non-sports card issues that had made it onto trading cards, the Lindbergh kidnapping was one that had not. Geez, that could have outsold "My Little Margie."

Luckily, that thought was the briefest of moments, as I didn't particularly want to visualize a card of Bruno Hauptmann being strapped into the electric chair, with the card caption reading, "New Jersey fries Nazi."

The kids' situation was going to be the challenge. Guilt or innocence was not the issue; what to do about their varying states of inebriation was the issue.

Their parents, and other affluent parents, were the root cause of the problem, so it was incumbent on them to use their political grease to make certain that nothing more than a slap on the wrist was administered. That would accomplish several things, if it came to pass: it would take the parents off the hook, it would not stigmatize the kids as felons, and the potential yellow sheets that would have otherwise followed them would be bleached white.

But it was never that simple, because there were many others in the community that would demand "punishment to the full extent of the law" either because they had young children who were potentially at risk from drunken teenagers, or they wanted their young children to stay on the straight and narrow because a handful of older kids got judicially nailed and became that generation's bad apples.

There were also community members with no children, or with grown children, who were not of a mind to put up with modern-day hooliganism, and one multi-day collection of headlines had the power to create the image that Hamlet was a law-abiding town and meant to stay that way.

To some, real estate values were about location, location, location. To others, it was about the potential gangster population keeping their noses clean, or, if they got bloodied, to have the book thrown at them.

That was a long way from the "give 'em a lecture and send 'em home" attitude of the permissive parents. In my tired condition, having done an eight to four during the day Monday, then home, then being called out again close to midnight for countless hours, I allowed myself the luxury that the eventual reality would fall somewhere between the extremes of slap on the wrist and lethal injection. I'd wind up testifying to having been at the scene and to having witnessed the cache of liquor within the vehicle.

The lab technicians from the county would testify to the varying degrees of blood alcohol intoxication, and a local magistrate would hand down some terms and conditions that resembled punishment.

But there was one other concern that was outside of the purview of municipal justice, and that was the recently shaped policies of the local school district. A number of parents, most likely those who would keep their children law-abiding, had petitioned the school board to hold children responsible in alcohol and "substance" related issues, as well as with regard to other prohibited activities, even when school was out or late at night in summer.

"Substance" somehow conveys at least slightly more dignity than "narcotics," and substance abuse is equally melodic when compared to gangbanger, crack-head, heroin junkie, or overdose victim. It's a matter of "kinder gentler" semantics. The Texas State Legislature, apparently all sleeping through the event, once voted to give a medal of honor to Albert DiSalvo for his efforts in population control.

Imagine their surprise when they found out Albert DiSalvo was actually the Boston Strangler.

Returning to the school issue, a policy had been established whereby any students involved in a caper like that of the previous evening would find themselves barred from extra-curricular activities for either two of the four quarters of a school term, or for an entire year. In this instance, with the juveniles all clearly underclassmen and equally clearly totally smashed, it allowed for the possibility that all five of them would be barred from activities for an entire year, beginning in September or even immediately, but a year either way.

Such a ruling would not have a heavy impact on the "Camaro Five" if all that was at stake was membership in the Library Club or the Audio-Visual Crew. But if it meant losing a year of football, wrestling, or, God forbid, cheerleading, then it was a far more serious punishment than "community service," in which the kids are dragged kicking and screaming to a local park and are observed as they plant—or likely *bury* would be more precise—a few flats of tulips.

In an affluent community like Hamlet, the students competed—if that's the correct term—for admission to Princeton, Bucknell, Notre Dame, Wisconsin, or Stanford, to name but a few of the iconic party sites where a higher education was also possible.

But all the affluent children in other communities were also competing, and because affluent children always got good grades or teachers were dismissed, the determining factor for admission was frequently the extra-curricular resumés of the applicants, and this event, when subjected to the scrutiny of the school's policy, was "risk" writ large.

That "risk" translated into the difference between Yale, Wisconsin, and Cornell and an institution that had a geographical note in the name and the word "State" in there as well. Yale was rarely confused with Southwestern Idaho

State, and everyone involved in this event fully understood the ramifications of possible school-related punishments. Every one, that is, except those still sobering up.

I'd removed my uniform shirt and was just about to hoist the t-shirt over my head when one of the probie officers, eagerly on duty because there actually was something happening, came running into the locker area screaming, "Decker, Chief wants to see you NOW!"

For a minute, and regrettably only a minute, I allowed myself the image that Pete Perfect had made page one of the tabloids, surrounded by a bevy of ladies of the evening, all covered in Pete's baseball cards and his cash.

The chief's urgent summons, however, was far more serious than any fast breaking news about Mr. Perfect's peter. It had been learned that Edwina Griffin, an octogenarian who had resided all her life in Hamlet and who remembered the first President Roosevelt, had been discovered, dead, about twenty feet in from the curb, in an ornate flower bed, on one of the local streets.

Edwina was—well, "had been"—not only a community legend, but also a community effort, of sorts, because she had been suffering from Alzheimer's Disease and was known for wandering away from her children's house at any time, day or night, dressed in a turquoise dressing gown bedecked with sequins. Community members knew, and either sympathized or empathized, and because of her long standing in the community, and her condition, she was always discovered, returned home, and nobody complained.

Except possibly Edwina, but that was by now somewhat understandable.

And just as equally moot.

Those perambulations were now at an end. She was dead—discovered almost by accident by a passing early-morning motorist who noticed the turquoise garment in the flower bed of a steep, well-landscaped front lawn of one of the town's more affluent corporate leaders.

The truly bad news was that there were tire tracks going from the road for about six feet onto the property where Edwina's body had been discovered. That immediately meant that the impounded vehicle carrying the five besotted youths would be checked for any traces of Edwina, just as Edwina's remains and garments would be forensically combed for any traces of the vehicle.

And, of course, if the tire tracks on the property were recognizable, and they matched the impounded vehicle, or if Edwina's autopsy discovered a litany of fractured bones, it was no longer a matter of someone being dumped from the Library Club for a year.

We had just entered "orange jump suit country" in less time than it takes to pronounce that destination. If my suspicions, and I was about to learn if they were shared by the chief, were correct, the issue was no longer five kids out joy-riding with alcohol provided by overly indulgent parents.

We were now looking at vehicular homicide and hit and run as the best-case scenario, and manslaughter as the worst. If the kids were too drunk to avoid Edwina, they would slowly be lowered into a cesspool.

If they had chased her with the car and killed her for laughs, a helicopter would drop them, weighted, into the cesspool.

Even for a veteran cop, it was too difficult to envisage. As a youth, thirty-plus years earlier, I had delivered newspapers to Edwina's house—where she lived before her kids had to take her in—and she would always regale me with history that she had lived through. After all, who else could vividly remember World War I?

As I re-buttoned my uniform shirt, I shared mental whispers with God. Please God, do not let this be a murder that these kids did.

Well, I might have made an exception for Pete Perfect, so he could no longer brag about the suckers he'd fleeced with his enticements of "spot cash."

It was a spot all right, but only a spot.

And now, I had to step out of the locker room and perform my sworn duties as a sounding board for Chief Shitfer-brains who had such well developed police skills that he could come upon three badly wrecked and twisted automobiles and pronounce, "Look's like there's been an accident here."

# The Five W's, But Not In That Order

The chief told me and everyone else within range of his baritone vocal cords to have a detailed report completed before we left for the day. Several of the others could write their reports and leave, as they were on the late night or early morning shifts.

I was on the 8 to 4, which meant I'd be staying. I could use the time before 8 a.m. to get the report completed and sent via e-mail to the chief, with blind cc's to a number of other agencies, which was now becoming, in the age of technology, normal practice. This new e-mail stuff was great because it meant we didn't have to face the boss when tendering a report. We just hit a button, and the report went. Chief Shit-fer-brains would then read it, presuming he *could* read.

The chief indicated he had to get ready for a press briefing regarding both the "alleged" drunken-driving incident and the discovery of Edwina Griffin's body. Originally scheduled to be held a few minutes after Edwina's tragedy had been learned of, it had been postponed so that it could be piped, "live" into the local schools.

To the chief, it was a perfect object lesson, but the rest of us did not necessarily agree. In his traditional not-so-delicate way, Chief S.F.B. told us he was planning to put the "hit-and-run" killing of Mrs. Griffin squarely on the drunken kids.

Jimmy Spaeth, the senior lieutenant who, at 57, was closing in on retirement, told the chief in no uncertain terms that he should make no such statement, as it could embarrass the department, the borough, and could do unnecessary—and perhaps inaccurate—damage to the children's reputations, and law suits aplenty would be forthcoming.

"How else can you explain what happened?" the chief asked Spaeth.

"All we have is five kids, liquored up, the body of an elderly female, and tire impressions on a lawn. *Nothing more.* The kids in the vehicle might have had nothing to do with the body that was found. Edwina could have been hit and killed by someone else."

"Or," added desk sergeant Mike O'Rourke, an Irish cop from a family of Irish cops, "a car—maybe the kids, maybe someone else-- could have swerved onto that lawn, scared Edwina, who spooked, ran, and had a heart attack. She was, after all, what, 86, 87 years old? At best, you'd have felony murder, but you do not have enough to say it was the kids."

"We know who did this," the chief insisted.

"Yeah, maybe," O'Rourke told him, mostly to calm him down. "But we need proof before we stand in front of cameras and convict people in the press. Do you think the governor of New Jersey is going to say that the kids did it before all the facts are in? Do you want to buck the establishment and possibly cost the department its reputation *and* its chance for future state aid? Do you want to be named as co-defendant in law suits if this turns out to be something other than what we claim to know?"

O'Rourke appended a thought to punctuate his statement: "And that muscle-car Camaro was not owned by a poor family, Chief. If you mis-speak and that family comes after you legally, all the king's horses and all the king's men…." and he let the thought hang.

Like we all wished the chief would hang.

I'd heard enough, so I turned around, went back to the empty detectives' cubicle, and started to put down facts.

Facts, not theories.

We knew who the five children were, but we could not statistically quantify their drunkenness without lab results. We'd have to say "believed to have been inebriated" or "allegedly inebriated" until the proof was available. We knew, within a couple minutes either way, of *when* they impacted on the light pole, because the time cited would be the department clock's time at the moment the call from a nearby residence was received and officers were ordered to respond.

We obviously knew *where* the event occurred, because there were not battered utility poles all over Hamlet, and if there were a silver lining in all of this, it was that kids *from* Hamlet were responsible. Had they driven another five hundred meters, they would have been in the town of Valley Grove, and their local newspapers would have used large letters to spell "Out-of-Towners" in their headlines.

We had a general idea of *how* it all came to be, although it was unclear if the statements made by the kids could be used in court because as they were shouting that it was all okay with their parents, the first officers were shouting back their Constitutional warnings. That confusion would definitely be a chicken and egg proposition for the parents and judicial authorities when push came to shove.

The "why" of the event would best be left to such data as could be researched from head-shrinkers. Why did kids feel the need or desire to drink and carry on, and do so at risk? What generational shifts caused parents to become so permissive, or was it a matter of surrendering to children that basically could no longer be disciplined?

Of course, depending on lab findings of the blood-alcohol levels, the possible tire-tread match, and the coroner's findings regarding Edwina, the "why" might be nothing more than an attempt at rationalization for the purpose of mitigating what could have been one or more ugly judicial sentences.

Take all of those considerations, and you should quickly understand that my report would be terse, since I was not first on the scene, and considering I had been off-duty, it would reflect badly if I had been first on the scene unless it was the utility pole that graced my property.

"Date of event: March 9, 1992. When I arrived at the scene [include name and exact address of residence where the utility pole was located], I found a 1988 yellow Camaro, New Jersey license plate 'VX CORP' approximately six inches from a utility pole that I measured, using Hamlet police equipment, and noted to be on the north side of Arlington Avenue, sixty-six feet from the corner where Arlington Avenue crosses Jefferson Street. I observed damage to the utility pole, which was numbered 'PL 0803—194' on a metal band that faced the street. I measured the height of the damage and found it to be 29 inches above the ground, and instructed the on-scene officers to take paint scrapings, which appeared to be yellow, from the pole. I noted that the cited Camaro had damage, which corresponded in height to the observable damage on the pole.

"The vehicle was ordered impounded by me, as it contained several broken bottles that had at one time held alcoholic beverages, and there was alcohol present throughout the vehicle, including on the inside of the windshield. It was impossible to ascertain, without extensive laboratory testing, which broken bottles might have contained the free-flowing substances in the vehicle.

"Officers on the scene immediately contacted Dispatch and reported the "VX CORP" license plate in order for it to be checked and yield the address of the owner, although it is common knowledge in the borough of Hamlet that the owner of the vehicle is _____." (Name not included because to include the name would reveal the identity of at least one of the juveniles.)

I did not think it wise at the time to put the license plate out on the air, for several reasons. For one thing, we knew who owned the car, although it had to be made official by computer bank search. Secondly, vehicle registration papers and insurance documents were available in the glove compartment, which I note was opened, either by the collision or more likely by the air-bag deployment. Because it was open, we did not need a warrant to search the glove compartment, where the cited documents had been, along with packages of condoms and glassine envelopes containing potentially illegal substances. Those were viewed by both county and local officers but "seized" by county officers for immediate processing in their sizable lab facilities.

"The five youngsters comprised three juvenile males and two juvenile females, although by statute their names must be redacted from this preliminary report but will be included in the Summary Report of Investigation. At the time of my arrival, in my personal vehicle, I noted that the two females were wrapped in blankets, and I was advised by Officer ____ that both females had been unclothed at the time he arrived on the scene. No further statements were made to me by on-scene officers, which I thought perhaps unusual, given the air temperature, close to 40 degrees, and the state of undress of the females. But I cannot report what was not said.

"One of the three males was partially clothed, wearing a New York Jets football-style jersey underneath a jacket. He was not wearing anything below the waist and was barefoot. The above-freezing temperature and the length of the football jersey meant that the officers did not have to wrap him in a blanket, or, weather aside, at least not to prevent him from appearing to be obscene.

A second male, still holding a bottle in a menacing way, would not surrender it to the officers and accordingly, I reached him from behind, grabbed the bottle, and as I dropped it and he bent to retrieve it, I was able to handcuff him. He protested loudly that he had done nothing wrong, as he was not driving.

"At that moment, the fifth youth, the tallest of the three males, shouted back at the handcuffed youth that he was not going to take 'all the heat' (his exact words) because he was driving. *At the time he made the statement, I was unable to understand if 'all the heat' meant all the blame for the damage to the utility pole or if some other code offense was involved.*

Investigation into other possible code violations is continuing.

"Because the juveniles' identities cannot be revealed in this preliminary report, the names of their parents can also not be immediately released. However, the senior on-duty officer, one patrolman and myself, having ascertained the identity of the self-confessed driver, and because his identity matched the address of the registered owner of the vehicle, it was decided to visit the residence, either to take note of any possible events "in progress," or as a courtesy call to let them know their Camaro would not be in the garage that night.

"This visit was made immediately after I served as an escort to the local hospital for emergency room treatment for the five juveniles.

"At that time, a party was still in progress, and alcohol was visible when the officers were permitted to enter the residence. There was some 'scurrying about' noted, but this could in no way be proven to suggest any attempts to hide or dispose of illegal substances. I would add, parenthetically, that there was no response from anyone present when the nature of the event was explained to the owner of the home, who also was the owner of the yellow Camaro. Responses were made anonymously, from the individuals present at the party, but they were not in English, and although loud, did not appear to be menacing. Neither I nor the senior on-duty officer felt it necessary to unholster our weapons.

"I had gone with the other two officers only because there seemed to be the possibility of an unruly welcome at the residence, but that did not occur beyond the owner eventually saying, 'So what? I'll pay for the [expletive] pole.'

"As a precautionary measure, I suggested to the county officer that we make a list of the makes and models of all the cars parked on the property of the residence, as well as those parked in front of the residence—an illegality after midnight, but more for curiosity's sake than to write summons in the larger scope of things. All told, I copied data from 17 vehicles quickly, and I then returned to my personal vehicle and drove four blocks, in haste, back to the scene of the alleged collision. I returned there in order to make certain that a 'crime scene' was not and would not be violated by curious neighborhood spectators. In addition, I was concerned lest anyone reveal the identity of the owner of the vehicle to media individuals, as we were not supposed to know who the owner was, and revealing his name, all things given, could have proved counter-productive.

"I checked my own observations of the removal of the five juveniles by EMT units with the officers remaining at the scene. The two unclothed but blanketed females had been placed in the first vehicle to arrive (which accorded with my recollection), and had been taken to Hamlet Valley Hospital, accompanied by Officer _____, along with a female EMT attendant and a male EMT driver. Their names will be supplied in a supplementary report. The second large EMT vehicle arrived just as the first was leaving, and the two males who had not 'confessed' to having operated the vehicle had been placed in that vehicle, with County Officer ____ and two attendants to be named in the supplementary report.

"I remained at the scene with a County Officer until a one-passenger ambulance arrived, and County Officer ____ and I escorted the alleged driver to the Hamlet Valley Hospital. He seemed extremely incoherent, insisting on being allowed to drive the ambulance, and at one point, attempted to force the issue by attempting to remove himself from the gurney to reach the driver's seat. He was restrained, using a minimum amount of force, and handcuffed—both hands—to the two rails of the gurney.

"At that time he protested the use of excessive police force.

"End of preliminary report."

*So much for the official side of it,* I thought, as I hit "send" to the multiple intended recipients, and then pushed my chair back, stretched, and pretended not to be tired. Sick and tired might have been a better characterization, because I knew that if our brilliant police chief, or the media—or both—linked last night's events with the death of Edwina Griffin, the situation would go way past ugly, and I was not looking forward to that.

At that point, in the eyes of the law, at least, the connection was not proven. If it turned out that the kids were responsible, it would be the ugliest thing to happen in Hamlet since one drive-by, drug-related shooting a few years earlier.

But that was a dead drug dealer, and who cared? The cops did not even know of his business until the search of his residence gave strong evidence of his occupation. This situation, however, was a medley of five kids, countless permissive parents, and one elderly lady who had once been, in better days, the talk of the town.

I shook the cobwebs out of my brain, or at least tried to, and focused on Edwina for a minute. In her situation, we knew the "who"—it was Edwina. We had a reasonable idea, but not proof positive, of the "where," but for all we knew to a certainty, she could have been killed, or died from exposure to the overnight elements, blocks away and been dumped in the patch of garden where she was found. "When," "how," and "why" remained unanswered, but the county medical examiner could give a pretty good idea of when and how, but the "why" would be the sticking point in the entire legal issue.

"Why?" was also the question I asked myself when I thought of the other event—the disappearance of Pete Rizzoli, baseball card shark to the rich and famous. I wasn't thinking about why he wasn't around to be found; I was also thinking why I should even care.

Then I remembered that I was wearing a blue uniform and also that because I might well have more insider information on Rizzoli's business affairs, it was possible that I'd get to do some consulting with the Melrose Police Department on that one and I just might learn a thing or two about how to get rich—honestly, of course, in the memorabilia business.

I doubted I'd really get the chance, but thinking about that was better than imagining Edwina Griffin on an autopsy table. As unpleasant as Alzheimer's Disease was, at least a "natural causes" death would be preferable to being sliced and diced and then repackaged because one's remains had become "evidence."

Oh, God: Can please I be ten years old again and have no bigger worries than my baseball card collection?

God gave me a definitive answer of "No, you can't Decker. Now get off your ass and get back to doing some police work. The people of Hamlet are paying you to do that."

That pretty much defines an all-knowing God.

# All Hell Breaks Loose

I decided to again attempt to change my uniform shirt before hitting the street for what I anticipated would be routine traffic patrol or to assist, as needed, at either of the two current sites of concern: the utility pole and the tulip bed where Edwina had been found.

Before I was ordered to do so, since the chief was outside running his mouth to the microphones and cameras, I began running the automobile license plates I'd written down a few hours earlier. I entered the plate numbers, and quickly got a print-out, which I then tried to make sense of.

The cars with New Jersey plates belonged almost exclusively to individuals with long Slavic names. The New York vehicles belonged to amorphously-named holding companies all located in Brooklyn.

Slavic names for the individually-owned vehicles; corporate names in Brooklyn for the remainder. My hunch: Brighton Beach. *Little Odessa.*

As I wrapped that up and dropped it into the detectives' basket for further investigation, I heard the beginning of the chief's remarks to the press, and in retrospect, I think I would have preferred to be on the street in a stinky blue shirt.

It's not as if the chief is a lousy public speaker. Well, he is, but it's mostly because he's a lousy public *thinker*. Somehow, his mouth always attempts to outrun his brain, and miraculously, the mouth always wins.

Maybe because the brain lost interest years ago.

In any case, he began by thanking a half-dozen "press representatives", mostly feature writers from the local shopper, but at least one journalist from the county newspaper, which boasted a circulation of over 300,000.

"I have a brief preliminary statement, and then I will try to answer your questions, but please understand that there are answers that I will not be able to supply because of certain protocols, or because either or both investigations are far from completed.

"Our Hamlet officers, aided by county officers, responded to two emergencies during the night. In the first instance, five juveniles, aged fifteen and under, were found in a vehicle registered here in Hamlet after it had hit a utility pole. The five juveniles involved were taken to Hamlet Valley Hospital where they remain, and all are in satisfactory condition. At this time, I have no information regarding any broken bones or any other serious injuries, but if they are in satisfactory condition, that would tend to rule out serious injuries."

The mouth then outran the brain when he continued, and editorialized: "I hope this is a lesson learned by our young people about the safety of seat belts at all times."

In point of fact, we had no idea as to whether or not the seat belts had been used, as air bags had deployed in the front seat, and the injuries, or lack thereof, among the back seat occupants made the issue of seat belts conjectural. What should have been editorialized, if an editorial was necessary, was about the alcohol on the scene, but that was treated almost as an afterthought.

"There was a good deal of alcohol, either in bottles or laying about from bottles that perhaps had broken upon impact. The driver was given a breathalyzer test."

I wondered why that mattered, since he was not a legal driver, but it wasn't my press conference. And, in point of fact, the blood-alcohol level of all five juveniles was tested at the hospital, because parental liability and potential criminality were involved.

"Approximately five and a half hours after the light-pole collision, the body of Edwina Griffin, an 86 year-old resident of Hamlet, was discovered in a flower bed approximately three blocks from the scene of the earlier crash I mentioned. As some of you may be aware, Edwina was an unfortunate victim of Alzheimer's Disease and had been known to the police department for her occasional wanderings at odd times of the day or night."

I had hoped he would not make that linkage between the kids and Edwina. But he did, so I buttoned the last button on the clean shirt and waited for the onslaught of questions.

As it happened, I would not have long to wait.

"Now I'll take your questions. Yes?" he said, pointing to the youngest of the reporters, a female whom I knew from the cop house to be about twenty.

"Is there any connection or do you suspect any connection between the two events that you described?" The question virtually restated the Chief's linkage only a moment before, but it was the opening he had been hoping for.

"If you're asking me if I think the vehicle carrying the juveniles hit Edwina, we have no proof of that at this time."

By saying "we have no proof at this time," the implication was clear that there would be proof. He might as well have started picking the jurors.

"Can you positively state that there is no connection whatsoever, Chief?"

"No. I cannot say there was a connection and I cannot say there was not. I can't even say for certain, without all the facts being known, that these events were unrelated to Watergate, fer Chrissake."

"And you cannot provide the names of the juveniles because of their age?" the county news journalist asked.

"That is correct, and I ask you to understand that the statute prohibiting the release of the names will be a ground rule in any further discussion."

By hinting at further discussion, he was again alluding to a connection between the two events, as the press was certainly not going to show up to be told the five kids had been sent home with aspirin.

The county news reporter was tape-recording the discussion, and paused briefly to turn the tape over. He then asked the critical question: "And where exactly does 'Billy' Vychon fit into all of this?"

You could hear the chief's angry response echo through headquarters: "Who said 'Billy' Vychon has anything whatsoever to do with this?"

"Chief, let's face facts," the reporter told him. "Some officers—either from here in Hamlet or county officers that you said were on the scene—called in the license plate 'V-X—C-O-R-P' and reporters hear those conversations on scanners that are perfectly legal to own. Secondly, I feel certain that there are a lot of people who know *precisely* who owns that vehicle."

"It had to be called in for the sake of a complete inquiry," the chief answered, trying to work out of a serious jam.

The journalist wasn't done yet. "And you know and I know and everyone here knows that the vehicle was a high-powered yellow Camaro that belonged to 'Billy' Vychon. Would you care to comment any further?"

"No!" And with that, the chief turned, red-faced, and walked back into headquarters, wishing once again he'd never played "meet the press" or that 'Billy Vychon' was not a resident of Hamlet.

Everyone did indeed know who 'Billy' Vychon was. His real name had undoubtedly, at one time, been a much longer Slavic name along the lines of (but not limited to) Vyachaslav Ivanovich Vaganovski—although I admit to exaggerating for the purposes of illustration. How or when it became shortened for Hamlet's purposes was not really known, except possibly to keep his house from catching fire because residents had not quite forgotten the Cold War.

What *was known* was that he was a ruthless bastard who threw his money around—and didn't that thought remind me of Pete Rizzoli—treated his neighbors, affluent in their own right, like dirt, and had a reputation for owning

VX Corporation, one of the nation's largest providers of pornographic films.

Thus, he was not exactly beloved in that God-fearing community, or what passed for one, and what I also knew was that it was his arrogant little bastard of a son that was driving—or had been pointed out by the others. I hadn't seen the kid in a couple of years, since he'd been picked up drunk at age twelve, but walking on that occasion. I can't say I recognized him in the ambulance, but in that darkened enclosure I might not have recognized Johnny Cash.

It did not take long for the news—and particularly the suspected linkage—of Vychon's car and the death of Edwina Griffin to spread through Hamlet like plague.

By the end of my shift, 4 p.m., there were no less than 150 cars making a four-block circle around police headquarters, and tying up all other traffic, as the headquarters building was only 75 yards from downtown Hamlet. As the cars passed the station, the gentle people among them honked their horns; the not-so-gentle people yelled obscenities; the really nasty folks made anatomically impossible suggestions.

The chief asked several of us if we wanted to get some overtime dealing with that crowd, and Jimmy Spaeth—bless him, told the chief in no uncertain terms that his ill-chosen words, hard on the heels of his ill-chosen desire to meet the press, was the root cause of the problem outside, and if he wanted it fixed, he could do it himself.

As for me, I got out of my uniform, finally, having completed Tuesday's work and knowing I had Wednesday off. I really could have used a couple of Bud Lights at that moment, but, and this is one of those decisions that often hangs on a thread, I passed; for the moment.

I got in my six-year-old Firebird clunker and drove to the Melrose Police Department.

Suddenly, the disappearance of Pete Rizzoli seemed like much more of a challenge than keeping the Hamlet townies at bay.

# Where's Waldo?

It was almost a blessing to drive a mile and a half from headquarters and see the sign that read "Welcome to Brentwood Bay," a town halfway to Melrose, and one which believed the beauty of its lake would have potential home buyers swarming into the area.

The 'bay' itself was a fenced off, "keep out or we shoot off your kneecaps" reservoir of sludge that fed the local water supply. One drive across that sludge after a storm and you bought stock in bottled water.

There quickly followed Running Hollow, a town without sludge or barbed wire to protect itself, but, if nothing else, the final obstacle before Melrose. If one missed Melrose, you were in New York State, and that was a place where gas prices were dedicated to paying off the national debt.

After traversing Brentwood Bay and Running Hollow, I reached Melrose, a community distinctive for very low taxes because its outlying areas were the homes to "corporate campuses," the steel and glass buildings where many a glassy-eyed CEO learned the fine art of making a shit-load of money. But low taxes were a good thing in these here parts, and an additional upside was that municipal facilities were among the best in the state, because before a new corporation got permission to desecrate what was once "Injun land," they had to promise to erect some new municipal structure.

Given that there was still a lot of open land in Melrose, I expected that someday, their "welcome to" sign would speak of "Melrose, the bucolic town with seven libraries."

Well, if nothing else, their police headquarters was magnificent, and we could have put Hamlet's P.D. in one corner of it, even though we probably had more bad guys in Hamlet.

Art Swanson was serving temporarily as desk sergeant, and he and I had been baseball card buddies in the late 1970s, before Arty decided he wanted to father enough boys to field a basketball team. A decade after we stopped comparing memorabilia notes, Arty was only one player short, but now lacked the cash flow for memorabilia.

Still, he was my best hope for a contact with regard to the Pete Rizzoli events, and my hope that he was just going off duty was not disappointed, as I was directed into the municipal headquarters "locker room and lounge," and I chided myself for not bringing a bathing suit or perhaps a jet ski.

"Decker!" I heard Swanson yell from a locker area at some distance from the entrance door. "Get out of Hamlet before the torchlight parade comes to stick a spike through Billy Vychon?"

"Yeah, something like that," I told him. "Got a minute?"

"For you, Decker, absolutely. I was going to call you again on this Rizzoli thing." At least that told me who had originally called.

"Let's go back to the bullpen," he told me. "Too many potential ears here," he added in a softer voice.

Clearly, fatherhood was doing wonders for Arty, as he looked terrific. He stood a solid 6'2" to my 5'9", but he outweighed me by no more than ten pounds. *Memo to self: get an exercise bike or meet up with a rich and beautiful nymphomaniac.*

Four kids, however, had given his hair the salt and pepper look that would have made him look slightly older than me, although I was about four years his senior. *Who counts?*

I asked about the kids, and, not surprisingly, his only complaint was that he'd had to take his card collection and get a safe-deposit box at the bank to protect them against little hands covered with peanut butter.

*Or boogers,* I suspected.

He asked me about my cards, and I told him I still had them and was protecting them so they'd put my kids through college.

"Kids?" he barked.

"Well, none yet, but I can dream, right?" *I better dream fast at age 44,* I reminded myself. "Now, if you can, tell me about Rizzoli, since we're discussing baseball cards." What he had referred to as "the bull pen" was ideal, as it was a large, well-appointed if casual dining area, but nobody was having lunch just after 4 p.m.

"Tough call, Decker. His wife came in here early last evening—yeah, Monday evening—to say he was missing. I was only here because I dropped Jack Banta off while his car was being fixed. Anyhow, Mrs. Rizz said he'd gotten a phone call sometime around noon on Thursday, that would be March 5th, and that he went through his usual routine of packing up a bag of flash cash and was talking to himself in terms of the treasures he was expecting to find.

That was the last she saw of him...."

I quickly jumped in. "Why did she wait so long to say something?"

"Apparently, it was not unusual for him to be gone sometimes for three, four days at a stretch, because he would drive—his old pickup, not one of his top of the line 'hey look at me, I'm rich now' sports cars, and if he was off to fleece some sucker in Maine, or Tennessee, Michigan—anywhere it could have been a long drive, he could be gone for days. Or maybe it was Manhattan and he decided to have a little hotel party and come back home with less cash than he left with, and some cards in the suitcase that he had put there earlier."

I had to ask the obvious: "Does it make any sense to fill a suitcase with cash and then drive that old rusty shit bucket that he drove when he actually was making a buck and a half a week before he struck it rich?" The "buck and a half" had only changed with regard to zeroes, as word in baseball card circles was that Rizzoli was clearing $150,000 weekly, or almost $8 million yearly, on his cards. He'd rolled over some card money into "blue chip" investments as well, but for my dime—and that was all I could offer, his cards were better than blue chips on Wall Street any old time.

"It makes no sense, but that was something that we did not want to confuse his missus with at the time."

"How concerned was she, Arty?"

"She was terrified, and that is putting it mildly. It was after my shift, but I came back to drop off Banta and to spend an hour breaking in a volunteer on the desk, and I was here when she came in—probably close to 9, 9:30. After she gently introduced herself, the floodgates opened and hysteria took over. Pete was dead; he was being tortured; mobsters might be holding him for ransom; an irate *former* baseball card owner was getting revenge. She came up with more scenarios in about two minutes than we could have plotted in two days. We tried to get specifics, but she was adrenaline drained by the time we got a word in. We did get permission for the feds to put a tap on the house phones, but the feds haven't heard much else, and now she's under sedation so that when she truly calms down, we might be able to get something from her."

I had to ask the obvious: "Did you put an APB out for the vehicle he was driving—it shouldn't be hard to spot."

"The feds did that, too, although the official lookout notice did not come across our screen yet. Can't explain that one."

"Any chance you'll need me as a resource person for that little session?"

"Good chance. I told the chief as well as the feds that you and I knew Rizzoli—at least in his 'poverty period,' and the only other cop I can think of that would know anything about him would be—what's his name—the guiny detective up in New River?"

"Butch?"

"Yeah, Butch. But he absolutely hated Rizzoli, so I don't know how much help he would be."

"Arty, we all got to hate Rizzoli. Everybody that had met him twice knew he was an arrogant, thieving prick who'd sell his family to Gadhaffi for target practice."

"Yeah. But at least he only pissed me off. He never burned me. Did he ever screw you out of anything after we stopped comparing collections?"

"No, luckily. I saw him lay a line of bullshit on someone once..."

"Just about any card dealer nowadays is peddling as much bullshit as they are cardboard," Arty interrupted me. "It's not a hobby any more—it's a business."

"Been that way for a long time," I told him, "but that's not the concern. If you think I can get inside this, it would help if you could tell me what you know."

"Off the record, until the chief says you're in, Decker."

"Understood."

"And I should add that with what's going on in Hamlet right now, pal, you may be the new chief there by 15 April. Your man really fucked up in front of the press this morning."

"Yeah. The chief is a screw-up and Rizzoli is an arrogant thief. So where are we?"

"Okay." But as Arty Swanson said that, his eyes and thoughts seemed to go somewhere else, as if he was being bombarded with new possibilities or insights.

"Like I said, I'd come back to work with one of those volunteers who works the desk when we're on overload. Carmichael was the duty sergeant of record—and awake," Swanson added.

I let him talk.

"Mrs. Rizzoli came in, trembling slightly, clutching her purse in what could only be terrified body language."

"Did you know who she was when she walked in?"

"Oh, yeah. She stood in for the big man at some charity deal we ran here at headquarters a couple years back."

"What was her story?"

"Simple. He got a call on Thursday, mid-day, then he put on his 'I'm going to make a killing in cards' face and took off with a bag full of money in the old clunker."

"I don't suppose anybody thought to trace the call..."

"We're not as unenlightened as your chief, Deck. But the call came in to one of those suitcase phones that Rizzoli always bragged about and made sure he used in front of his influential friends. It will take days to trace that call, if it can be traced, because there's always the possibility that the call went *from* a suitcase phone *to* Rizzoli's suitcase phone. It's damn near spy stuff, but if that is how the call came in, it can't be traced, period. These phones are essentially very expensive walkie-talkies.

I tried a different approach. "Let me ask you this, Arty. Does Mrs. Rizzoli have the look of someone who would be married to a ton of money, or is she just the a basic tired, frumpy housewife?"

"She is no 'looker,' Chris," he told me. "They got married before he hit the baseball card lottery. At the same time, though, she's no frumpy housewife because as you might suspect, they live in large splendor and they have servants to take care of the chores."

"Could he be out just having a party, and he'll come home when he's done?"

"We thought of that," Arty told me. "But the idea was vetoed because it just did not seem logical that someone with all that money would risk an action that could spell 'divorce' and he'd have to split his ill-gotten gain, all of which he gained after they were married."

Swanson paused for a minute, and his eyes became fixed at an uncertain point in space. At the same moment, someone gunned an engine and left rubber in the street outside the P.D. Arty continued, "Yet he could be hiding a whole lot of cash as well as extremely valuable cards, in reserve, just in case. Since the feds are already listening in, we might want to have a look at his tax returns. Do you think he would declare all his income, Deck?"

"Most folks would not," I told him. "But you can't just go out and buy the estate he lives in, plus all those high-priced cars, and pretend you're getting by on $60k per year. He has to be declaring some of it."

"Well, maybe..." Swanson began.

I cut in. "What if her appearance is a charade? What if she had his ugly ass deep-sixed last week, and now she shows up, frightened housewife, what-happened-to-my-meal-ticket look, when in fact she knows what he is worth, how to turn it all into cash, and get away with it? She might not be able to buy high-priced talent to whack Mr. Pete Perfect, but she damn well could afford to do it on consignment."

"We," I continued, "or at least you and your guys, Arty—have to talk to someone that knows them well as a husband and wife, and not as the memorabilia millionaire and his frump."

"Yeah. While she's sedated, I'll suggest to the chief that we canvass the neighbors, although living up there in that gated enclave, the neighbors might not even know who their neighbor is. Ain't no poor people in that neighborhood. In the meantime, I'll try to get you fully inside this deal, and I promise you that you'll enjoy working with Chief Porterfield a helluva lot more than that imbecile in Hamlet."

I started to say something, when the door to the bullpen opened and a Melrose officer yelled in, "Decker?"

"Yeah, here."

"There's been a messy incident down the road in Hamlet. Rumor has it that Billy Vychon took his kid and flew out on their private jet to some exotic place that does not have an extradition treaty with the United States. That, in turn, caused one helluva traffic mess outside Hamlet police headquarters."

"I'm off duty," I told him.

"I know that," came the answer, "but you might want to go back down there and make some points with the people on the promotions board. This is going to get ugly before it's all over."

"*Going* to get ugly?" I asked rhetorically. I winked at Arty Swanson and headed for the door.

"Take care of your '52s," he yelled, as I started to accelerate.

"Get Mrs. Rizzoli back in here, Arty, and call me when you do. If she offers a reward for his discovery, let's make damn sure she pays off in mint cards."

"Deal, Deck. I like your mind..."

# Ah, But I Was So Much Older Then; I'm Younger Than That Now

I vaguely remembered the youthful officer who had rousted me from my mental masturbation with Arty Swanson. That kid had been on duty on a windy, threatening Saturday afternoon a couple of years earlier when a few local Melrose kids decided to kick a soccer ball around on one of the town's recreation fields.

I was in a Hamlet supermarket at the time, and one blast of thunder—easily the loudest I had ever heard, knocked the lights out throughout the entire large shopping area. I abandoned my cart full of items that would give a health-food afficionado a bad case of hives, and headed for the exit, making my badge obvious in my left hand and my newly-purchased Glock slightly less obvious as I held it at my side in my right hand.

There was not going to be any looting while Hamlet's finest was on the job. Luckily, the lights came back on within about ninety seconds, so I was headed for my junk-food basket when an announcement was made that sounded somewhat ominous, at least in its wording: "Attention shoppers! Important announcement! Will anyone in the building who is a member of any emergency units—police, fire department, emergency medical personnel—please contact your respective commands immediately. Repeating..."

*Respective commands? Was I about to be deployed?*

My innate sense of sarcasm disappeared when I called "my command" and was told to haul ass to Melrose, and when I got there, just follow the sirens and flashing lights.

The young officer who had rousted me from Arty had been the first one on the scene at the soccer field after the lightning strike that for reasons known only to the Almighty, had targeted that soccer field. Two of the youths had been electrocuted by the blast and appeared slightly discolored, because the worst burns were internal.

Two other kids had gotten away with having their rubber cleats melt into the artificial turf. If they'd been wearing metal cleats, they, too, would have been covered with sheets. And at least on that occasion, nobody made any orchestra jokes based on the fact that the two survivors had proven to be good conductors.

But the young cop took it damn hard, spitting his guts up all over the turf, but at the same time taking on a new dedication to protect not just the kids of Melrose, but everybody.

So when he told me something was going on in Hamlet, I had no reason to doubt him, although I did seriously doubt the stated content of his message.

Vychon, Jr., was not about to be released from custody, so the likelihood was that he was still in the hospital, handcuffed to the gurney. Unless some of daddy's goons had kidnapped him when he conned the officer on duty to let him take a potty break. Still, unlikely.

And Vychon, Sr. was not about to flee the country without his son and the rest of the brood.

Still, something was happening. I had a flashing light in my aging sports car-wannabe, and a toggle switch connected to the horn turned it into a siren, so I headed south, to Hamlet, "Code Three."

I had traveled about a mile and a half when a barricade became visible where the "keep out" reservoir bisects Brentwood Bay. Two police cruisers, lights flashing, were directing all vehicles to turn right and cross the reservoir, but not to enter Hamlet.

Huh.

Since no traffic was coming north, I pulled out, passed the few southbound cars waiting to bitch out the officers before turning, and I pulled to a stop and got out. One of Brentwood's boys recognized me and backed up his cruiser so I could get through, but in my rear-view mirror, I saw him return to his position blocking traffic from going further south. The lingering aroma, if that is the right word, of ozone was still present in the air.

Unless they had all roads blocked, and there had to be two-dozen ways to get into Hamlet, what was the point of this, and why block the roads?

It was about the rumor. The townies had literally become the characters in an old "Bride of Frankenstein" movie, in which the good people of Frankensteinville, all carrying torches, ascended the mountain to put an end to the evil "groom" in the cinematic classic.

By the time I reached the vicinity of headquarters, I found I had to abandon my vehicle on the front lawn of the largest bank, size-wise, in Hamlet, and jog-trot four blocks to headquarters, where I learned that some connection—not proof, but some manner of unstated connection, now tied the yellow Camaro, owned by the dreaded pornographer, to the death of Edwina Griffin.

The driver of the Camaro, Vychon, Jr., had been taken from the hospital and brought to the municipal building for a preliminary hearing.

And the townies had become a lynch mob. About two dozen had been arrested, although how the eight officers on duty on the 4 to 12 shift would have had enough handcuffs was unknown to me at the time. County and state police had been called in, and there were no less than twenty police vehicles, lights blazing, surrounding the headquarters. Cops, now in riot gear, were guarding the front and rear doors, as well as the basement parking garage, whose door could easily have been locked from the inside.

As I arrived at the scene, slightly breathless, I checked in with the 4 to 12 platoon commander and he told me to grab riot gear and pitch in.

*Doing what?* I wondered. The townies had retreated a bit, and it was now just a demonstration of anger quite a bit short of Tienamin Square or the October Revolution of 1917 in Petrograd.

After perhaps fifteen minutes of tension-filled watching and waiting, the front door of headquarters opened and Harold Benson, the local magistrate, appeared. The Chief was alongside him, with a bullhorn, but I laughed heartily inside because if the chief tried to utter a syllable, the crowd would have drowned him out like the home crowd at a football playoff game in a domed stadium.

Judge Benson, somewhat frail and 50-ish, although he looked older, still in his robe—perhaps to look magisterial, took the bullhorn, and after fumbling with the keying mechanism, spoke softly: "People, please. You know me. I'm Harold Benson, and I've been the magistrate here in Hamlet since 1968. Perhaps I've even seen one or two of you in there," and as he said that, he jerked his left thumb over his left shoulder. Without illumination, Benson was speaking with only the traditional front lights on the headquarters building, and moonlight. Luckily for Benson, it was cloudless after the passing and fatal thunderstorm, which also meant cooler temperatures, and that may have kept some of the potential ugliness home for the evening.

"Today's events are tragic, but the final word on exactly what happened is not yet known, and will not really be known until it is presented to a Grand Jury at the County Seat, if necessary, or if a jury is chosen here in Hamlet to hear a criminal complaint.

"No such thing has happened yet. The driver of the vehicle that allegedly hit the light pole has been brought before me and I have ordered that he be held, without bail, as a material witness."

That brought a round of epithets from the crowd, who were hoping for an immediate guilty verdict. And sentencing.

"It has to be that way, ladies and gentleman," Benson continued. "A determination still has to be made regarding exactly what crime or crimes may have been committed; then, depending on that determination, a second determination will be necessary to decide if any of the parties involved will be charged or tried as juveniles or adults."

That brought one response of "Punish them as adults!" and a muttered agreement followed.

"I ask that you please, for the sake of the reputation of Hamlet and its good people, return to your homes and let the judicial process work as it is designed."

I was personally moved by Benson's words, and I think the crowd was also, but in an extreme example of bad timing, the garage doors opened and two officers manhandled a hooded individual into a van, which then made haste to jump a curb and squeeze through a convenience store parking lot before disappearing from sight.

At that, the crowd surged forward again, and I was expecting a hail of rocks to be thrown at headquarters, to be answered by tear gas.

Neither event happened, but the van with the hooded individual did not make anyone happy; and in retrospect, I think it guaranteed that Benson would have to recuse himself from any further deliberations, as he seemed, at least to the crowd, to be tainted by letting himself be a shill for police tactics.

I knew Harold Benson and I doubted that he'd ever go for such a bait-and-switch ruse, and I found that to be true when I finally got inside the building, as he laid into the chief for the cheap and unnecessary theatrics.

Something—I can't say what, exactly—drew me back outside. I sat down, about ten feet from the door, on a rock adjacent to a monument that was dedicated to Hamlet police officers who had died. There were only six or seven names on the bronzed monument, but I knew them all. The one at the top of the list had fingerprinted me and all my classmates when we were in second grade in the spring of 1955. Scared the living hell out of me.

Seeing that sergeant's name reminded me that in 1955—and the thought came blazing into my head that 1955 was Koufax's and Clemente's rookie year on baseball cards—the Hamlet police department was the Chief, also since deceased, and four or five officers, plus a few "specials," who directed church traffic on Sunday.

There weren't any "Saturday churches" in Hamlet, if you gather my demographic drift…

I also remembered, seeing those names, that I could recall times when I sat on the giant rock in the park—the place where baseball card dreams were made or broken—and I could see *both* of the Hamlet police vehicles parked near the guard booth at the main intersection in town.

Now there were sixteen vehicles, and thirty-two officers, four sergeants, plus a half dozen higher ranks.

Where had it all gone? How had it changed?

I could only tell myself that the world had changed. I had taken on the job in 1974—1975, and now, seventeen-plus years later, I was half way between my forty-fourth and forty-fifth birthdays. And also about three-fourths of the way to a cushy retirement.

*Retirement? I'm still a kid!*

My parents were both gone for a decade, I was still working hard, and I was still collecting baseball cards. Long gone were the days when I sat in my tree-hut, built by my father, and a very serious structure, which gave me a peaceful place to read my *Superman* comics and all the spinoffs. Gone were the days of going down to the ball-field and spending hours playing one pickup game after another. Now I drove the well-worn Firebird and worried about gas prices, when there was a time that coasting down a long hill on a bicycle was an incredible high.

My age really was showing, and I decided to get the hell away from that monument before I either got more maudlin or before I pulled out the Glock and joined the names on the bronze.

My youthful reverie, which had included Pete Rizzoli, without whom no consideration of baseball cards would have been complete, was shattered when I walked back into headquarters.

The first thing I saw was two county officers leading Mike ("Mikhail") Vychon from an interrogation area into the one holding cell we had in the building. Vychon looked as if he had aged ten years in the few hours since I'd seen him, and his shock of black hair was a stark contrast to the orange uniform he was now sporting but which clearly did not resemble the Baltimore Orioles.

*What the hell?*

I went around the desk, well above shoulder height, and asked one of the many volunteers on scene, "Didn't I just see him leave in a van?"

"That was one of the county officers, hooded up to fool the crowd," I was told. "The Chief wants Vychon here, and he'll be guarded around the clock until all of this has settled."

I didn't think it was a good idea at all, given the ugliness of the crowd I'd seen, and if they learned the truth...well, some local contractor was going to make a sizable amount of money rebuilding the headquarters site. Beyond that, the county had much more serious facilities and manpower for guarding ugly felons, including a twenty-five year old who had murdered a seven-year-old girl in 1973 as she tried to deliver Girl Scout cookies on a quiet street in Hamlet.

I wondered if the townies would have been so angry if Vychon, Sr. had made his fortune in baseball cards and not skin flicks. Hmm.

I truly felt my age and my mortality for the first time in my life. As much as I wanted to go back to the tree house and read the adventures of Superman, I finally realized I never could.

I silently said a prayer for one more hour in that tree house with Clark Kent, Lois Lane, Jimmy Olsen and Perry "Don't call ME Chief" White.

Didn't happen.

Damn tough pill to swallow.

# In The Town Where I Was Born...

I should have gone home, eaten, and made two lists: the first, of the as-yet-unknowns in the matter of Edwina Griffin's likely death by auto; and the second, possible scenarios in the disappearance of Pete Rizzoli.

Instead of going home, I walked a couple of blocks to "Lee's Tavern," the local shot-and-a-beer dive where true drinkers gathered daily. The less serious imbibers met later in the evening at "the Cornerstop," a watering hole where men and women gathered to get to know each other for a few hours and hopefully never again. The Cornerstop boasted far more genteel decorations and appointments, and the food, while not gourmet, was delicious and plentiful. And for a couple bucks, you could get a Coke or ginger ale served to you by a barmaid who could out-hoot Hooters any day.

The shot and beer crowd had lived in Lee's since time immemorial, and I felt a part of that tradition, as I'd been at my father's side in the 1950s and 1960s when he single-handedly paid off the mortgage on the place.

Despite that, I must have been the generation that genetics passed over, as I was not much of a drinker. That first beer always tasted good and quenched my thirst; the second beer made me question why I had enjoyed the first one, and the third beer re-acquainted me with the gutters outside, where I left behind whichever were my two most recent meals.

If Lee's Tavern had for any reason taken a second mortgage, they were shit-out-of-luck if they counted on the next generation of the Decker family to pay it off.

Still, it was an informational hot spot, as a high percentage of cop cases got kick-started from local gossip, and at least Edwina's case was center stage in Hamlet on that early Tuesday evening.

Fortunately, I had earned enough respect in Hamlet that I was not greeted with the catcalls that usually follow local flatfoots who set up personal quotas for traffic tickets, or the like. And I certainly was in better favor than the officer who used to sit and drink with his buddies at Lee's, and when they left, he'd make an excuse to go outside and write each departing buddy up for drunken driving.

The buddies did not stay buddies long, and the officer involved, zealous to move up the food chain, had to escape Hamlet for a federal law enforcement career to avoid a lynching. In his federal career, he made even greater enemies and he was hidden away as a guard in an American legation overseas. Since his enemies could not get at him, they cut the brake-fluid cables on his son's car and the boy was pronounced dead on a state highway.

Moral to that story: Don't create arrest scenarios. Only act upon the ones you stumble into.

The crowd at Lee's was subdued and there was only a semi-silent buzz when I arrived, instead of the usual one-end-of-the-bar-to-the-other rancor that was commonplace. Not surprisingly, I was questioned at length by the curious patrons but there really was not much I could tell them except that procedures were being followed etc.

That seemed to soothe the savage beast. The best question came from a stunningly beautiful and youthful woman—one of only two in the place, and she had the dubious distinction of being married to a local politician who was old enough to be her grandfather.

She was his trophy, which she knew. He was her cuckold, which he didn't know.

She asked if anyone was considering filing negligence charges against Edwina's children for letting her wander about as she did.

Damn good question, and I was unprepared for it. Falling back on the old ploy of taking a long swig on the beer, I eventually told her that since nothing had been done previously with regard to negligence, it would be a difficult challenge at this point to suddenly blame them for something that had been long-standing.

She could not understand, and neither could most of the remainder of the crowd, how Edwina's caretakers, which amounted to her fifty-plus year-old daughter, her husband, and their children, could not keep Edwina inside the house, using some kind of electric door mechanism, or at least a serious picket fence with gates that could lock.

I didn't have to answer the question. One of the local landscapers, known affectionately in the community as "Knucklehead," piped up that because of Edwina's medical bills, medication, and occasional need to be baby-sat, they were at the end of their resources, and he further suggested that they would finally have a life again now that Edwina was gone. Apparently, cutting lawns and shoveling snow had made him an economist. Notwithstanding, I planned to stay friendly with him, on the odd chance that he'd be appointed as the next chairman of the Fed.

Somehow, I don't think his message was well-received, as most people that I knew who talked about aging were roughly split on Alzheimer's. Some swore they didn't give a damn and that someone out there would care for them, while others said they'd either blow their brains out or get their cars going as fast as possible and find some immovable object.

I didn't ask for a show of hands as to who had guns handy, in order to blow their alleged brains out.

Know your audience...

When it was noted that the "little Vychon bastard" had been taken away, I kept silent, knowing he was still in Hamlet custody, awaiting the results of all the tests. Privately, I suspected that the results would arrive at or shortly after midnight, and any necessary judicial process and/or prisoner transfer would only occur after that time, while Hamlet slept and readied itself for a typical Wednesday, whatever that entailed.

Still, if this bar crowd had been jurors, Bob the Builder would already be selecting lumber for the gallows. There was no doubt in anyone's mind as to what had happened to Edwina Griffin, but one could almost perceive a reverse judicial psychology: Edwina's 'murder' was suddenly the vehicle with which to be rid of the Vychon family, whatever it took.

I also suspected that those offering opinions, while only a fraction of a percent of Hamlet's feelings, were pretty much the norm, and I equally suspected that I shared those sentiments. While I did not admit to it, I also fully believed the evidence would point in the direction that the boilermaker crowd was convinced of.

Ah, Hamlet. This tavern, and the baseball cards I opened herein, the gum I wolfed down, and the Bonomo's Turkish Taffy that followed the gum, all were a part of my very fiber.

But I knew things had changed. Whoever said, "you can never go home again" was wrong.

You could go home. You just might not like what you found there.

# Book 'im, Danno

I walked out of Lee's Tavern to find what had suddenly become an overcast, dreary night in which the moon now chose no longer to make an appearance. It was the kind of night on which the world could easily end, if anyone cared.

I decided to walk back to headquarters, and my immediate instinctive reaction was to swill down a handful of breath mints, as booze-breath and on-duty cop are not a good combination.

The crowd around headquarters had for the most part dispersed, but I noted a couple of vehicles each with two antennas, meaning that they were radio equipped, suggesting either law enforcement or media, but either way, they were not Hamlet vehicles. I reasoned that if they were law enforcement vehicles, young Mr. Vychon's goose was cooked; if they were media vehicles, the press boys were waiting for the Vychon recipe to be produced.

Either way, it had the smell of a lynch mob, which, if you are unfamiliar with that olfactory sense, is akin to having a bad case of sinusitis and being in the men's room at a bus station. It's not to be confused with the smell of fresh-cut grass or the warming return of spring.

Satisfied that my breath was safe, I walked into headquarters and immediately saw that O'Rourke was back on the desk—and busy. He was a little surprised, I suspected, that anyone off duty would be crazy enough to come back to the vicinity where only overtime beckoned, but he quickly jerked his head toward the door to the bullpen, which told me that something was in the air.

And it wasn't fresh-cut grass.

It was an unusual sight, to say the least. The Chief, looking tired and years beyond his actual age, was sitting with two of my fellow Hamlet officers and three or four County boys, who were undoubtedly hearing the cash registers that signaled either overtime or comp days.

"Decker," he announced. "Shag your ass over here and join us."

"So?" was all I said, and then the chief just cut loose with a recitation that I suspected he had already rehearsed with the other officers there.

"It can't get much worse, Deck," he started. "The County Medical Examiner and the County Prosecutor—not an assistant—are on their way here, which means we'll be having indoor fireworks later tonight."

"Is there any way that their visits are exculpatory?"

"No such friggin' luck," the chief replied. "Baby boy Vychon's ass is so cooked he will be lucky to celebrate his eighteenth birthday.

I kept quiet—an event likely to make the Guinness Book of World Records.

"Let's start with the Medical Examiner," the chief went on. "Edwina's autopsy, which, for evidentiary purposes was filmed—a first for this entire county—found that she had broken legs, pelvic bones, a couple of ribs, and a fractured skull. It suggests, at least to the M.E., that she was facing away from the vehicle that struck her, and that she whiplashed backward, fracturing her skull on the vehicle. Some blood stains were found on the very back of the car."

We had not seen them in the pitch darkness of the accident site, but then again, we wouldn't have looked for blood stains anywhere except on the hood even if we had had any idea there might have been someone hit by the vehicle, and we would have otherwise searched only for such blood stains on the inside of the vehicle, from its occupants.

Rather than let 'himself' tell me I wasn't doing my job in finding the bloodstains, I stated the obvious: "So Vychon's car hit Edwina. Do the tire impressions match?"

"They match perfectly," he said, "but it gets a lot worse."

"One of the passengers in the car—one of the two girls—became seriously sober and gave a statement that all of the occupants had seen 'the old lady'—her words—walking along, and they put the car in neutral and revved the engine to scare her. When she brushed them aside, they put the car back in drive and went after her."

After a pause, filled by nothing but silence, he added, "They fucking murdered an old woman."

"That will take the jurisdiction out of Hamlet," I answered, stating the obvious, "but only if that witness had the lowest blood-alcohol level and can be considered reliable. The car may well have killed Edwina, but not necessarily in a pre-meditated scenario. That kid knows the town wants Vychon's head on a platter, and she may be doing one helluva Scheherezade."

"The County Prosecutor will be issuing a statement at about 10:30, or at least a little while from now and just in time for the Eleven O'Clock News, that the yellow Camaro, recklessly driven by an underage youth who has been identified, was steered in such a way as to strike and kill Edwina Griffin. The defendant is going to be tried as an adult...."

I waited.

"And the prosecutor is going to charge one count of Murder One and ask for the death penalty. That little bastard is facing the needle."

"He won't get it," I said.

"Probably not," the chief said, uttering a sigh that signaled disgust. "But I suspect the prosecutor's strategy is to force Vychon and his high-flying legal team to focus on the sentence, not the issue of guilt or innocence."

One of the county cops piped up. "That legal team has helped Vychon beat any number of porno charges over the last decade."

"Yeah," the chief answered, "but porno is not the same as running down an old lady. A porno case, with twelve jurors, almost comes with a built-in guarantee that one or more of the twelve find porn to be harmless. Murder by vehicle is another matter."

I could never recall hearing the chief so lucid, so direct, and with such analytical clarity. Maybe he was going to retire on a sudden burst of good-cop sense.

I needed more. "Is there any way you can get the porn king out of the closet as far as all of this goes?"

"The prosecutor intends to make it known that the parent of the driver of the vehicle, a Mr. Billy Vychon, is going to have his legal team present for the arraignment of the driver. He will also be announcing that there will be a Grand Jury empanelled to determine if 'accessory to murder' charges should be brought against any of the adults who got the kids liquored up and gave them the car keys. How does that sound?"

"Music to my ears," I said, smiling for the first time in almost two days. "So what's next? Has anyone considered some kind of plea deal that will save the kid's skin in return for Daddy changing location?"

"The press conference. Edwina's physical condition will be stated in general terms, and the tire impressions, and blood traces, which will only be linked to the 'suspect vehicle' will be included in the statement, lest there be any 'lingering doubt' about what happened."

"I hope the statement by the girl is going to be kept quiet," I said, with some urgency in my tone. I then added, as an afterthought, "And I hope the statements from the higher-ups are not so all-encompassing that they prejudice potential jurors and make the prosecution a challenge."

"That's not our worry, Decker. As for the girl's statement, it will be kept quiet, at least until Vychon speaks to the press, most likely tomorrow. If Vychon, Sr. denies anything and everything, we'll have a salvo to fire back."

I sat back and pondered the impact—no pun intended in any way—of all of this. A kindly old woman who had been in Hamlet since 1906 or 1907 had been killed by a car-full of drunken kids who had adult help in getting smashed. The victim had so many broken bones that the medical examiner probably lost count, and a witness would state that the striking of the woman was intentional.

The only wiggle room might be that it could be argued that the witness was too drunk to fully understand what was happening and that the vehicle striking Edwina might not have been a pre-meditated event.

I'd heard enough, and I wanted to let O'Rourke know that I was scheduled for a day off the following day, but if need be, I'd arrive for some generous overtime. When I got back to the front desk to brace him on that matter, he indicated we needed to talk privately and asked one of the volunteers to cover the desk.

It would perhaps be fair to say that I had damn little room left in my system for surprises at that point, and whoever passed the unwritten law that things happened in three's had never been a cop in Hamlet.

O'Rourke quickly came to the point: "Are you aware that Nick Sweeney, the probationary kid from New River, is carrying on with some long-distance bimbo from Moscow?"

"No, I wasn't aware," I told O'Rourke, "but as soon as you mentioned the capital of all that is evil in the world, a bell rang. What is going on?"

"He's been on nights, with Sullivan, learning the ropes. And he's been bragging that he met some delicious Russian honey in an international dating magazine, and he's talking about trying to bring her to America."

I was shocked. "How the hell does he think he can get her out of Russia? And is he too stupid to realize that international bride magazines are just less-challenging ways to gamble away money?"

"Sully said he sounded serious. He's got forms from the Immigration and Naturalization Service, and he's about to hire an attorney."

"He'll need an attorney in short order if even one of our busybody townies learns of what he's up to, at least after last night."

O'Rourke looked squarely at me. "And he'll need three quarters for the parking meter as well."

"Which, uh, parking meter is that?" I was not aware of any in Moscow.

"The ones on the street in front of the unemployment headquarters down the road a piece. The chief will fire his ass on general principles if somebody—anybody—even whispers the words 'Sweeney' and 'Moscow' in the same sentence."

"I like the kid," I told O'Rourke, "so it won't be me."

"I like him too," O'Rourke said, "but Sullivan hates his ass."

*It only takes one,* I thought. Then, to O'Rourke: "Got any quarters? ... I probably have a couple." I said, dejectedly.

# Appointment Confirmed

I walked in the door at home a couple of minutes shy of 10:30, which meant I'd been gone, and ravenously hungry, for almost twenty-four hours.

Before I could even reach the refrigerator or the microwave oven, the phone machine was blinking a message.

"Deck, it's Arty. Nine a.m. tomorrow, here. We're going to have another chat with the lady who was hysterical last night. Your presence is strongly requested. Please call me at home if you can't make it."

I knew exactly what Arty was saying, in cop-speak. He wasn't about to put anybody's name out there, but I figured there was not a line of hysterical women in the Melrose police department on the previous night.

What I didn't have was a completely thought-through set of questions I would need if I was allowed to do more than listen.

I popped a TV dinner in the micro and headed to my office to get a yellow pad and start ruminating while meatloaf, undoubtedly from a cow that appeared on a 1950s western like Range Rider or Sky King, warmed itself.

Putting the culinary concerns aside for the moment, I began to write:

Item 1: Make a list of questions. *Good start, Decker; you're on a roll.*

Two: Assuming Mrs. Rizzoli would walk the Melrose Police through the scenario with less hysterics but the same specifics, was there anything she could think of that made this call to her husband, or this "card-buying trip" different from any of the others?

Three: Did Pete take anything with him that would have indicated the nature of the trip? Did he usually take snacks, and did he do that this time?

Four: Did he take his passport, if you know? *Stupid question, but it has to be asked.*

Five: Does Pete have any enemies? I almost choked while writing that, as I would expect to be handed a phone-book-sized list.

Six: Was his attitude typical of such baseball-card buying trips?

Seven: Was he dressed for colder weather than was forecast for Hamlet over the next couple days, if he paid attention to such things. Or did he pack articles to suggest he was heading south?

Eight: Do you have any idea—even an approximation—of how much money he would have been carrying?

Eight, part two: Do you have access to the place in the house where he keeps cash, or does he maintain a safe-deposit box locally? Would he have needed to make a bank withdrawal to have enough cash? These questions were really for the Melrose cops to follow up on his bank records, or the Feds would, assuming they were sitting in.

Nine: How often, if ever, does he return with the cash and no cards?

Ten: Did he take the suitcase phone with him so that you would be able to reach him in case of an emergency?

Eleven: Foolish question, but file it under "long shot": Do you know where he buys the gas for his vehicle, and does he have a gasoline credit card?

Twelve: When he makes ordinary purchases—groceries, garden stuff, restaurant meals—does he pay cash or use a credit card?

Thirteen: I know this is personal, but does he take any medications, and if so, did he take them with him?

Fourteen: Are there any friends or acquaintances, north, south, east, or west that he might stop to visit if he was in proximity to where they lived? Long shot again, but when you have no information, you have to dig deep to get some—any—information.

Fifteen: I may have asked this, but did he give you any idea of what exactly he was going out to buy? If he was on the hunt for a Honus Wagner rarity, at least some folks who owned them would be known to the people who write sports-collecting magazines.

Sixteen: Was his vehicle in good running condition?

Seventeen: Was there a chance he was going to stop and pick up a business associate, in a manner of speaking, to help safeguard the 'spot cash'?

Eighteen: Did he carry a weapon of any kind? And if so, was it registered, on the odd chance that the weapon's serial number suddenly appeared on some nation-wide telex?

Nineteen: *Nineteen, dammit.* Enough. Set the alarm for 7 a.m. and continue this in the morning.

Twenty: Eat the cold meat loaf...

Did you ever have one of those near-exhaustion moments when, if someone asked your name, you would have had to take out your wallet to answer the question correctly?

That was me. Tired, dirty, and ready for the next day.

What I wasn't ready for was the next phone call.

# EVERYBODY'S TALKING AT ME

I knew it was headquarters by simply viewing the caller i.d. number. I truly did not want to pick up that phone, and given my state of "well beyond tired," I was not sure I could have picked it up.

The message kicked in after four rings: "Decker, O'Rourke. Shag it out if you get this. There will be some interesting things said to the press at midnight. Out."

"Out." I didn't know if it meant I was out of luck, out of sleep, or soon to be out of work based on the obscenities currently swirling in my head, to describe our chief of police.

*A midnight press conference? What is this, Woodstock?* The smart money had been that the politically-correct words would be said at 10:30 so they could still be warm news at eleven.

But midnight? To me, that translated to, "We're having a press conference, but we damn sure don't want the local folks to know about it, and there is going to be crap coming down that you just won't believe. ... And you aren't likely to hear it, because it will make the 4:30 a.m. news and be ancient history by 7 a.m." The kids in school will know all of it before the adults will.

Something was definitely up, and would I be Mrs. Decker's son if I went back to sleep and missed all the fun?

I need to make a confession here, and it's something I certainly did not say to Chief Shit-fer-brains when I was interviewed for my current job. I'm a creature who needs his sleep. Some cops can go for days without sleep, then tuck in for seven hours and be raring to go.

Not me. I need those seven hours on a daily basis. Four hours and I can do an excellent "incoherent rage," and with two hours, I can be a wreck on the highway. It was now 11:30 pm, Tuesday, and the last time my brain rested was 6:30 a.m., Monday.

A fine recipe for disaster.

Leaving home behind, I drove the obligatory mile and parked in the convenience store lot, as they probably were not doing volume business in lottery tickets or coffee and bagels at this hour, and whatever business they were doing was courtesy of the Hamlet Police Department.

O'Rourke met me at the door and was looking past me, to the main road going by, as if he were expecting something. What he was expecting was a crowd to show up, and I figured the townies were too adrenaline-drained from the earlier activities in the day, so maybe—just maybe, it would be a quiet, business-like press conference.

If such a thing were possible.

At the stroke of midnight, Judge Harold Benson again emerged, and I was behind him as he stepped out into the still-dull night. He quickly explained that the services for Edwina Griffin would be held in the local funeral home on Thursday afternoon and evening, with burial services set for Friday. By even bringing her funeral into his comments, he had in essence recused himself, as he had, howsoever subtly, expressed a sense of loss. *However, this is not why I'm here. Please, tell me, this is not why I'm here.*

Benson continued: Sufficient evidence had been received in order to convene a Grand Jury at the County Seat, with those plans also scheduled for Thursday." In the meantime, the County Prosecutor was planning on seeking an indictment for pre-meditated murder, with the defendant, the driver of the Yellow Camaro, to be tried as an adult.

Further, because the case was seen as including an adult defendant, the defendant's identity could be revealed. He was Michael Vychon, a resident of Hamlet, born August 16,

1977." *I'm betting I was the only one there who realized that was the day that Elvis actually left the building.*

Or that Baby Vychon was really only fourteen years old, and would not turn fifteen for over five months, assuming he lived that long. But more than that, the lowering of the age somehow, to me at least, dented the credibility of the witness—the young girl—who stated they had steered at Edwina. *If a fourteen-year-old kid would really do that, hell, I'm in the wrong business.*

The 'suspect,' as Benson modified his wording, was being held in the County Jail without bail. Three of the other juveniles would be arraigned on drunk and disorderly charges in the morning, but in the meantime, had been released to their parents. The fifth defendant was being held as a material witness, place and reason unstated. *That had to be the girl who ratted out Vychon as having driven the car to slam into Edwina Griffin.*

Being held as a material witness seemed a little harsh or perhaps Draconian, but then I remembered that many of those license plates at the Vychon residence showed up possibly as "Little Odessa," and the prosecution here was taking no chances that Vychon's gorillas would go after the female witness, who, it would be later learned, was simply in a private room in the hospital, with her parents nearby. But not closer than the guards.

"That is all that can be known at this hour, but the investigation is continuing, both into matters that have been discussed as well as to such parental permissiveness that brought about this horrible tragedy. I hope you will understand that as an officer of the court, I cannot answer questions. Thank you."

*Nice touch, Harold.*

Our next contestant was the chief, and he simply made an announcement, and it stunned virtually everyone, both inside and outside police headquarters. "Mr. Billy Vychon has requested the opportunity to make a statement, and we have acceded to his request. Mr. Vychon."

Billy Vychon looked tired and stooped, and if sympathy had been his goal, he would have been a smash hit. He stood about 6'1" tall, and looked reasonably solid for someone just about my age. I duly noted that he was clean-shaven for the event, and it had to go without saying that he was dressed professionally and well-coiffed for the occasion. No salt or pepper yet in his deep-black Slavic locks, and his eyes still had the power of persuasion necessary for his chosen line of work.

He reached into his suit-coat pocket and for the briefest of moments I imagined he was going to produce a Makarov, the pistol of choice for those from behind the Iron Curtain. To my supreme disappointment, he took out a pair of black-rimmed glasses and unfolded one sheet of white paper.

He began to read, and with a somewhat hesitant Slavic intonation, "My name is Billy Vychon and I want to speak to you from my heart this evening. I grieve alongside all of you over the loss of the lady who was killed. As for my son, I will give him the best legal defense that I can afford, and I want to assure everyone that my attorneys will also cooperate fully with the police and the prosecutor to determine how these children were given the alcohol which caused their drunken condition, and who was responsible for allowing them to be driving a vehicle illegally.

"I will also make myself fully available to investigators. I have long known that my occupation has brought offense to some people in the community, and last Friday, only three days before this tragedy, I thought I had taken steps to correct that matter. On Friday, March 6th, I divested myself of all holdings in the adult film industry and will have nothing further to do with it. I have no immediate economic plans, but I may do some investing in older items—what Americans call 'antiques.' ... And what you call 'collectibles.'

"I deeply apologize, and Mrs. Vychon certainly joins me in that, to this community for what has happened. This is America, not Soviet Union, and there will be justice. I'm so sorry," and with a quiver in his voice, "thank you all."

*Collectibles?*

So while his son is going to be collecting the hatred of every inmate in the County Jail, because someone who runs over an old lady intentionally is not going to make many friends, Vychon, Sr. is going to start a business collecting.

*Collecting what?*

I stumbled back to my car approximately ten minutes later, and believe me when I tell you, after that performance, I was wide awake. So, as I drove the few quiet blocks home:

Twenty-one: Suggest to the Detective Bureau that they find out everything they can about Vychon before the Feds decide they'll tell us only what they want us to know and then slam the door on the resources.

Oh, yes, and Twenty-two: "Mrs. Rizzoli, are you planning any manner of reward for the safe return, or "information leading to" the safe return of your husband? And will you redeem the reward in baseball cards?"

*I promise not to put them in the spokes of my exercise bicycle. Even if I can find it.*

# On The Road Again

I'm generally a creature of habits, and I'd have to include my alarm clock behavior in that category. If I had lucked out and fallen asleep at ten or eleven in front of the TV, I'd have had no need for an alarm clock.

But at 1:30 in the morning, wide awake but needing sleep, the time-piece was a useful gadget.

Once upon a time, I had it set to play the 1960s music that was the most special thing about my first car. I made sure the alarm clock was far enough away that I had to get out of bed to silence it, and it became a challenge of awakening totally and playing, literally, "beat the clock."

I could get to the alarm before Paul Simon finished "Hello, Darkness, my old friend," or before Dylan or McGuinn could actually ask the Tambourine Man to "play a song for me." But what was the fun in that? Why race to shut off music you love? As a result, I often fell back to sleep enjoying peaceful music.

So I tuned in to a rap station and fell over furniture, shoes, coke bottles, and occasionally a dog to get that noise out of my cobwebs. After all, who wants to start their day knowing that all women, beautiful or not, at the end of the day, were "ho's"?

I knew for sure at least some were not.

Finally, I compromised and settled on opera as the best vehicle. The LED read-out would go from 6:59 to 7:00 and "the fat lady" would start warbling—and I knew it was not because an athletic contest was out of hand.

On this day, however, with the prospect of finding out the deepest trade secrets of Pete Rizzoli, I was awake and splashing water on my face even before the fat lady donned her helmet.

Five hours' sleep in two days. I could have stashed all of Rizzoli's money in the bags under my eyes, and if I didn't get near some decent shampoo soon, my gentle auburn locks would go Kojak on me. I could at least take comfort in the fact that it was my day off, and after learning all about Pete Perfect, I would have the luxury if lounging in the shower for a couple of hours.

One more detail before I bolted: I went to the smallish, combination-lock safe hidden in the house, and opened it, simply so I could take a look at the "iconic" 1952 Topps Mickey Mantle card. *Would someone really kill for that?*

I put it away. Yes, someone would kill for that.

I had all the questions bouncing around in my head as I drove north to Melrose, reminding myself that I had to be well-behaved and focused, because I couldn't risk embarrassing Arty Swanson, and since the Feds would probably be sitting in, they would be looking for any excuse to simply take the case over and shut Melrose—and me—out of it.

There was also the possibility of some reward bucks.

And although my scheduled appointment was the previously-cited 9 a.m., it's axiomatic in police work that if you are supposed to be somewhere at a certain time, that you get there well early.

It's a survival technique to arrive there first.

Not that it was an ambush; I just wanted to see Mrs. Rizzoli's arrival—would she drive her own vehicle, or be driven by the servants?

Would Feds be showing up in quantity?

So, I had to slog through the morning school traffic, which meant cars, pedestrians, and even some bicycles in or out of their designated lanes.

But I got there, parked, sat and waited. At 8:50, a woman whom my well-tuned cop antennae suspected was Mrs. Rizzoli, arrived in a shiny, newer model BMW, which I doubted was lacking in any extra amenities. I probably should not have been surprised that the New Jersey "vanity plate" on the vehicle read "MS Pete."

I let her get inside the door of the municipal building and then I got out, brushed some lint off my suit, and headed inside. It was cool and brisk, and at that hour I might have benefited from a topcoat if I'd had one, but, well, I couldn't wear a heavy cop jacket over a suit, so I prayed for warmer weather by the time I'd be leaving.

Good chance, as the sun was out and there were none of the ominous clouds from the previous day.

Once inside, I was asked to show my credentials by a cop who knew me, which I treated as a formality, but I understood also that there would be "security." He did not ask if I had my service weapon on my person, as he either assumed I did, or he strongly doubted I was going to shoot a key witness. But it nagged me that for security purposes, the question was not even asked.

That seemed surprising, since there was no "security" in the parking lot. *Or was there?*

I was ushered into the conference room, where five males and Mrs. Rizzoli were already seated, with a desk volunteer serving coffee and cookies. She seemed mid-50-ish, and drawn-looking. Her sallow skin, an upper lip that would have benefited from electrolysis, and tired brown eyes exaggerated her actual age. Still shapely, but these events were not going to benefit her figure. Perhaps seven figures, though....

The Melrose chief, Ed Porterfield, a well-educated and well-spoken antithesis to his opposite number in Hamlet, was equally well-groomed and could have been a corporate CEO in a distinguished blue suit that had never been on the rack, and his tanned features and salt and pepper hair with not a follicle out of place was a constant reminder that after all, he was chief of police in a corporate town. He had a welcoming smile, which demonstrated a fine dental plan and crisp blue eyes that command attention. I had no doubt that when he cashed in his chips, one of the corporations would provide him with a well-paying sinecure as "security consultant." And headquarters would be well protected.

Also present were Arty Swanson—no surprise there, two Melrose detectives named Jack Banta and Mitch Somerville—both very *chic*, well-dressed, and youthfully vibrant. Corporate taxes can buy that kind of staffing. I had no doubt that they were both educated or they would never have passed Chief Porterfield's muster.

The final individual, besides me, was an FBI Special Agent who was introduced as Kevin Longwell, working out of the Melrose FBI resident agency. He was not as *chic* as the Melrose crew, and at the approximate age of thirty, I wondered whom he was friendly with to be in a resident agency. He seemed too well-tanned for this time of year, suggesting a salon—not to mention ego. Slick-backed hair made him look like he was about to audition for *The Godfather*, a bit of an oxymoron for a law enforcement geek, but often the hunter resembles the fox. And on that subject, resident agency personnel almost invariably travel in pairs.

I suspected his partner, whoever he or she might be, was on the business end of ear phones listening in, at a discreet but visible distance, to the Rizzoli's telephone. I briefly tried to imagine what kind of "cover" they had for that, and then allowed for the possibility that he or she was sitting in a phone company office miles distant. Or a chimney sweep truck, just up the block.

Either way, I was certain that with Rizzoli's money, it was already a high-profile FBI case, and they would be taking no chances.

And then "Chris Decker" was introduced, a local officer who knew Pete Rizzoli and had done business with him with respect to his collection of memorabilia.

I was waiting for questions about my collection, but that would have been very bad form with Mrs. Rizzoli present. I figured that subject would come up after her departure from the interview.

After some brief "let's win this one for the Gipper" pep-talk remarks from Chief Porterfield, the well-dressed but not in uniform police CEO asked Mrs. Rizzoli to walk through the events again.

She repeated the essence of her late Monday night story, stating that her husband had gotten a call at roughly midday on Thursday, now six days past, regarding the possible purchase of a baseball card collection.

"Are you certain it was specifically baseball cards?" Detective Banta asked.

Mrs. Rizzoli thought for a moment. "I'm sorry. I assumed it was baseball cards. He does buy all kinds of sports collectibles."

*Collectibles...* I heard a tone sound in my head and I thought briefly that I'd become one of Pavlov's dogs. Focus, Decker.

"So he got the call, and he got ready to go and look at whatever it was that was being offered."

This time the FBI agent interrupted: "Roughly how many calls like that would your husband get in, say, the span of a week?"

Mrs. Rizzoli seemed to get a little tense as I read her body language when she heard the phrase "your husband," but it passed. "Some weeks he got perhaps five calls, some weeks perhaps as many as fifteen. I am only guessing, of course, because I was not privy to all his calls and, of course, he used the phone to sell items as well. But based on conversations we had regularly, he'd tell me that someone called with, for example, 'a complete set of last year's cards,' which would be worth a couple bucks, and Pete would remind the caller that he only bought premium items, at premium prices."

"So what would be your best estimate as to how many serious calls, when he would take an amount of cash with him, putting aside the lesser-valued calls?"

"Probably two, on average." *That didn't sound like much in the grand scheme of things, but it meant he got to bid on and/or buy 100 serious collections each year.*

Detective Banta again: "And would these calls come through on your house phone, or on the 'suitcase phone' that you described the other night?"

Mrs. Rizzoli seemed to take that question as something of a challenge, but she at least had an answer. "We have a private line for personal conversations—friends, relatives. There is no business done on that line. Pete has a business line—the one advertised in all the sports publications—and that is the line that he would be called on if this was a buy or sell situation. Then—"

"Are you able to tell the two lines apart?" Detective Somerville asked.

"Oh, yes. The house phone and the business phone have different ring tones. Then there is what you called the suitcase phone—I don't know the technical name for it—it's a bauble that Pete bragged about, like so many other baubles, and that would only ring when he was doing business with someone he knew very well and had that number because Pete gave it to him."

Now, Chief Porterfield phrased the question: "So that would mean that the Thursday call, at mid-day, was the last call that you are aware of on the suitcase phone, and it is fair to suspect that it came from someone Pete knew very well?" I thought, Porterfield was being careful to say 'Pete' and not 'your husband.'

"Yes, I guess that would be true, and I'm sorry I had not thought of it."

FBI agent Longwell asked the question that I knew would come up: "Mrs. Rizzoli, we at the Bureau would like your permission to review all of the incoming and outgoing calls for perhaps the most recent three or six months. We would ask that you sign a form to that effect."

"Certainly, if it will help."

*It might not help the FBI or the Melrose blues, but it was damn sure going to be a godsend to the Internal Revenue Service.*

Porterfield, re-focusing events: "So, we know of a call, mid-day, Thursday, on the special phone, which at least suggests that it was from someone known to Pete. Right so far?"

"I would think so."

"Fine. Do you have any idea how many individuals would have had the number to reach Pete on that special telephone?"

"I would only be guessing," she answered. "See, we got married almost twenty years ago, when he was working in an auto body shop. We needed both incomes—I was a waitress—to get us by. Then Pete got lucky with the card business a few years later, and at that time, I was very much aware of his business activities, because he wasn't initially inclined to hire an accountant—I think he was fearful that someone would go public with the extent of his, uh, profit margin, but he was taking great personal pride in his success. So there was a time when I knew that, for example, he'd bought three complete and mint—always mint/perfect—sets of cards from the early 1950s. He'd tell me what he paid, and I'd keep track, but he'd also tell me that he expected to sell them for a certain price, and that price was usually very well above what he paid. In that sense, I knew his business.

"But then it literally exploded in the mid- to late-1980s, and there wasn't even time to discuss all the wheeling and dealing. We were close as husband and wife, but he sometimes just handed me sheets of paper with expenditures, either from a purchase or a show he traveled to, and I continued to do his bookkeeping, until he became so very important that he wanted to brag about his personal accountant. And by that time, he had a lot of well-heeled friends in the memorabilia business, and I could not keep track of all of them. But still, only a handful...well, perhaps as many as twenty...could have called him on the suitcase or briefcase phone."

My turn to speak: "Mrs. Rizzoli, two questions. Did he take the phone with him when he left, and could you give us any data—names, locations, type of memorabilia involved, with respect to those perhaps twenty individuals?"

She looked at me directly for the first time. "He took the phone. I probably could give you information on some of his business associates, but I can't and won't pretend that what I could give you would be a complete list of names and items that were specialized in."

"Fair enough," I said. "Could you call him on that telephone right now?"

The room became frozen in time. It was as if nobody had asked the obvious question in the previous days.

Finally, the spell of absolute silence was broken, and she replied, "Yes, of course. I have the number here. But I tried to call him on Sunday and got no answer," and as she said that, she reached down alongside her chair and pulled up the briefcase that had been resting there.

"The number is....."

Chief Porterfield pushed a desk phone toward her. "We don't need the number right now, Mrs. Rizzoli. Would you mind making the call?" *The feds have that line tapped, so what will this prove?*

"I'm sorry, I didn't think that I should, because federal authorities are involved, but, ... certainly." She looked at the paper in front of her, and pushed the appropriate buttons while Porterfield asked if she would put the call on speaker-phone.

The phone rang... and rang... and rang... and with each ring

Mrs. Rizzoli seemed to fade, like an old sepia photograph. Her features sagged and a certain hopeless resignation came into her eyes. A voice said, "I'm sorry, the number you have reached is no longer in service." Then she swooned, which is close to a faint, but not quite. There was nothing staged in her behavior, so in that moment, she was eliminated, in my mind, at least, as a potential suspect.

I looked down at my pad and scratched off the question about a possible reward.

The odds were 100 to 1 that Pete Rizzoli would not be selling any more sports memorabilia.

# Never Ask The Question Unless You Know The Answer

The room was a collage of emotions, all of them stifling. And the problem all stemmed, of course, from my willingness to violate the first principle of the legal trade: Never ask a question that you do not know the answer to. I had assumed that if she called the unique phone line, it would be an answer or no-answer situation. Maybe her missing husband was in a location where such phone reception would not be possible.

But nobody, myself included, expected what we had heard.

The FBI knew that they were tapping at least one phone that was now dead, but probably no more or less dead than the phone's owner. But the FBI had also told the local authorities *nothing*, which was only possible if the line had been taken out of service in the last few minutes, or if the FBI was responsible for taking it out of service. I reminded myself to share this thought with Porterfield on the odd chance that the nature of FBI "go it alone" mentality had not occurred to him.

Mrs. Rizzoli then began to respond. "Oh, God. Oh, God. Jesus, Mary, and Joseph. He's dead. I know he's dead. When I heard that recorded voice on the phone...it's like people say, 'Someone walked on the grave.' What can I do? What's going to happen to me?"

Porterfield was as comforting as he could be, but his tenderly expressed suggestions to remain calm, "because there are many possible answers to this," fell on deaf ears.

One EMT attendant, the police matron, and Detective Somerville helped Mrs. Rizzoli up and took her from the conference room to the Chief's office, where she could sit and collect her thoughts—if such a thing were possible.

That left Porterfield, Jack Banta, one Federale, Arty, and me.

Porterfield quickly focused matters: "Anybody?"

Nobody wanted to be the first to say something along the lines of what seemed obvious, so Porterfield turned to his immediate left, to Arty Swanson, and just said, "Arty?"

Swanson shook his head sideways before saying anything, then offered up the obvious: "The fact that the phone line is no longer in service is a whole lot worse than if a ransom note had arrived."

Porterfield agreed. Then it was my turn, since I was next to Arty. "Officer Decker, although you have not been intimately privy to these events, you're here because you knew Mr. Rizzoli. Do you have any thoughts to share?"

"With all due respect, Sir," I began, speaking with more solemnity than usual, "there are a number of possibilities that have to be explored.

What we know is that Pete Rizzoli got a phone call six days ago, and he packed up cash, and left home in an old pick-up. Ten minutes ago, that was all we knew, although we may have privately had suspicions.

"Now we have to factor in that Rizzoli's phone is no longer working. There are innocent explanations for that, although they defy logic."

"Like what?" Special Agent Longwell asked.

"Hypothetically, let's say he was going in the direction of, say, Lake Erie. Somewhere in upstate New York, Pennsylvania, or where New York and Ohio meet up. I have no idea and neither does anyone else in here where there is a hugely valuable collection of baseball cards to be had."

"Make your point."

"My point is that this card-buying trip could have taken Rizzoli into some potentially hazardous weather site. I had planned to ask his wife if he took any form of clothing that would give us a clue as to where he was going. But let's hypothesize cold for now. He gets a flat tire in the old truck. He's in the middle of friggin' nowhere. It's dark, so he gets out, takes his bag of cash and his fancy phone and starts hoofing it to the nearest anywhere he can get help, because he is not likely to be able to make a call from the middle of nowhere. He slips on unseen ice and drops and breaks the phone. He sprains an ankle, or breaks an arm. He's hurt and the phone is dead and he's got too much pride—and too much business greed to admit a failure, so he gets himself patched up, then the truck, and off he goes. That would explain the delay and the dead phone."

But I wasn't quite done. "Has the FBI run a routine check of hospitals for a patient, most likely on an emergency basis, named 'Pete Rizzoli'?"

Longwell stayed silent.

"Possibility number two is that he has gone somewhere to start a new life…something he's been perhaps planning since he made millions in the baseball card market. He's put funds in very private accounts—hell, Switzerland for all I know, and he's taken the remainder of his cash on the pretext of going out to buy cards. He drives the truck to some previously chosen and well-secluded location, where a waiting limousine collects him and takes him, his cash, and possibly the most valuable of his baseball cards, to JFK Airport, where he flies out of the country. The, uh, hold on, the fourth question on my list was, 'Did he take his passport with him?' Has the FBI checked passenger manifests for 'Pete Rizzoli'?"

At that point, I began to suspect that Special Agent Longwell and I were not going to become good friends, exchange Christmas cards, or be invited to our respective daughters' weddings. Especially the latter, since I was, sadly, childless.

Longwell verified my hypothesis by getting up to leave, while I continued. "The third possibility that comes immediately to mind is the worst-case scenario. An awful lot of people out there are aware that 'Pete Perfect' carries around wads of cash to buy gem mint baseball cards in order to resell them. All that would be necessary would be for someone to call him up, act like some real yokel who has a house full of valuable stuff, and lure him out. That, of course, would involve the cooperation of one of the twenty possible people that Mrs. Rizzoli spoke of, but it's very possible, because whether or not you are aware, Chief, Rizzoli made an auditorium full of enemies with his wheeling and dealing. He knowingly bought a cache of cards here or there worth a million or more and paid two cents on the dollar.

Someone out there could have sought payback." I concluded.

"Are you suggesting that he was lured out to be separated from his money?" Porterfield asked.

"Yes, and then dumped in a hole, somewhere in the vast hinterlands of these United States, where he would never be found. His money is untraceable, and if he had cards with him, hey, one Willie Mays card in mint condition looks just like any other Willie Mays card in mint condition.

"He could easily have been set up in just such a way," I went on. "The 'yokel' could even be one of his twenty possible insider contacts. Act like you know nothing about cards, whet Rizzoli's appetite, and take him for his cash and hide the body. That same person could then, in a moment of consoling Mrs. Rizzoli, con her out of the remaining cards she's holding at the same kind of prices that Pete paid."

"But wouldn't she know the value of them?"

"Sure she would. But with him out there 'missing,' with the passage of time, she's going to realize that he's dead and gone, and it's because of the way he did business with baseball cards. And when that day arrives, she'll be happy to part with them, and get by on what she sells them for, plus selling off his sports cars, maybe even the mansion. The time would come."

"Sounds like you've been planning this yourself, Decker," the chief said, but with at least a smirk if it was not a smile.

"Planning, no. But once I saw him in every imaginable publication holding up wads of cash, I knew sooner or later that some skell out there would try to take advantage of his *projected* generosity. I also meant to ask his wife if, for protection against this very idea, he took a business associate along on such trips, or, if he carried a weapon, because its serial number might someday turn up."

With a very serious look on his face, Porterfield tented his fingers together and looked at me like a father about to lecture an errant son: "How many questions did you bring with you, Officer Decker?"

"Twenty."

"Then let's us play twenty questions until Mrs. Rizzoli is able to speak to us again, if she is able to at all, today. Decker?"

I was on the spot, but it was a good spot to be on, as I was being put on point in front of Melrose detectives and one temporarily absent Fed. But question number twenty-one was beginning to nag at me.

*What was Billy Vychon saying to his son at this moment?* It seemed like a fair question at that point, because I think if we had voted for scenarios numbered one, two, or three, Rizzoli would have gotten number three unanimously, and the search for his unmarked grave would go on forever.

Vychon was still very much alive.

And very Russian.

I could see the sign posted on a busy thoroughfare in Brooklyn: "Welcome to Brighton Beach, population 44,328. Half of them Russian mob members or illegal Russian immigrants."

Welcome indeed.

# There's Gold in Cardboard

By virtue of having been put on the spot, so to speak, it was my police sense that got me through the next few minutes. Luckily for me, as I was gathering my notes and wits, Arty Swanson interrupted to address Chief Porterfield: "Mrs. Rizzoli brought that briefcase in with her. She may have brought materials in order to help us with this uh, investigation. I think we should ask if she will permit us to have a look at what is in there."

Porterfield rose and hastened, wordlessly, out the door and to his office.

After a delay of a deadly silent two minutes, he was back. "Mrs. Rizzoli is breathing oxygen under the watchful eye of an EMT technician and her blood pressure is stabilizing. She may or may not be coming back in here today, but she has given tentative permission to view the contents of the briefcase."

After a pause, Porterfield concluded, "Tentative in the sense that we can review the contents, but we are not to copy them." Another pause. "Anyone here have a really good memory for details?"

Arty Swanson looked at the chief and jerked his thumb to his left, meaning me. Porterfield asked if I indeed had a good memory, and I told him that for baseball cards and values, I did, but that both this event and the tragedy in Hamlet had drained my mental facilities slightly.

We then quickly reviewed my as-yet-unstated questions, taking no more than five minutes. Some had already been touched upon, and what drew attention initially was my question about where he kept his cards, and, by extension, his money. I stated that this was critical because if he had intended to leave and not return, a lot of the cards and money would have—or could have—been removed prior to the Thursday phone call.

How much he left behind for Mrs. Rizzoli's survival would

In one of those "come quickly, Watson" moments, I almost blurted out, "Wait! The first thing is to find out when that suitcase phone-line was turned off, as well as where and how, if that is possible."

Porterfield nodded almost imperceptibly to Banta, who got up and walked out.

We then went back to my list from the previous day—a moment in time when I allowed myself the suspicion that Rizzoli was still alive. Most likely he wasn't, so I shared my curiosity about credit cards that could also possibly track him, so that would be followed up by the Melrose detectives or the FBI—if Longwell decided to return.

The only remaining question dealt with attempting to get to his baseball card acquaintances, and see if any of them could be squeezed. I think I convinced Porterfield that someone had to know something, particularly since the Thursday call had been made to a phone that had a very limited clientele.

When I finished, I pushed my papers away and sat back a little. Porterfield also sat back and looked at the ceiling. "You certainly came prepared, Officer Decker, and if Mrs. Rizzoli had been able to face those questions, we might know more than we do now. But that's academic. I'm going to call the borough administrator and have him contact your chief in Hamlet, as I'd like his permission to deputize you; one, so you can officially indulge your memorabilia expertise on what may be in that briefcase, and two, so that you can consult, as needed, on this investigation. You may well be needed as a witness in this matter, and it would be more advantageous if you were at least temporarily on staff here. I hope that makes sense."

It certainly did make good sense. I wanted to thank him, say I was flattered, but that I had open cases still pending in Hamlet. But those desires were overridden by a far greater desire to see what was in the briefcase.

The chief had the professional courtesy to leave the room to make the call, although I doubted he went to his office. In his brief absence, Arty asked me for my 'best guess.'

"I don't have any guess, Arty," I told him. "But the answer is simple math. If the lion's share of the cards and cash are gone, then Pete Rizzoli is now living it up in some foreign paradise, which has generous banking laws. If the inventory and the bank accounts show no vigorous activity, Pete Rizzoli is dead—dead and buried. The only clue we will ever have is that his truck will be found—as a tease, to let the world know that Rizzoli was beaten at his own game. But wherever that truck is eventually found, you can draw a circle on a map with a 500-mile radius, and Rizzoli's remains are buried outside that circle.

Arty pondered my deductions and I could see that he was weighing both sides of the argument, just as Detective Banta began to ask me a question, which, happily, was interrupted by the return of Chief Porterfield, now with a loosened tie and looking like he'd splashed some water on his face.

"Art Swanson, you will witness this swearing-in." The Chief then deputized me and didn't even bother with the handshake. I felt a little bit like a Christian, in early Rome, who'd just been told he was being elevated to the status of 'performer' in the Roman Coliseum.

Undefeated hungry lions.

Porterfield reached to where Mrs. Rizzoli had placed the briefcase, and as he pulled it to him, he pointed to Banta and told him, "Lock that door."

Porterfield was clearly a man of his word, more visionary than the idiot I worked for. By locking the door, no one would interrupt the study of the briefcase.

I took a long swig on my Pepsi and then pushed the can and its remaining contents clearly out of harm's way. My safety concern was not lost on Porterfield.

Porterfield drew out all the contents of the briefcase and began working from the top of the pile down.

The first item was a photograph which showed Pete Rizzoli, flashing his traditional shit-eating grin, in front of hundreds of boxes of unopened cards.

"Can you tell me what these are, Decker?" He passed the photo to me. I moved it to my right so that Arty and I could both look at it.

"Stop me if you think otherwise, Arty," I began, pointing to the pile that reached from the floor almost to Rizzoli's thigh, and amounted to about five rows of forty boxes. "Those, I can say for certain, are 1952 Topps."

"And if they're the right series, those boxes would contain as many as 300 Mantles," Arty added.

"Giving them what value?" Porterfield asked.

"Assuming they were not kept in a wet basement or a humid attic, 300 1952 Mantles could have a value of between eight and ten million dollars."

"Are you sh--... are you kidding me?" Porterfield asked.

"Noooo. If there are, let's say, 200 unopened boxes there, and I'm only identifying them from photos I saw of the '52 Topps when they were being sold, that means 25,000 cards, or about 250 of each card, but the Mantle card was double printed—allowing for 500 of them. The Mantle was the most valuable, by far, but the other 24,500 cards would average at least $100--$200 each, for an additional $2.5 to $5 million. But that would have to be the high series of the '52's. If they were any other series, you're looking at 25,000 cards, brand new, worth about $25 each or just over half a million. Plus an incremental value for the stars in the lower-numbered cards—Berra, Feller, Robin Roberts, Duke Snider, Gil Hodges, Johnny Mize, and I'm sure Arty could name others.

"Of course, if you market them as "unopened packs" each pack would go for $1,000 or $1,500, because it might have a Mantle in it. In that scenario, 200 boxes equals almost 5,000 packs, so that lands you somewhere at or above $5 million—without even having to peel a wrapper.

"Any way you slice it, it's a windfall, and from my experience—and I say this because Mrs. Rizzoli is out of the room—Pete Rizzoli did not spend much above $100,000, if that, for that haul of cards. And that's just one variety. These smaller boxes to the left of the 52's, the camera's left, they have to be from somewhere between 1948 and 1951, because those cards were much smaller in size than the 1952s, which were the first-ever larger-sized cards. This stack is labeled by Bowman, the issuing company, but it's 1951 or before." I looked more closely, although I was straining my eyes.

"The rest of these are after 1952. They're identified from the two companies that competed up until the end of 1955; and I know this pile is 1956 Topps, because I earned a full box from my third-grade report card, and I'll never forget what it looked like. The rest of these are newer, up to maybe 1959, 1960, but unopened boxes from any of those years are worth their weight in gold, and it's typical of Rizzoli that he'd want to be photographed, grinning, with this haul."

Porterfield looked at Arty then me. "What is all of it worth? Just that picture's stuff."

"My guess," and I said that to Arty more than to Porterfield, "would be somewhere near $30 to $50 million, but that's misleading. For one thing, this is an older photo of Rizzoli. My guess is that it was taken in 1984, 1985, and the value of those cards would be about half of today's estimate. Secondly, there is no way to accurately value the boxes of '52's, because the possible difference in value between early series and the last series is massive."

"And," Arty jumped in, "Rizzoli was known to wholesale cards out to selected dealers who would then owe him huge favors. See, with, well, the 1952 Topps Mantles, you can't just dump 300 mint cards onto a table and expect to sell them at full price as if they are scarce. It's the law of supply and demand, and sometimes, Rizzoli's bragging that he found a new cache of rare stuff—well, it made the stuff less rare. So he probably would have wholesaled 250 of those Mantles, if he did anything with them, over a period of maybe six years. Six, Decker?"

"Sounds right. And he would have sold the other fifty or so for the going price, over the course of those six years. I once saw six or seven gem mint, Pete Perfect Mantles on one of his tables maybe four years ago. Maybe five years—Atlantic City."

Porterfield seemed stunned. "Is it even remotely possible to consider that one human being would consider a kidnapping or commit the murder of another human being for a baseball card of Mickey Mantle?"

"For what is in that picture, Sir, people would wipe out an entire village..."

Porterfield mumbled to himself. "Murder. Motive: Mickey Mantle. Means.... Means? How? I'm not even sure I want to know what else is in this pile in front of me,"

his face changed and he looked up with a true copper's grin. "But for the sake of justice, we do need to take a look...."

# Back in the USSR

Before Chief Porterfield even dared to look at the next item in the pile of papers taken from the briefcase, there was a knock on the conference room door.

"Yes?"

"Phone call from the Hamlet police for Officer Decker. He can pick it up in there if you want."

"No, he'll take it somewhere with privacy. Thank you."

Porterfield then turned to me. "Unlock the door on your way out, and we'll close it behind you. If you have to leave, or if it will be a long call, please let us know. Otherwise, we'll wait a few minutes before proceeding."

I thanked the Melrose chief, got up, walked to the door (remembering to unlock it, as it's so hard to walk through locked doors), and was met by the police matron outside. I then heard the latch click back in place.

"You can take the call in here, Officer Decker. Line two."

I walked into what was probably a press office, although why Melrose, before the last couple of days, would need such a thing, was unknown to me. Still, nice touch... press office. Money.

"Decker."

"Deck, it's Nick Sweeney. I'm the probie who rides with Sull—"

"I know who you are. What's up?"

"The detectives have absolutely hit the wall trying to learn anything about Billy Vychon."

"Do they think the feds have the information and have sealed the files?" I asked.

"Nobody has given any indication of that. It all started this morning. Vychon went before Magistrate Benson to request a bail hearing for his son, but he got nowhere with that idea. Benson's no jerk, either. He told Vychon he understood, and I quote, 'a father's need to be with his son at this time,' but he told Vychon that there would not be any bail until he felt confident that the boy would not be 'threatened by local vigilantism' if released. He may have been waiting for Vychon to promise that his goons would protect the kid."

"Vychon is too smart for that, but it was clever."

"Benson then told Vychon he would take the bail request under consideration in the next few days, but he also ordered Vychon to surrender his passport, and his son's. Here's the kicker: Vychon said that nobody in his family had a passport.

"That sent the detective bureau scurrying, and there is no record of Vychon having a passport, or, for that matter, of his existence on earth prior to 1985, when he initially filed incorporation papers for VX Corporation."

"I can't believe he doesn't have a passport," I told Sweeney. "What name was used on the incorporation papers?"

"Two words: Billy Vychon. Address in Hamlet. He opened his account in the midtown bank after the incorporation papers came through, dropping $150k for openers, and as a corporate entity, he could do that. If he had done it as an individual, the IRS would have sent a SWAT team to his house for the sheer hell of it."

"Are there any bank records in the name of Billy Vychon?"

"None before the corporate filing. And once he got in business, he made hefty bucks. Several million, in fact. To get all the details of who, when, and how, we're trying to get a subpoena to present to the bank officials."

"Look," I said, "I can't tell the Detective Bureau their business, but they need to get his tax records, and immigration records from the years, oh, 1982 to 1985—if such things even exist. Where was Vychon's place of birth listed in the incorporation papers?"

"Wait a minute, I have it here. Born, June, 1950—making him only 41, well, almost 42, and Union of Soviet Socialist Republics. No specific date in June, and no city listed."

"Crafty bastard. Still, if he brought the family here, he had to have financial resources, and nobody accumulates wealth in Nizhny Novgorod or Pskov. He had to have Moscow money behind him."

"Listen, I'm busy here. Share my thoughts with the suits and I'll be back there before I go off duty. We have to be able to follow Vychon's trail from birth to this morning, with no gaps in the time-line. Follow me?"

"Yes. I'll pass your message along." Click.

Huh. Vychon sprang from the earth of Hamlet as he was almost middle-aged. Neat trick, but not impossible for someone with cash. And the bastard's trail is safer than it would have been in 1985, because the Soviet Union is now officially gone.

*But not forgotten.*

I rattled it around in my head as I headed back to the conference room. Billy Vychon: now a self-pronounced respectable antique dealer, having saved himself from the evils of pornography. Smart money says he brought some Russian treasures with him, and thinking on it, even smarter money says he fenced some of those treasures in Little Odessa to receive a new identity and set up his "adult film" business.

I headed back to the conference room to learn more about the now-officially 'missing' Pete Rizzoli.

# The Taxman

After I hung up from Nick Sweeney, the probationary Hamlet officer who would be served up on the altar of all things anti-Russian after the heat died down, I looked at my watch: 9:50 in the a.m.

It seemed impossible that only an hour ago, I'd watched a well-dressed terrified woman exit from her BMW with a briefcase under her arm.

She had made the walk from her car to the municipal building as Mrs. Pete Rizzoli. I could only wonder if she would walk back to her car thinking of herself as 'the widow Rizzoli.'

I didn't have much time to ponder the question, and lacking sleep, I wasn't as mentally sharp as I prefer to be, so I pushed my private "caution" button as I knocked twice on the door to the conference room and simply said, "Decker."

Detective Banta opened the door to let me in, saying, "Not bad news, I hope."

"Is there any other kind?" I answered, with a shrug of the shoulders intended to convey that this was, after all, police work, an occupation that carries with it a minimum of good news.

Chief Porterfield looked at me as if my presence signaled the ability to resume looking at the briefcase contents. It clearly need not have been a concern, as the next few items were the family photo album and would not shed light on any crime except, perhaps, the offense of a woman marrying a sub-species of homo sapiens.

A wedding picture. Not exactly royal nuptials, as the bride was not wearing a bridal gown and the groom was decked out in a sports coat, not a suit. Polyester pants, once nearly *chic* on golf courses, and plastic loafers, forever *chic* in senior citizen homes, rounded out the picture.

But, as we knew, times changed, and the next few photos were Pete Perfect with each new sports car, or at card shows, or being made up for some television appearance that I had blessedly missed. The make-up artist should have won an award for turning the greasy creep into something that almost looked human.

*It's not nice to speak ill of the dead,* I reminded myself, but in the same moment, it hit me that in my subconscious, Pete Rizzoli was indeed dead—dead and buried. Possibly submerged; or dissolved.

After the photo-montage, which must have been a challenge for Mrs. Rizzoli to compile in her fearful state, Porterfield turned several sheets of paper, then separated them from the pile, suggesting they were one entity.

"Tax returns," he said simply. He spread out five sheets of paper in front of him, as a virtual signal that we should gather around.

The documents were the 1991 earnings returns, which meant they were being readied for submission at this point in 1992. Banta immediately noticed and stated that they were 'rough' data, as the entries were in pencil, the tax form 1040 was not signed by Mr. or Mrs. Rizzoli, and it bore no co-signature of an accountant/tax preparer. Either way, it was a significant document, because it gave us a very clear insight into Mrs. Rizzoli's state of mind, and if she was scared enough to share her personal taxes, she had clearly passed 'terrified' about two toll booths back.

"I wonder who printed those numbers," I said aloud, although in that moment, it didn't make a huge difference.

Skipping past the address and 'exemptions,' we got to line 7, 'earnings.' Zero. Arty thought that was ridiculous, but Rizzoli didn't work for anyone. His income would be further along, under 'Business income or loss,' and there were no entries between 'earnings' and 'business income.' There, however, Rizzoli had claimed $4.7 million and change, although he could not attach form W-2, but rather a 1099 prepared by his accountant—in essence, he was telling himself how much to declare. Still, it seemed like he was owning up to a lot of business.

There were some marginal adjustments between lines 12 and 22, 'total income,' but even with the adjustments, it was still just a tick above $4.6 million. I couldn't wait to see Schedule C.

Under 'Adjusted gross income,' there were deductions, undoubtedly accountant-driven, and Mrs. Rizzoli, it would seem, was paying tuition (and fees) to some college, so that put the adjusted gross income just a year of my salary below $4.6 million.

Line 40, 'itemized deductions,' was just over $2 million, and that would require scrutiny of schedules A and C.

Two exemptions on line 42 did not change the picture much, but the Taxable Income was still just midway between $2.5 and 2.6 million. That meant that the 'Tax' owed was $861,640. *This guy is a national resource...* I had to adjust myself to the current situation: *Rizzoli had been a national resource....*

There were some adjustments to that amount, each of which would have required the attachment of a separate form not present in this accounting of things. To me, that suggested that this was not the work of Mrs. Rizzoli, but an account, who would have said, "Show them this, if they need to see something," and handed over the basics.

There were changes in 'Other taxes,' which included 'Self-employment tax,' (no form), plus a notation that Rizzoli had paid quarterly taxes—four times a year, which is probably why they're called 'quarterly taxes' of $200,000, so the amount owing was just over $50,000.

For reasons best known to whoever put this packet together, Schedule C was next, and while it revealed sizable expenses as outlay for the baseball card business, no federal auditor would challenge it, given that the income more than doubled the outlay, and the taxpayer owed Uncle Sap almost a million bucks.

The oddities came initially in Part III, 'Cost of goods sold,' where Rizzoli claimed a starting inventory of over $10 million, purchases totaling more than $1 million, and a closing inventory in the range of $8 million. That change in the value of inventory was considered "Cost of goods sold," and would be subtracted from 'Income' on the front page line for 'Income,' reducing the total. But just from one photograph, admittedly a few years old, we knew Rizzoli had to be holding a lot more than $10 million in inventory.

*Or was he?*

'Expenses' were another curiosity and a good place to pad expenditures and lower the eventual tax burden. Advertising costs were listed at over $500,000, and considering how many times I'd seen Rizzoli's ugly mug in sports publications, I could not doubt the amount as much as I deeply wanted to. Car and truck expenses were minimal, and in the baseball card business there's damn little that will depreciate beyond the calculator used to compute the ill-gotten gain.

If he had lived long enough, I suspected Rizzoli would have bought a corporate jet, and written off, as depreciation, the jet, the hanger, the gate fees, insurance, and pilot cost. The flight attendant would be probably written off as entertainment.

Rizzoli's insurance was staggering, because to insure 'collectibles' amounted to about $20 per thousand of value, which meant it would cost $20,000 to insure $1 million, and Rizzoli had that many times over. Someone needed to have a chat with his insurance man, preferably while holding a warrant or a subpoena. Or both.

Legal and professional services, office expense, travel, meals, and entertainment rounded out the staggering costs of being the king of baseball cards.

But 'other expenses' caught my attention at least. Rizzoli claimed three storage facilities. One, in virtually an extension of Melrose, and only two blocks north of where I'd bought cards long ago from Harry, who lost his cards to a thief and died of a broken heart.

The second storage facility was in Rye, New York, which made a certain amount of sense, because that was 'money-country' and those folks, if collectors, would be well serviced if Rizzoli could just visit his nearby storage facility and then play show-and-tell with his valuables.

The last entry troubled me deeply. "Brooklyn, N.Y." Brooklyn, although it still housed thousands of Dodger fans, despite the Bums' departure thirty-six years earlier, did not seem like an ideal location to store valuables. Too much crime in the area and too little likely business.

Huh.

That single sheet of paper left me troubled, but Schedule A only compounded the felony—pun intended. Rizzoli claimed over $35,000 paid in sales taxes in New Jersey—no doubt to update his sports car fleet. The next line, 'real estate taxes' showed an entry of just over $46,000.

That is a lot of money in real estate taxes, even for a mansion. Even for Melrose. I made a mental note to discover how much his house was valued at and how the tax figure was arrived at. Porterfield had enough clout to get that information from the local assessor's office. It seemed high, but it could have been a lot higher…unless the appraiser paid a visit, chatted up Rizzoli as "Pete Perfect" and got bribed with some cards. Shadier deals have been done.

The next eye-popper was 'home mortgage interest,' and at $131,000, it meant his monthly mortgage *interest* was just about $11k, with an additional $4k-plus, per month, in property taxes. Monthly. Plus the principle, of course, and that's an amount of money that is tough for a cop to break down into components.

But what was odd was that with an income of $4.7 million, minus what he claimed as expenses, he even had a mortgage. Why pay $131,000 in interest when you have the resources—and then some—to pay off, or at least pay down—the nut. It was not as if 1991 was Pete Rizzoli's first year in the chips. I knew from hearing him brag at the National Card Show in

Parsippany, New Jersey, back in 1984, that he had just bought "a 'modest' 18-room house, indoor pool, indoor bowling alley, and five car garage." He might have mentioned that it also had an elevator, but I guess he didn't want to rub it in. After all, Rizzoli was the stereotype rags-to-riches parvenu, and he would have had an elevator in a one-story home.

The only reason, and I kept it to myself among that gathering, planning to share it privately with Arty, that he was paying interest and not paying the whole thing off, was that maybe he *was* accumulating and keeping cash to start a new life. And unless he had been heavily insured prior to last Thursday, Mrs. Rizzoli would definitely pass out again when she discovered her mortgage obligations as a widow.

Still, it troubled me, and I was surprised that Mrs. Rizzoli, who had to sign all the papers as his dependent, didn't raise the issue. If we got to talk to her again, it was certainly an item that I planned to introduce into the conversation gently. "I heard that you have a bowling alley in your home. Do you bowl? Oh, and why didn't you pay the place off?"

Maybe I was drowning in self-pity because I'd never see that kind of money, except on someone else's tax forms. Or I was angry that I never really had the chance to tell the bastard what I thought of his larceny. Or that somewhere inside me was a clot of sorrow over Edwina Griffin, the wonderful lady who had once been on my paper route.

Or maybe I couldn't get past Rizzoli having a storage locker in Brooklyn. Not a crime, but it niggled at me.

It seemed like something that desperately needed to be followed up, and it occurred to me that I might be damned surprised by what I'd find in that storage locker.

The corpse of Pete Rizzoli, for one thing; and/or the gun that killed him.

No fingerprints, no serial number. The handle wrapped in gauze or tape, with neither empty cartridges nor bullets remaining.

Just death, or, perhaps nothing. The life of a cop.

# You Don't Need A Weatherman To Know Which Way The Wind Blows

Blessedly, when I returned to the conference room, a coffee break was wildly in progress, so I hadn't missed anything that might provide a revelation of some sort.

Equally blessedly—or so it seemed, we were within sight of completing the items that Mrs. Rizzoli had brought with her in the briefcase.

I had no knowledge of whether she would be returning, and if Chief Porterfield knew, he didn't think the information was important enough to share with me. If she did not return, the fate of the briefcase's contents were clearly an issue that had to be addressed, but luckily, that was not my call.

Returning to the contents, there were a few more photographs, but each, in turn, merely reinforced the already-known fact that only a banquet hall would be large enough to contain Pete Rizzoli and his ego.

There was also a small, rectangular receipt for a safe-deposit box located in the bank no more than 250 yards from where we were sitting. The receipt indicated that the box had been opened on September 27, 1989 and had cost $25 annually. To me, that suggested a small or medium-sized box, but certainly not something big enough to hold a Rizzoli-sized inventory of valuable cardboard.

This time, I spoke up, suggesting to the chief that he get a subpoena for the bank records of that box, and a warrant to find out what was inside it.

Porterfield wasted no time, ordering Banta to get in touch with Judge van der Kamp and have the documents signed and sealed, and to take someone with him to the bank to find out the answers.

Banta looked as if he did not want to leave, since there was one remaining document—a stack of paper that looked like a raw manuscript, and we knew it contained Rizzoli's known inventory. But Porterfield invoked the maxim that a kidnap trail goes cold after 48 hours, and that 48-hour period had ended at mid-day on Saturday.

And today was Wednesday. Banta replaced his tail between his legs and left, leaving the world of baseball cards to Arty Swanson and me. Arty got the assignment to re-lock the door.

"Well, gentlemen," Porterfield intoned as he pushed the stack of spiral-bound pages away from his immediate grasp, "we have come to the point known as 'nuts and bolts.' Forgive me if I lean heavily on your expertise in the matter of sports collectibles. I do have some knowledge of antiques, but not collectibles."

*Antiques...collectibles. I heard the Pavlov's dogs' ringtone again.*

Before we got as far as page one, there was a knock at the door and Arty unlocked it, admitting FBI Special Agent Longwell back into the proceedings. It occurred to me, as I'm sure it did to Arty, that despite Longwell's renewed presence, the composition of the room really hadn't changed.

FBI agents didn't collect baseball cards; they collected 'meritorious service awards for overtime work.' *Try finding a price guide for those items, pal. Better still, look for loose change in your pay envelope.*

Arty dragged the card inventory across the elegantly carved table top that dominated the room, slightly elevating the spiral binding so as not to scratch it. Mentally comparing it to Hamlet's equivalent, which was a folding flea-market table, I quickly realized the importance of having a modicum of well-appointed corporate headquarters in town.

The document, untitled, was clearly an inventory of various sports collectibles, as there were notations for football and basketball cards, but no non-sports cards. There were also a few pages at the back for things like World Series and Super Bowl rings, autographed baseballs, plus checks signed by everyone from Babe Ruth to Connie Mack, to Geronimo, for all I knew or cared.

I knew those items fetched hefty prices, because there had not been conventions at which Connie Mack or Babe Ruth sat all day and signed autographs, and the only autograph I could imagine for Geronimo would have been on some government document that took Indian land. Still, the law of supply and demand was involved in the value of the signature, even if on a fraudulent document.

But Rizzoli's holdings were massive, and the first 20 of the total 211 pages made it clear that his Schedule C listing of $10 million as inventory was a complete and utter fraud. The inventory was chronological, and there were cards or sets that went back to 1887, plus the early 20th century treasures of Honus Wagner, Ty Cobb, Eddie Plank, and Napoleon Lajoie.

There were sizable holdings of the Goudey cards from the 1930s, and as the card sets edged closer to modern times, the volume of items only increased.

A sample would be what I recalled from 1957: "Complete sets, 11; 9 Mint, 2 ex-Mint; rev., 12/91; BB. Below that would be individual cards of value from 1957, usually starting with Mantle and working through the litany of established stars, and the major "rookie" in that pile was Brooks Robinson, a ball-player who was not only a superstar on the field, but off the field as well.

Rizzoli had taken care to note that the listing in question—the line only for 1957 sets—had been revised in December, 1991, suggesting he had not sold any of them in the last two or three months. "BB" seemed obvious, although, as I mentioned, there were football and basketball sets. But a football set would not have been followed by Mantle, Mays, Clemente, and Brooks Robinson, and the 1957 baseball set would not have included Gino Marchetti, Roosevelt Brown, or Norm Van Brocklin, although I suspected that with the Dutchman's arm, he probably could have pitched for the Cubs.

Then again, so could my late lamented mother.

The inventory was truly mind-blowing, and although I kidded myself that I had put together one of the better collections locally, my one-each, non-mint cardboard did not belong in the same sentence with what Rizzoli had in his possession, but I had to remind myself not to be hypnotized by what was there, but to see if I could identify what was *not* there, or if there was an anomaly.

Certain sets of cards had either variations or errors—the 1952 Joe Page/Johnny Sain reversals, some color variations in the 1962s, a couple of oddities—albeit cheap ones, in the 1969s, but all of those were there, and noted.

What I didn't see was the 1959 set of Ted Williams cards, which should have been standard fare for most collectors, nor did I see the 1963 Fleer set, a limited item because of inter-company law suits, but a set with a rarity in number 46, a Joe Adcock card not widely printed. It was not in league with the 1952 Topps Mantle, or any Mantle for that matter, but it was an oddity that a dealer would pitch to collectors.

Why Rizzoli had none of those—or listed none of those—was unclear. Maybe they just didn't strike him as "mainstream." Maybe they were simply give-away sets for high-roller collectors.

On one five-page flip through, I mentally added up 750 early Mickey Mantles, and with those cards alone, you could have bought any house in Melrose, or put a good down payment on the city of Melrose, but I was still looking at the gold when I needed to find the pyrite.

As we flipped through, entertaining Porterfield with our insider-knowledge chatter, I began to notice that only some baseball sets—clearly baseball because individual players or subsets were noted beneath them--, while all "revised" at some date, did not include the 'BB' notation.

Huh.

When we finally got done adoring someone else's wealth, even if the owner most likely was fish food, Porterfield asked us what it all meant. Arty simply said it amounted to more potential money than most people would associate with baseball cards, a judgment I considered reasonable and sound, particularly since it lacked the braggadocio associated with the former owner.

"Millions?" Porterfield asked.

"Possibly closer to a billion in today's dollars, but less than that when purchased," Arty said.

Porterfield looked at me. "You agree?"

"Without hesitation," I said. "However, they're baseball cards for the most part, and while extremely valuable, they are not quite the same as, say, gold. When times get rough, people will invest in gold or rarities—very valuable postage stamps or coins, but I'm not yet sure that baseball cards are perceived in quite the same way as the upside-down airplane stamp. Still, if the economy is healthy, and Rizzoli only wanted to sell enough to pay all his bills and keep himself up to his ass in hot cars, he could hold onto ninety percent of what's there, and in ten, fifteen years, yeah, what was left would absolutely be a billion dollars."

Porterfield looked away, to an unfixed point in space, as the realization of what he was dealing with truly hit him. He said, quietly, and perhaps to himself, "And an inner city kid will kill another inner city kid for his lunch money."

Then, to us, "Would this guy really go out to buy this stuff with a suitcase full of cash?"

"Oh, yeah," Arty said. "Decker and I have seen him operate, and I think both of us thought at one time or another that one day…." and Arty let that thought trail off.

Porterfield looked at me, but I just nodded, adding stress with the my eyes.

The chief picked up the phone and asked about Mrs. Rizzoli, who apparently had been taken home in an unmarked police vehicle. Apparently, she had asked that the briefcase be maintained in the safest possible location until she could come back for it.

Porterfield informed Arty that the two of them would witness the placement of the materials in a municipal lock box, after which it would be placed in the building's vault. An off-duty officer would be paid overtime to stand guard at the vault, as a courtesy to Mrs. Rizzoli, already being treated like a widow…

Porterfield stood, and looked briefly lost for words, but eventually offered me his deepest thanks for spending time helping Melrose with this "issue", as he styled it. He asked me to remain for just a moment while he and Arty put away the contents of the briefcase.

Five minutes later, he was back, sans Arty, who was temporarily standing guard at the vault. "Decker, I respect your expertise. I still have a few years before retirement, and I enjoy this job, so I'm not leaving any time soon. What I'm trying to say is that if you get tired of working in Hamlet…." and *he* let his thought hang.

"I'm very flattered, Mr. Porterfield, but I don't think I'd want to go back to being the probationary officer."

"Nothing of the sort," he told me. "It would be a lateral move, and I can assure you that the salary and benefits here are more appealing than they are in Hamlet."

I told him I'd think about it seriously, but for the moment, I had to focus on the events right in front of us—the possible vehicular homicide murder of a woman in Hamlet, and the Rizzoli issue, which I told him I thought was a dead end.

He got my drift, and shook hands, thanking me again. While I was still pressing the flesh, Detective Banta returned, almost breathless. "I got a look inside that safe-deposit box. About a dozen rounds for a Glock 9 millimeter, and two keys."

"Any ideas what the keys would be for?" Porterfield asked him.

"They were just keys…."

I wanted to validate my current resumé with Porterfield, so I asked Banta, "Did you photograph them or dust them for prints?"

"Fuck."

I realized Porterfield and Banta might need a moment together.

I got back to my tired looking, salt-covered vehicle that was begging for a wash after the winter's toll, and thought that the world had been different when I parked it.

But that was inconsequential compared to what I knew was a missing piece.

"BB": Baseball? Bad buy? Maybe those initials stood for a dealer that was being targeted to buy those cards, although I couldn't think of any "BB" at that moment besides "Bobby Babe," the sticky-fingered friend of my youth who introduced me to the infamous 1952 Topps Mickey Mantle card. I didn't have any idea at that moment where "Bobby Babe" was, but the odds seemed thin that his possession of a card almost forty years earlier would make him a Rizzoli marketing target.

Maybe "BB" was there because there was also a basketball set available from that year, as obviously, basketball would also be "BB."

Too late to check that one now, so I stopped in my tracks and tried to remember where I'd seen "BB" listed, and whether or not those listings would have to be separated out from basketball.

No, that was no answer. It would have been simpler to just put 'baseball' or 'basketball' and leave it at that. So why the code?

Maybe "BB" was a place. Burbank? *Hollywood investors?*

No, not baseball, and not Bobby Babe.

*Brighton Beach.*

I literally froze in my tracks.

# A Tale of Two Cities

The sun was making one final attempt to break through the typical overcast March day as I drove back to my house in Hamlet. My brain was firing questions faster than answers were arriving, and I really only knew three essential facts.

One: It was still my day off. Two: My mind was totally exhausted. Three: My body was in worse shape than my mind. My mind was still the, well, the tired-battery calculator. My body was the roll of paper that was stuck somewhere in the gears.

I knew I had questions, but did I have answers? I pondered that briefly and realized I did have answers, but I wasn't yet sure what the questions were.

Sometimes, not always, but sometimes, that is how police work succeeds. The plan was to get home, make a list of "Rizzoli" questions and information to seek, and then a list of "Vychon" questions and records to seek.

The smart money was decidedly on the side of getting some answers to the Rizzoli items and getting a serious stonewall on the other side of the issue. After all, Vychon only existed from 1985, although he'd been born in the middle of 1950.

Arriving home, I abandoned the car in the driveway and foolishly went in the door that was virtually next to the phone, and sure enough, the light was blinking wildly.

I was hoping it was in reference to an overdue library book, or perhaps a charity seeking a donation for the cure for leprosy.

No such luck. It was Sweeney. "Decker. I know I just spoke to you up in Melrose, but there are people getting ugly near Vychon's place, so the chief is putting officers there, round the clock. You're set to be on days tomorrow, but you'll have the Vychon watch from midnight to eight. Call in when you get this."

Obviously, I could claim ignorance, because Hamlet was a town that was essentially an east-west collection of road stripes. I lived on the eastern extremity, in the modest dwellings, but Vychon's manse was on the exact opposite end of town, where they frequently petitioned to have our zip code unlisted.

I sat down and started making a list entitled "Rizzoli."

Phone records, especially the suitcase phone; bank records—as much as for financial doings as for the dates when he visited the safe-deposit box that contained the ammunition and the two unknown keys; the VIN number on the truck he was driving; insurance figures if he had the good sense to insure his inventory; the inventory itself—would it match the print-out that we read, or would it be deleted? I also needed to know, since he owned ammunition, if he was the legal owner of a weapon. If so, where would he have gone to practice with the weapon, and when—particularly most recently? Which of his co-card dealers could Mrs. Rizzoli identify, and what was the particular specialty of each, if that applied?

Then I worked down to the little details: his blood type; did he have any known aliases, or, if needed, would he check into a hospital as "Pete Perfect"? Did he have any credit card history with rental cars, as leaving in the truck and then renting something was an option not yet considered. Who had been his credit references when he was just getting into the big money?

Most importantly: Had Mrs. Rizzoli been contacted by anyone, and if so, why was she withholding the information? He had gotten the call and left on Thursday. It was now

Wednesday. Could there have been a call before the feds put the tap on the line? Would Mrs. Rizzoli ignore a ransom threat, and say, or at least think, *Shoot the bastard and be done with it!*

Not counting that option, there still existed three possibilities: he was living it up in some foreign country and planned to remain there, he was dead, or he was living it up somewhere in the US and planned to come home and tell his wife some interesting story.

Kidnapping for a ransom payment seemed remote after seven days, but it could not wholly be ruled out. During my police science studies, I had read up on kidnappings, and it is not, as some might suspect, the easiest crime to commit, as there are several variables that are not common to, say, bank robbery.

If Rizzoli had been kidnapped, and assuming it would have been someone or some group with decent intelligence, how would they do it?

In answering that question, I realized it could be a time consuming process, and that would be why we were in day seven of the event, when that amount of time usually means a funeral is in the offing.

Hypothesis: Rizzoli is called to some location at least 150—200 miles away from Melrose. He gasses up the truck and takes off with cash. He arrives at the designated "meet" location, most likely a residence—rented by a cash payment, temporary, so it couldn't be traced, and is met by multiple well-armed gunmen.

The ransom, of course, could be in the form of cash, but most likely, in baseball cards, as they're much harder to trace than Franklins.

But how?

Hypothesis: A ransom call to Hamlet. "Mrs. Rizzoli. If you want to see your husband alive again, have your domestic staff pack up every piece of his collectibles inventory that you can put your hands on, plus such cash is available. Do not make a withdrawal from any bank to do this, and do not make the authorities aware of what is happening. You can feign concern for your missing husband to prove your anxiety, but nothing more.

On Saturday night, fill the interior of a vehicle with small boxes, weighing no more than thirty pounds, with the good cards—and we know what they are. Park the car at the front door, but in a parking space, of St. Thomas Aquinas High School in Melrose. Leave and do not return Should the authorities try to follow anyone, the boxes will be tossed out and the explosive devices will be detonated, and your husband will be executed by attaching jumper cables to an industrial battery and his testicles, causing a painful electrocution. A video of that event will be sent to the FBI, local authorities, and national networks and will undoubtedly go viral, so it is in your best interests not to attempt any deception.

"We have thought of everything. You should think of your husband only. Cards can be replaced. Husbands cannot." Click.

If that was someone's plan, I thought, it was a damn good one, although I allowed for the possibility that several better plans might exist, or something foolishly simplistic would have been tried.

Still, I figured Rizzoli was dead, and probably pre-deceased Edwina Griffin.

As my mind reached that name, I realized I'd be tired and needing a thorough cleansing and a shave in order to put in a courtesy appearance at her wake, scheduled for Thursday—possibly after sixteen straight cop hours, eight at Vychon's manse and eight on the street. She had been a very warm and gracious lady to the community, and had treated me very well when I delivered her newspaper, even giving me history lessons.

Rizzoli, on the other hand, was now probably "history," and nobody would miss him. If there were indeed a wake, it would feature his widow and a collection of drooling opportunists.

Did I just say "history lessons"? In my tired state, I had to actually ask myself the obvious question.And there was the key to Vychon, or at least one possible key—right in front of my tired cerebral cortex. He was born in 1950 in the Soviet Union. At that point in time, the mentally-decaying Josef Stalin, fearing that he was being slowly poisoned by his attending physicians, was planning for the kind of purge that he had unleashed in the mid-1930s when he butchered the Red Army top brass so ruthlessly that when the Nazis arrived in 1941, it was being led mostly by former corporals.

The 1950s purge was to have been a 'doctors' purge, but it never really got going by the time Stalin shuffled off the mortal coil in March, 1953. What if 'Vychon' had been the son of a well-to-do physician of some rank in the Soviet Union? The father certainly would have tried to get his son, or sons, or sons and daughters, out of the Soviet Union before that purge began.

But where, and how? A medical conference somewhere outside the USSR. Little 'Vychon' was bundled up and smuggled out. Who would check the items a doctor was taking *out* of the USSR? Bringing things in was another matter... but it was possible.

That somehow triggered a *Goldfinger* image in my head. In that mid-60s James Bond classic, Auric Goldfinger, played by the sardonic Gert Frobe, plotted to break into Fort Knox. Not to steal the gold there, but to vaporize it with a cobalt and iodine nuke. The net result would have been that Goldfinger's holdings in the precious metal would vastly increase in value.

Would some card dealer or a consortium of such dealers destroy Rizzoli's hoard to make his or their own holdings that much more valuable? It seemed ludicrous, as it amounted to destroying hundreds of millions in order to increase the value of a few million. Baseball cards were not, I reminded myself, the gold in Ft. Knox. But at least I was considering all scenarios, far-fetched as some might appear.

There was the rub. Since the mystery call came through on the "special phone," it seemed like an inside job. Would someone have wanted to keep Rizzoli alive, just so he could no longer brag endlessly about his wealth and what it had bought him, or would they just put a bullet in his ear and dump him in a shallow grave?

Baby smuggled out of Russia, perhaps. Baseball cards as ransom, perhaps.

But where did those two paths cross when my thoughts kept coming back, again and again, to Brighton Beach?

When I figured out the answer to that, I'd be able to determine, with some serious help, who Billy Vychon really was, and what had really happened to Pete Rizzoli.

It was definitely time for a lone-overdue nap. I imagined dreaming of Soviet baseball cards.... "Vladimir Gruchenko, second base for the Sverdlovsk Sea-Otters."

Maybe I was just losing my mind.

*What mind?*

# Don't Shoot The Messenger

I woke up at twilight, face down on the dining room table, a pile of notes for my pillow. Not REM sleep, but it would have to do.

Twilight reminded me that it was not yet Daylight Savings Time, so it had to be about 6:15; the bad news was that I'd now have to be awake for about twenty-four hours straight, and no phone call had come in to change that. Which was the good news.

Was Vychon's place still a target for townies, and what was the dynamic going on over there? Had he withdrawn his goons, his "safety perimeter" or had he just equipped them with rubber bullets or stun guns?

One thing was for certain. Short of something on the scale of the Normandy Invasion, no group of townies would reach his front door alive, and I felt certain his windows were shatter-proof glass. Perhaps opaque as well, on the odd chance that one of his "adult features" had been filmed within. There's a thought: *Heather does Hamlet. Starring "Peter" O'Toole.*

On that note, I realized I had to know what was going on, so I quickly cleaned up, put on a clean uniform, and dashed out to grab dinner—a polite euphemism for greasy junk food—at the place where the garbled speaker takes your order.

An hour later, now gassy and still tired, I arrived at headquarters. Before I even had the chance to look up and see who was on duty at the desk, Chief God-help-us came through the door that led to what was laughing called the "squad room," but which in no way resembled the real squad room I'd seen hours earlier in Melrose.

"Enjoy your day off, Decker?" the chief asked.

"Oh, yeah, sir. I got to visit a real police station and even touch some of the wanted posters." I tried to sound like a young child on a school trip to some exotic site like the post office.

"And did we learn anything?"

"Maybe a lot, maybe a little." I did not want to say too much more, as I doubted that my boss gave the proverbial rat's ass about Pete Rizzoli, and if I offered my suggested that Vychon had been smuggled out of the Soviet Union to avoid Stalin's purges, I'd probably be asked, "Who's Stalin?"

It was a collection of memories just like that which caused me to regret that the chief had not stayed in school a little longer and maybe try to finish sixth grade. He was unique in the sense that he was arguably the only cop who ever hit the street and could not do basic arithmetic. He would look at a parking meter with fifteen minutes remaining, then look at his watch, which would say 12:15, then take out a small pocket calculator and compute the fact that the meter in question would expire at 12:30.

To him, that was rocket science. And he was in charge of law enforcement for 8,000 souls.

I did tell him, or perhaps remind him, that I'd been up to Melrose to consult on the Rizzoli deal.

"Yeah. Porterfield called and said you were a smart cookie," he said, as I waited for the other shoe to drop.

"Well, get this, Decker. You're back in Hamlet, and we have got a dead woman and five juveniles who were drunk off their asses, and several parents—identities unknown as yet—who gave them the alcohol and keys to kill a Hamlet resident.

"The local town trash has come clean that his son did it—but he exonerated himself and even said he was going out of the porno business and he's changed his ways. You can never come clean when you use dirty money to establish what you pretend is a clean business," he editorialized.

"The Grand Jury meets tomorrow, and you'll probably be called as a witness."

"Shouldn't I know that officially by now?" I asked him, "And if so, I'm not going to look spiffy clean after eight hours of watching Vychon's property."

"Catch some sleep when things get quiet," the Chief told me.

I desperately wanted to change the subject, since I couldn't change the current venue: "Will I be going to court in a municipal vehicle, or will I be putting in for mileage on my own car?"

"Decker, you're getting eight hours overtime to keep that Russian bastard safe and sound. Don't try to set my ass on fire over a couple bucks." I knew I could get under that man's skin—then again, his skin was thinner than thin-crust pizza, and the pizza was probably more intelligent.

"So what, exactly, am I supposed to do at Vychon's tonight?"

There will be two patrol cars, one at each end of the property. You'll have one and Cobb will have the other. Other squad cars will come by from time to time, for appearance's sake, and so you can get coffee and not piss on Vychon's plants. The county will also send cars to the neighborhood."

"And if someone tries something stupid?"

"Arrest them for whatever they were doing," he answered, like a commander telling the troops they were about to storm a fortress.

"Okay, I get it. You there—you're under arrest for trying something stupid. You have the right to remain silent; if you give up that right, anything you say may wind up in the funny papers tomorrow."

Now the chief was pissed. Put another way, I'd succeeded. "God dammit, Decker, sometimes you're too smart for your own good."

"Forgive me, chief, but that's not quite accurate. The problem is that sometimes I'm too smart for *your* own good."

"You're on at midnight," he said, storming away. "Maybe Grand Jury tomorrow morning. And don't fuck it up."

I looked up at the desk and the volunteers on duty had been laughing so hard the tears were running down their faces. I shook my head at the lunacy of the whole thing, and reminded them that Edwina Griffin's wake was the next day, and if they had not planned to attend, it would be a nice touch if they did. "The bigger the turnout, the bigger the headline on Friday, and publicity like that can only put more heat on the little bastards responsible."

That was the first time in about fifteen minutes that I'd said something that made any sense.

At that moment, the static of the in-house radio crackled. It was Banta, the Melrose detective calling in: "Decker there?"

I bounded behind the desk and keyed the microphone. "Yeah, this is Decker. What have you got?" *Rizzoli's body, perhaps?*

"We got a response on the all-points bulletin on Rizzoli's truck. I sent them the VIN number. But get this—the truck was painted, hastily, in three stripes of red, white and blue; that's the story on the exterior. Inside, there was no body, no obvious traces of blood, but a lot of booze, with a number of broken bottles."

"Is this one on you, or are the feds helping?"

"It's the feds, because it's out-of-state for us. But I know what you're thinking after dealing with that knucklehead Longwell this morning. He's the exception. Because Melrose is literally on the New York State border, we get a lot of over-the-line situations, and the feds put a residence agency right here in town. And those guys will bust their collective asses, particularly on a high-profile case like this, 'cause if they fail, they'll be back in a traditional bureau office, and that means a transfer, packing, moving—they don't want that. So they'll cooperate fully."

"Will they tow the vehicle to an impound garage to do a microscopic search for forensic evidence?"

"Yes, if the VIN number on the vehicle matches. Wait a minute, Decker. That truck is older than the use of VIN numbers in vehicles. How the hell…?

"It's a Rizzoli deal. He probably bought a newer model and had it customized to look like the older vehicle. He worked in that kind of sheet metal/auto body shit before he struck it rich."

"We'll be certain to have it checked," Banta told me.

"Okay, get back to me if the VIN number matches; one more thing, Banta."

"What?" with some urgency in his voice.

"Where was it found?

"Literally underneath the eastbound end of the Brooklyn Bridge, by the docks just beneath the overhang of the Gawanis Expressway. Maybe the location is not totally unusual, because Rizzoli had a storage locker in Brooklyn."

"Yeah, and I suspect he's in it. Or he was in it, but didn't like the company, so he decided to swim one night in the East River. Okay thanks."

Click.

*Yeah, Rizzoli had a storage locker there, but there was also a well-known neighborhood nearby that had more Russians per square mile than Stalingrad.*

*Shit.*

# Rich or Poor, It's Nice To Have Money

Ordinarily, in the evening hours of a Wednesday night, I'd be watching some cop show on TV, or a video tape of some earlier cop show if tonight's broadcast fare got bumped for something less interesting than good guys always beating bad guys.

This, however, was no ordinary Wednesday night, and with the possible discovery of Rizzoli's truck, my gut was telling me that the next twenty-four to thirty-six hours were going to be of critical importance.

And I would have only police radio for communications from midnight, a couple hours away, and four p.m., when my regular eight-to-four ended.

And part of the last two hours of that shift would be spent at a funeral home mobbed with Hamlet residents paying their respects to Edwina Griffin. I could only wonder if such a presence would take pressure off the Vychon residence, or add to it.

We would have the answer to that soon enough. In the meantime, I needed to know what was going on out there, and was the perceived danger to Vychon still enough to require that we protect one Hamlet citizen, despised by all the others, from all the others?

You cannot always look for logic in police work.

My locker usually held a few cans or bottles of heavily caffeinated soda—usually that bilious Mt. Dew, disgusting, but it was loaded with caffeine—for long shifts, so I went to the locker room to retrieve my evening necessities, planning to stop at the convenience store for snacks. As I passed the Chief's office, I heard him pronounce, "Your newspaper can quote me on this, word for word. I will be here at headquarters until this situation is cleared up. That should be after the Grand Jury meets tomorrow, but that's the best I can hope for."

A promise is a promise, I thought, so rather than drive my own vehicle out to Vychon's neighborhood before I went on duty, I took the chief's car.

Vychon resided at the extreme western end of Hamlet, a town that stretched, if you will, approximately three miles from its eastern and western borders, and slightly over a mile-and-a-half from north to south. It meant that for all intents and purposes, everyone knew everyone else. At least Vychon had the benefit of some separation, as he lived in a subdivision where the homes were built on two-acre or more parcels of land, and each house sported a somewhat different design in how the brick or the stucco fronts were presented. But all of them screamed big bucks.

Vychon's digs were no different, except that the house was probably the last one built, as it backed up to a serious hill, and the builders probably made it one five-acre plot to help sell it, particularly with a county road rising seventy-five yards well behind the back of the house. The road itself was magnificent. Joggers used it frequently, as it opened out to a beautiful view of all of Manhattan, from the bulge of buildings in mid-town to the two magnificent towers at the lower end. The joggers used it because it provided a great excuse to pause, empty the water bottle, and enjoy the view.

I felt confident that one of Vychon's guards, liveried in the carriage house north and west of the main house, kept an eye on such comings and goings, and the goon-in-chief made sure that his sentries were well-armed and well-versed in the ability to scare the hell out of a trespasser simply by invoking the guttural Russian language. If one of them pointed an AK-47 and simply said, in Russian, "Hamlet is a very lovely town, is it not?" it would turn most mortals to stone.

Vychon's house itself was splendid, and probably would have sold for somewhere in the neighborhood of five million, but in a way unremarkable—at least as far as houses that elegant went. When I arrived there, I found two police cars parked about 200 yards apart, both on Vychon's side of the street, but not adjacent to his property and facing each other. I parked right in the middle between them, approximately 300 feet from each, as Vychon's property had decent frontage. I chided myself mentally for not hitting the town assessor's office for a site plan of the residence, but with 400-plus feet of frontage and property that went at least 500 feet deep, that would account for my five-acre estimate.

Driving the chief's car in the dark meant that the two patrolling officers would not hurry to meet me, so I had a chance to take in the view. Not many lights on in the house, although the carriage house was well lit, but what made the visual exceptional was the lighting that was placed on the landscaping. Clearly, it had been well designed, and different colored lights gently highlighted each copse of shrubbery, trees, or flowering foliage, although none was flowering in mid-March. For the briefest of moments, I wondered how a "typical Russian" would landscape a home, but I reminded myself there were very few homes like this in Mother Russia. Beyond that, what could you do—trees are trees. The only Russian touch I could think of would have been to have a few recalcitrant peasants hanging from the trees, and that visual was enough to remind me why I was here.

I got out of the chief's car, and the two patrol units put their lights on and realized it wasn't the chief out for a look-see. Both jogged over to find out what was going on, and there was not much to report at my end, except that Melrose was reporting the possible discovery of Rizzoli's truck.

Both cops noted they hoped there had been a body found within, but I had to disappoint them.

The night itself was cold and cloudless, the second factor being responsible for the first, as clouds will at least hold in some of the day's warming sun. But no clouds, no heat, a chilly night. And it seemed odd, with some form of precipitation—rain, possibly sleet, possibly light snow, in the forecast—despite the absence of clouds.

The two officers had come on duty at four, and would be done at midnight, when I officially came on duty. Apparently, from the time they came on, until an hour after dark—say, 7:15, the locals had come by and had decided to protest by throwing partially empty or totally empty—why waste?—liquor bottles on Vychon's property. The soft, almost spongy composition of the lawn, made softer by the very gradual spring thaw, prevented any bottles from breaking, and a driver, pitching a bottle over the roof of his or her vehicle, was not about to reach the house itself.

Still, we had a duty to protect our citizens, and it would be bad press if some young busty porn "actress" were to be knocked even more brainless by a hastily thrown bottle of Stohley. Or, God forbid, if her limo was dented...

*Pavlov's bell rang again.* Liquor bottles being thrown on the lawn—a protest against what had happened Monday night, when the juveniles got liquored up and most likely killed Edwina Griffin.

Rizzoli's re-painted vehicle, found abandoned, with no body, no trace of blood, but, *broken liquor bottles.*

This wasn't coincidence by any means. It was the sudden realization that stage props were involved.

It damn sure wasn't coincidence, Decker, I told myself.

It was evidence.

And it had to be secured, and scoured for prints or any possible forensic evidence: DNA on the lip of a bottle? A human hair stuck to liquid on a broken bottle? One fingerprint, please, and please don't make it Rizzoli's, because we knew he didn't commit suicide.

Finally, evidence.

Maybe.

# Show Me The Money

I bade a quick "adios" to the two duty officers and told them they most likely would not see me coming back on duty at Vychon's modest dwelling at midnight.

I hit the siren through town and made the eight-minute ride in about three minutes. Good thing, too, as the chief treats his car like he treats his wife: low mileage, and no speed. Shit, that buggy needed to have the exhaust pipes cleaned out. The wife probably has the same needs.

Hearing the siren, everyone at headquarters was expecting *something*, and naturally there was disappointment when the only thing that came through the door was me.

"Playing cop again, Decker?" the chief said, by way of greeting.

"Well, if you're playing Chief I guess I can play cop. Oh, yeah. I am a cop. And before you say anything, you have to get me off that midnight-to-eight shift at Vychon's. I need to get up to Melrose and we need to wake up the county forensic unit before the Grand Jury convenes tomorrow."

"Have you completely lost your mind, junior?"

"No. I think I can make a possible connection between our drunken juveniles and the disappearance of Pete Rizzoli in Melrose."

The chief suppressed what might have been a hearty laugh. "Are you thinking that the kids, who could not get their car out of Hamlet without killing someone and taking down a light pole, kidnapped someone? Or are you just hunting for the reward money?"

"What reward money?"

"All over the news this afternoon, Decker. Mrs. Rizz-what's her name has offered $250,000 for 'information leading to…' what were you doing, sleeping again?"

"Yeah, chief. If I don't get at least two hours a day, I get cranky. Now get me off the midnight to eight and maybe I'll have something intelligent for you to tell the press after Edwina Griffin's service tomorrow."

"I should bring you up for insubordination," he fired back.

"Suit yourself, when this is over. I got it figured, chief, and now you have informed me that Mrs. Rizzoli—*the widow Rizzoli*—is going to hand me the reward bucks. Now, do you want this settled in the next day or two, or do you want to read ugly headlines for months?"

"You know what you are, Decker?"

"Yeah. I'm a cop, not a house-sitter. Change the shift and I'll see you at 7:45 a.m. for the platoon-shift change. And thanks for letting mc use your car."

Before I said that, I took careful notice that the chief was not wearing his service revolver, an item I doubt he had fired more thanonce a year to qualify for the job he currently held.

I then turned to the volunteers on the desk and told them to let Melrose know I was on my way up there in a few minutes, and to wake up Arty Swanson if necessary, and have him alert Chief Porterfield. Then: "And connect me with the county forensic people."

That call came through about thirty seconds later, and I said I'd take it at my desk. I knew the chief would be listening, but it was okay, because I wanted him to.

From habit, when I reached my desk, I took out my gun, removed the clip and the round in the chamber, and put those items, plus my handcuffs, in the right-hand top drawer of my desk, which I then locked. There was no reason for doing it, but it was a habit.

Full-time. I was only a wise-ass part time. And the buzzing in my head became much more clear as I heard again

Porterfield suggesting he wanted me on his police force in Melrose, and for a lot more money. And probably a lot less crapola.

I was finally connected to the county forensics office, but the only person on duty there was the officer who would process such items as had come in during the night. The worker-bees had left the nest and gone home. Still, he might know something.

I introduced myself and told him I was dealing with the hit-and-run vehicular homicide that had occurred in Hamlet two days earlier. *Was it really only two days?*

He acknowledged that he knew about that investigation.

I told him that we'd had the vehicle and everything in it taken to the impound garage for forensic analysis. Could he tell me anything about results?

He could only say that the vehicle was at the location where I hoped it was, and almost before he got that out, I asked him if everything was intact.

"It's urgent, and I have to know—were the liquor bottles and the pieces of glass processed? And please tell me they're still present."

"Yeah, that's all here, because we have to return to you everything exactly as we got it. I have no information that anything was processed. It's just broken glass, shards of glass, and some sticky labels."

"Great. That's all we need. Listen carefully. The FBI is in the process" (I hoped and prayed) "of impounding a vehicle in Brooklyn. It also contained, for reasons I cannot fathom, broken liquor bottles, which, since one broken liquor bottle tends to look like another, I assume might not draw attention. I need to have the best forensic person you have got make an in-depth comparison of the bottles and shards of glass from both vehicles. As I said, the FBI is involved, so lean on them if they don't lean on you."

"What's it all about—we usually just process for prints, and a lot of those small pieces of glass won't have prints."

"I know. I know. But suddenly we've got an outbreak of broken liquor bottles here in Hamlet, and I'm betting my badge—literally—that there is a connection to this second vehicle I mentioned. If and when anything is done—and please, this is a murder investigation—leave word at the Hamlet police headquarters, and make sure it gets to Chris Decker, D-E-C-K-E-R. Okay?"

"Okay, chief. If it's a murder deal, we'll bring in some people for overtime. But we damn sure better see some results, you know?"

"I know the drill. Look for any—*any* anomaly. There's got to be something between the bottles in the two vehicles. Meanwhile, I'll round up what we've got here—another collection of liquor bottles, but most likely unrelated—on a large expanse of lawn in Hamlet, just in case."

"Getting right on it, Decker."

"Thanks. Owe you big time." Click.

Six minutes after I had divested myself of my cop gear, I gathered it all up again and girded myself for battle. It was a strange feeling, but this was one of those moments when I made sure the gun was fully loaded and I was carrying extra ammunition.

I had no idea whom I was going to shoot. Or why. Just wanted to be ready.

Then I hopped in my own car and sped back out to the Vychon neighborhood. I met with the same two officers as I had not long before and suggested to them to pass the word that when the eight-to-four group comes on, one shift after they left, someone should tell the junior officer, maybe a probationary officer like what's-his-name... Sweeney, to clean up all the bottles from Vychon's lawn and to treat each bottle like evidence. Hint: Don't smudge the prints, if any. They may have value.

I also suggested that if anyone came out of the house to clean up the small array of potable containers, that the cops on duty should try to dissuade them from doing so, as they might have fingerprints that would tell us who put them there, and they'd be doing us a favor, blah, blah....

They understood. They also understood that this was more than about someone throwing liquor bottles on somebody's lawn because they were pissed off about something.

Then to Melrose.

There was only one sleepy officer on the desk when I walked in, but the guy had enough juice left to tell me that Banta was in the detectives' bureau and that Arty Swanson was on his way in.

Nothing was said about Chief Porterfield.

Huh.

I asked Banta for an update, and he told me, almost breathlessly, that the VIN number on the truck that was found was a match to the number we were looking for.

Arty Swanson looked tired, but it was not an exhaustion tired, rather a boredom-tired, as he had sat guard, not stood guard, alongside the vault that contained the Rizzoli briefcase from the moment it went into the vault, approximately 10 a.m., until he went off duty at 4:00 p.m. He could have had a more exciting day watching balding men get haircuts.

I commiserated with him, telling him I was so tired I'd have to look at the nameplate on my shirt if asked who I was. Still, and understandably, he wanted to know what was so urgent. I asked Banta to fill him in on the vehicle found in Brooklyn, and if nothing else, it damn sure woke Arty up. As he thought through the implications, he kiddingly said he should consider buying more life insurance because, after all, he also had a collection of baseball cards.

I knew what Arty had, and even between us, we didn't have the kind of stuff that Rizzoli would have donated to an orphanage; like Bosnia.

And taken a tax write-off.

Still, it germinated an idea, and I had to have at least some input, so I asked Arty, "If you were going to call Rizzoli, Mr. Pete Perfect, with the idea in mind that you were going to clip him, what would you wish he was carrying, a suitcase of cash, or boxes of cards?"

Arty pondered that for a moment, and I interrupted him to suggest that he consider my question from the standpoint of someone looking to make a score, not necessarily a card-collector.

"Tough call, Deck. You and I both know he's gone out the door, or to card shows with his little suitcase full of cash, and I have no doubt that he had six figures in $100 bills with him."

"As opposed to the value of cards?"

"Oh, shit. The cards would be worth ten, twenty, thirty times as much—if someone could take them off him and find a legitimate way to get them out on the street. And that assumes that he was taking cards to sell, because he wouldn't leave home with cards if he was going out to make a purchase—in those scenarios, he's the impoverished soul."

" Yeah, understood. But you would choose...?"

"The cards. Hands down. Are you thinking...?"

"Not thinking, Arty. I know it. I can feel it.

Tomorrow morning, as early as it can be done, we need subpoenas for Rizzoli's three storage lockers. We—well, you and Banta and whoever else is able—need to get inside them and find out what is in there, or what *was* in there but isn't there any more. I think someone took him off for his cards, not his cash."

"But," Arty began, taking a moment to form the thought, "wouldn't he have cash with him either way?"

Arty's thought hit me. "Yes, dammit. He'd have the money for bragging rights. Let's say someone called him and wanted to buy—not sell a shitload of high-end cards as a hedge against inflation or whatever. Rizzoli would take cash along so he could say, "Look, your offer for the cards isn't nearly enough. See this? This is cash. It goes where I go, and I earned it by charging the right price for perfect-condition cards. You want the cards, you have to bring serious cash."

"And he'd lose the cards and the cash, and they'd both be untraceable."

Arty looked puzzled. "The flaw, if there is one, is… how would he take a small fortune in cards to sell? Is there anyone out there with that kind of cash to buy, essentially, a business? Could Rizzoli manage that from a storage locker in a pickup truck?"

"Which is why we have to know about those storage lockers Porterfield has enough clout for subpoenas, no?"

"Absolutely. He'll certainly get one for the local site. We may need a federal judge for where were the others—Brooklyn, and ….?"

"Rye, New York. But the local one is critical," I reminded him.

"Yeah. Okay. That's no problem. Now, tell me this. When we break this wide open, how are we going to split the reward bucks?"

"Let's worry about that *if* we break it open," I told him, adding, "and I guess I was the last one to know there were reward bucks offered."

"I think we're damn close," Arty said, almost in a whisper.

It was just as well that it was a whisper, because at that moment, Detective Banta entered and it was clear he had something to tell us.

"The feds got the vehicle—the truck—to an impound garage, and apparently someone—you, Decker? told the local county forensic people to check the broken bottles and glass against the broken bottles and glass in the Hamlet vehicle from the other night."

"Yeah, that was me," I told him. "There's an anomaly there somewhere."

"Well, I talked to the Assistant Director of the New York City FBI office, or perhaps I should say that he talked to me, and he wanted to know what the hell was going on."

"It's a simple forensic request," I said. Almost to myself.

"That's not it. Did I tell you that the truck was painted?"

"Yeah. Red, white, and blue. Did it have 50 stars also?", I asked, not meaning to sound patriotic.

"No. That's why the FBI's big man called. It was red, white, and blue, but the blue was *light blue.*"

Arty didn't get it right away, but I think Banta had been told, and it hit me immediately.

"Those are not our colors. Those are the flag colors of the Russian Federation."

Total silence. You could have heard a mouse, wearing sneakers, walking on strawberry Jello.

"Who do we know from the Russian Federation?" Banta asked, phrasing his question in such a way to suggest he clearly knew the answer.

"And why are people throwing liquor bottles on his lawn at all hours of the day or night?" I answered him.

*Because I now knew the answer.*

*$250,000 worth of it.*

# All Quiet On The Western Front

As I left the Melrose Police Department, it seemed as if the temperature had dropped eight to ten degrees. But it wasn't any reflection on the thoughts that had come together in the back-and-forth between Banta, Arty, and myself.

It was just colder. So, since cops on duty are supposed to be supermen by only wearing their uniform shirts, I put on my cop jacket, since I was not technically on duty.

It was still cold, but once in the car, things warmed up, and there is nothing quite like an efficient car heater and a potential $250,000 reward to add some extra fire.

I didn't want to go back to the Hamlet P.D., and the idea of home, where I could probably make up some flow-charts that would resemble the subway lines in New York City was appealing, but somehow, I had at least one stop to make first: Vychon.

Heading home would have been a straight line, due south from the Melrose P.D. Vychon's property meant going west and south, and his property was as far from "home" as the Melrose P.D.

Still, I was drawn to it. I'd have settled for the "moth to the flame" because at least the flame would be warmer, and when I looked ahead to the eight-to-four shift with a detour to pay my respects to Edwina, the chill only settled further.

I stopped about mid-way to Vychon's at Eli's Deli, a proximate dining spot to a nearby community college, that stayed open until about 2:00 a.m. and whose major menu item was rather direct, if honest: probably no botulism. Salad dressing adventurous.

I picked up three containers of soup and some buttered rolls for myself and the boys on duty, and arrived at Vychon's at 11:45 p.m., just as the other two cars were getting ready to roll. The guys reported all quiet, and wanted to be back to the P.D. by midnight, so they thanked me for the deli goodies and left, knowing that another boring shift would arrive in a few minutes.

Vychon had decided to abandon porn for antiques and collectibles, and Rizzoli had probably spun off the mortal coil, leaving a huge void in the collectible market. One opening created, one opening filled.

Huh.

The soup was warm and tasty, but a little salty, so as I stood alongside the car in the street, I reached behind the driver's seat for a can of Mountain Dew, to wash down the salt. Great recipe for warmth, Decker: Hot soup and chilled Mountain Dew. I should have just ordered a cup of sodium to go with a splash of caffeine.

As I reached into the car, a pair of very upscale porch lights came on—perhaps the real estate brochures would cite them as "front entrance torches," as if to announce the presence of, or the arrival of a person of great importance.

I was not to be disappointed. It was Vychon, casually dressed and with a leather long-coat, reminiscent of Hitler's SS, thrown over his shoulders for warmth, and he was ambling gently in my direction, with something in his right hand that proved elusive to his landscaping lights.

Since I was hunched over and not fully visible, I put my hand on my automatic and unclipped the fastener that kept it in the holster. For the briefest of moments I thought, *Geez, if I get to shoot the bastard, I'll be the hero of the town. Maybe even get to keep the deposits on all the liquor bottles on the lawn.*

No such luck. Vychon was holding a bottle that was just slightly larger than a standard beer bottle. Perhaps some exotic European or Russian liquor. As he got closer and I got my hand away from my gun, I could not make any better diagnosis than it wasn't any traditional American beer.

"I see you are studying my drink," he said to me, and I noted that he said it in better English than when he made his press statement. *Why would he put on the Slavic accent for that moment? Sympathy? If so, he wouldn't be getting any from me.*

When I didn't say anything, he continued, "I would certainly have offered you one, but I strongly believe you are prevented from taking a drink when on duty."

"I got it covered," I told him, holding up the can of Mountain Dew.

"Yes, the great American beverage," and after a pause, "You were one of the officers involved with my son."

"Yes, I was."

"Can you tell me—"

"I cannot say anything because the matter is still under investigation. He was treated fairly and in full accordance with all New Jersey and American Constitutional legal proceedings."

"I did not doubt that. In Soviet Union he would have been beaten, and even before the matter of the old woman was learned of." *Why is he talking about 'Soviet Union'?*

Silence. Then Vychon spoke again, "I know you cannot say very much, but will he be treated fairly the rest of the way?"

"For his sake and your sake, I can only hope so. I heard your comment about losing your son. Clearly, he is in serious legal jeopardy. But the worst-case scenario is if he winds up in a prison, because younger persons do not always simply pass the time in a prison."

"Yes. It is just so in Soviet."

I could not resist. "Have things changed now that it is the Russian Federation? After all, the simple colors of the flag there are much more peaceful than the belligerence of the red flag with the hammer and sickle." I desperately wanted to get Russian Federation *and* the color scheme into the conversation.

"Officially, things are much better. But that is the official verdict. Unofficially, the economy is in pieces, because it is only a few years since the Union of Soviet Republics disbanded." After a pause, "And the judicial system, top to bottom, is being handled by people who would be more suited for slaughtering livestock."

*Or political prisoners,* I wanted to say.

"But," Vychon added, "he is here, and I would sell off all the holdings in my new business if it would aid his situation. If he loses this fight, I will lose him forever."

"The new business being antiques"– I left the 'and collectibles' intentionally unstated.

"Yes. I long ago grew tired of the film industry, but I had hoped to give it some dignity, if that is possible. In Soviet Union—forgive me, please, I say 'Soviet Union' because I have never been in Russian Federation, and what I knew was 'Soviet Union'-- the adult film business is worse than the gulag. Women are taken off the streets and forced into all manner of unnatural acts; after that, they are too emotionally scarred to return to their families or former occupations, and they wind up as little better than drug-driven street whores. Children are common in such films, and there is no concern for such things as there are here. If someone were to watch the Soviet films, they would see a collection of dying drug addicts, or people dying from sexual diseases. It is horrible, horrible." Vychon exhaled a long breath, and the steam brought me back to the climatic conditions.

I was surprised at his humanity, if that is what it was.

"Do you have any interest in antiques, or does the police salary prohibit that, and I do not mean the statement as an offense."

"No offense taken." I wanted to keep him talking and learn something—anything—before the midnight boys arrived.

"Antiques have never been my thing," I told him. "But I do have a small inheritance, which I devote now and again to *collectibles*."

"Yes, there is a big market here for such things. In Soviet Union, what is there to collect but memories of poverty in childhood and learning how to pay homage to puppet dictators?"

"You must not have had that problem, being from a medical family." This was not just putting the toe in the water, but the entire foot, and in the pond full of hungry alligators.

"What is this? Medical family? Where is this information?"

"It's common knowledge," I told him. "I can't remember where I heard it—perhaps one of your actresses said something along those lines." *The alligators can smell the toe.*

"But how much belief would a porn-lady be given?" The question seemed more solicitous than threatening.

"Ordinarily, not a great deal, but your profile seems to fit the pattern."

"Profile?" he asked, as if I was the now-defunct KGB and not the almost-defunct Hamlet P.D.

"Yeah. Born, June, 1950. Korean War started then, and 'Uncle Joe,' as Stalin was known in America, was warming up to purge doctors. American police believe that anyone currently in America with limited background—like yourself—born between, say, 1940, and when Stalin died in early '53, was probably smuggled out of the USSR by someone who feared the doctors' purge that Stalin was supposedly planning."

"You are very well educated for a policeman," he told me in a voice dripping with skepticism.

"It's basically a survivalist technique, nowadays. Besides, I hope some day to teach police science, so...."

At that moment, two police cars rounded the large bend about 500 yards south of Vychon's property.

"Ah, the late shift is here," Vychon intoned, as if announcing the soup course was now available for the diners.

"And that means I'm off-duty and going home," I told him. "I'd be glad to accept that drink you offered me, now that I'm off duty."

Oddly enough, or perhaps out of desperation because of his son's situation, he handed me that bottle. I said my thanks and then, "Nice talking with you. *Da' zvedanya, Tovarich Vychon.*"

Vychon's body language became very stiff, and I think he truly thought that his former KGB, now known as the FSR, but equally unpronounceable, had planted agents in America's small towns. *"Shto eta?* he asked. *Ti gavaru par Russkie?"*

*"Nim noga,"* I responded, letting him know I could speak a little Russian. Actually, little enough to say 'hello,' and 'a little.'

He continued to stare at me. Did he have a beeper to alert his goons?

"I may be back to see you about collectibles," I told him. "Just between us, there's a sizable reward for a local collectible dealer who's gone missing, and I plan on having that reward land in my mailbox."

"Then please do come back, when this is all done."

*"Da. Spaceeba."* The least I could do was thank him for his generous offer, if it were generous. "I hope things work out with your boy."

"Thank you," he said, reverting to English as he turned towards his front door, some 120 feet distant.

*Don't thank me yet, pal,* I thought to myself. *I've now got your fingerprints on this bottle and I'm going to find out who you really are.*

As he ambled westward, I got in the car, made a quick U-turn, spilling some of the contents of the bottle I'd laid sideways on the front seat, and slowed to watch him go into the house. As the door opened wide, I got a good look at the entry foyer.

Filled with luggage.

Somebody was going on a trip.

*Yeah, I'll be back, Comrade.*

*With a search warrant.*

*And handcuffs.*

# Just The Fax, Ma'am, Just The Fax

*Luggage?* What did it mean and what could I do with the information?

As soon as I got out of sight of Vychon's property, I pulled over, put the car in neutral and sat for a minute to weigh the options. There was, after all, nothing whatsoever illegal about having one's luggage stacked in the entry foyer of one's home. Or about handing me an open bottle, unless half-consumed hootch could be considered a bribe.

On that note, it would be interesting in court for an attorney to drag it out of me as to how I got the bottle with possible usable prints and possible DNA.

With respect to the luggage, no arrests could be made for "packing luggage with intent to skip out," since only Vychon's son was in any legal hot water. Of course, if it was going to be the son to skip out, somebody's butt would be in the sling for getting the luggage ready. At the very least, I somehow had to alert the chief in order that the round-the-clock watch, ostensibly to protect Vychon's property, would be continued.

Other alternatives presented themselves, at least some of which could be considered innocuous: Recent events had been traumatic to the point where someone in the household simply needed time away. That was possible, but it seemed as if I'd seen a lot of luggage for a quick getaway.

It might also be feared that an officer of the court with a warrant—and here, I propose myself as a candidate—would discover that some of the household staff were in the country illegally, and they were going to make a run for it. I'm not aware of any current laws against illegal immigrants leaving the country, and Hamlet damn sure does not enforce federal immigration statutes.

Still, if it walks like a duck....

I knew this information would meet, at best, with laughter and derision from Chief Dorkmeister, and at this point, he was dealing in the area of tunnel vision regarding the actions of Vychon's Camaro accident in Hamlet. The Camaro was all he cared about. Rizzoli was another town's problem, even if it did, as it now seemed, overlap with Hamlet's investigation.

I considered leaving a message at the desk for Arty Swanson and Detective Banta in Melrose, but first thing in the morning would be time enough. If that luggage, and someone carrying it, was going to depart the Vychon household, the only thing we could plan to do would be to follow it, and we'd have been damn obvious doing so in the middle of the night.

I again stopped at the Hamlet P.D., and spoke to the ranking officer. I explained that the bottle that I was holding at the very bottom had been handled by Vychon, and we needed the FBI—or Interpol if necessary—to run the prints and such DNA as might exist on the lip of the bottle. We'd know a great deal if we knew who and what Vychon really was. I stressed the urgency to him, and the equal urgency that the chief be avoided with this issue if possible.

I decided the best thing to do was head home, put my still-unanswered questions on paper, and get some sleep before a lengthy Thursday shift which involved at the very least a visit to the services for Edwina Griffin, and a sit-down with a Grand Jury.

I was too tired to bother putting the car in the garage, and stumbled into the house needing some additional drink to wash down the salty soup from Eli's Deli.

I flopped down on the couch with a pad and pen and started my "unanswered questions."

Did Pete Rizzoli rent a car anywhere since the previous Thursday, approximately at mid-day?

Was his passport used in that same time span?

Were any of his potentially many credit cards used, and that should also be cross-referenced against cards in the name of "Pete Perfect," because I felt certain that some credit card would have his ugly mug for advertising in return for the "vanity" credit card.

Did he have the new "E-Z-Pass" for highway and bridge tolls, and was it used? Were any toll booths on bridges between New Jersey and New York equipped with camera monitors, and did Rizzoli's truck show up on any of them, and if so, where and when?

Was anyone named Pete Rizzoli treated in any hospitals within a 75-mile radius of Melrose? That radius would reach to the border of Pennsylvania, the Jersey shore, Riverside on Long Island, and Kingston, New York.

Were there any morgue slabs containing "John Doe's"?

Could any firearm application or firearm purchase be tracked to Rizzoli, since he did have unexpended ammunition in a safe-deposit box?

Did any gun with matching serial number turn up in any police activity?

*I knew I could have started a new list with this entry, and entitled it "Damn unlikely."* Of course, if Rizzoli had taken a gun and met with foul play, nobody smart enough to take Rizzoli down would be caught with that gun. Equally obvious was the fact that nobody was going to send divers into any local rivers on the chance that a rather small handgun *might* be there. With police budgets shrinking, divers would not have been sent into the water on the odd chance they would have found a Russian tank. Or submarine.

*Or missile.*

I thought I was done, and a sigh was my body's way of thanking my brain for its willingness to shut down. Unfortunately, I realized I was not done, and that I'd only considered one of two possibilities.

Vychon was the other. Suddenly, list two was born.

Besides educated guesswork and corporate statements that revealed nothing more than the obvious, what did we really know about Vychon, and, more to the point, what recent activities had he been involved in?

He claimed not to have a passport, but I knew that was true only in the sense of his Americanized name, "Billy Vychon." I was certain he had at least one passport, if not more, and most likely from Eastern European countries just now freed from the Soviet yoke.

Ditto for his family.

His goons undoubtedly had enough friends in Little Odessa to be able to stitch together a get-out-of-jail-free card at will, so they, too, seemed beyond reach if a crisis should develop out of all of this.

Except for his besotted son Mikhail, I'm not certain we knew of any other family members' names. His wife's name was not on the incorporation papers for his "adult film" industry, and could have been "Nikita" or "Leonida" for all I knew. Women in Russia were wives or whores, fighters or God knew what.

Back to work: Were there any financial clues that could be relevant? Unusual activity with credit cards, bank accounts, safe-deposit boxes? Had anyone at any time since the accident had a look at Vychon's federal and state tax records? Seemed unlikely to discover without federal warrants, and all that would be learned would be with regard to "Billy Vychon" and "VX Corporation." I had to believe he had serious assets in his real name, on the odd chance that something—or someone, Edwina Griffin for example, would cause his assets to be frozen. But then again, the cold in Russia made people used to frozen assets, to a point I'm sure they pretend to love. While they move to California.

Anything that could be learned about that side of the problem would not only be helpful—hell, with the Grand

Jury set to convene in a few hours in the County Seat, the questions I was concerned about would demand answers. But who would demand them? Not anyone from Hamlet, but perhaps the Assistant District Attorney or the D.A. herself, since this was clearly a high-profile case.

Edwina Griffin, who was to be waked a few hours after the Grand Jury convened, had made it a high-profile case in the broadest sense. Had it just been drunken kids and a utility pole, it might have been very different, although with the goodness of the pious people of Hamlet pitted against the pornographer, it might have been high-profile either way.

Still—answers were needed.

Yesterday.

Other ideas flirted with my brain but only stayed as long as most of my recent female relationships, and I realized I needed some sleep. I climbed out of the clean uniform I'd donned seven hours previously and quickly fell asleep on the couch, with visions of reward bucks dancing in my head.

Unbeknownst to me, the FBI had been busy working over the two "suspect vehicles" for want of better cop terminology. On this side of the river but about eight miles from Hamlet, the county unit which had taken apart the Camaro had made their lab available to the feebs, and their counterparts did likewise, poring over an exotic truck in a Brooklyn-based, non-federal forensic lab.

When I learned the results at headquarters at 7:40 a.m., hours later, I could take comfort in the fact that it had been my insistence that both vehicles be checked. Ordinarily, only the truck, having crossed state lines, would have drawn federal attention. And even then, only scant attention, because the feds liked to stick to high-profile cases, and I doubted that they knew how high-profile Pete Rizzoli was in the world of baseball cards. Or that baseball cards mattered in the grand scheme of things.

The feds, truly short sighted at times, loved to run down bank robbers, whom they considered public enemies number one in all cases. They also nosed around what they called "suspected terrorist cells," but that never amounted to anything even remotely equaling "scrutiny."

Clearly, they were out of the loop, because for all the noise and hoopla, a pair of masked men with guns in a bank would usually leave with less than $50,000, and the silent bank alarms would betray them quickly, giving the feds two "perps" and a fleeting headline. The very same federal agents, however, had no understanding of the collectibles market, on a par with virtually any other high-end specialty markets, and I'm sure they had no idea that Rizzoli probably had at least 200 cards each valued at $50,000 or more. If they had, 250 agents would have been temporarily transferred to the Newark, New Jersey office.

That is, of course, if there was any suspicion that a crime had actually been committed.

With typical FBI efficiency, the preliminary results—a polite FBI euphemism for "we'll do more if we damn well feel like it"—were faxed to both Melrose and Hamlet, and the folks at the desk knew I'd be interested, so I got to have a look-see while the chief was napping in his office. I was told his nap started at 2:00 a.m. But, the desk folks insisted, he *was* napping; not sleeping.

The paint on the Camaro had matched the paint on the utility pole. No surprise there.

The dent on the Camaro was at the same height as the dent on the utility pole. Ditto.

There was an "unpronounced" dent—perhaps impression would be the better word—on the rear of the passenger side, suggesting that Edwina Griffin had possibly been struck by the rear of the car, perhaps in a skid. That could mean she was struck accidentally, as the car perhaps skidded to avoid her, and not intentionally. That could save one or more juveniles some serious prison time—if accurate.

Clothing was found inside the vehicle, and it was just enough to flesh out the outfits of the five semi-naked juveniles. No other clothing was evident.

Routine papers were found in the front seat as a result of the air bag deploying. Included were the car's registration and New Jersey insurance card, as well as the driver's license for Boris [mnu]? Petrov, presumably one of Vychon's goons who usually drove the car. From the name, I figured, *probably Russian.* That made the "goon" designation so much more easy. It would not hurt, I reasoned, to run down "Boris Petrov" as well, although that name, in the Russian Federation, was about as common as "Joe Smith" here. What seemed odd was the absence of a middle name, which in Russian is called a "patronymic;" everyone has one and everyone uses them. It should have been something like "Boris Ivanovich Petrov," meaning Boris, son of Ivan, and he would be formally greeted as "Boris Ivanovich." Not in our records, however.

The liquor bottles, or what remained of them, seemed to draw the most attention and create the largest inventory of items. Once the smaller shards of glass went through a strainer to eliminate them as either hazards or carriers of fingerprints, what remained were portions of seventeen bottles, which contained what was believed to be fingerprints from eleven different individuals.

That would most likely, but not absolutely, mean the five juveniles, and, by careful subtraction, six other people. They could have been the retailers who sold the potables, but they also could have been the telltale fingerprint impressions of the adults who supplied the booze, and that meant a search warrant and a subpoena to fingerprint the household staff at Vychon's, and any individuals I could recall from the party visited after the accident, or from my list of vehicles and their owners. As it happened, I didn't know anyone at that party, and I figured I could grow old without being crushed by that disappointment.

Suddenly the luggage took on serious significance.

Almost as an afterthought, I read the remainder of the New Jersey fax. There was a list of the various brands of alcohol determined to have been in the car, some with only partial labels, and, where possible, any identifying marks on the labels were included.

It didn't seem to mean much without some basis of comparison. What did seem strange was that although most of the labels were common brands of liquor, there was one listing for "Vodka: Bolzov."

I was aware of the basic Russian vodkas, even to the higher priced items like Stoli. But Bolzov? Someone has to be kidding with that one.

With only a few minutes to go before the morning muster, I took a quick peek at the fax from Brooklyn. Four likely sets of fingerprints, maybe more. The truck was, liquor aside, clean as a whistle—not a print, a drop of blood, a human hair—nada.

It reminded me of a question one moron had asked at the police academy over twenty years ago. DNA was just getting unveiled at the time, and this simpleton asked how far back it actually went.

"To friggin' Cro-Magnon Man, for all I know," the instructor said, "but they didn't use it for evidence."

Clearly, the Brooklyn feds couldn't either, if there wasn't any.

The second fax identified nineteen bottles of one form or another, and I'd already forgotten how many were in the first, so I rechecked.

Seventeen. Nineteen and seventeen. Wait a minute, 1917 was the Russian Revolution. Is this a bad joke or an ugly coincidence? Or perhaps a reminder that history majors did not necessarily make the best future law enforcement officers.

As I pondered that and the platoon sergeant yelled for me to get my ass into the squad room, I quickly scanned the rest. I wanted to compare the batch numbers of identification marks found on the Brooklyn bottles, and I was surprised to see that there was a notation that the truck wasn't as much "painted" as it had been treated to stripes of red, white, and light-blue graffiti.

Huh. That made the painting a far less "in-your-face" event than simply a random act of violence. I made a mental note to try to contact precinct commanders in Brooklyn, the largest Russian community in the US and the place where the truck was found, to ask if such graffiti were commonplace.

Then, the standard litany of liquor brands, plus, at the very end, "Bolzov Vodka," with a question mark after it. Were they as confused about it as I was?

Time to get the riot act read to us before we hit the streets. I flipped the papers onto the dispatcher's desk and told the volunteer on duty to make sure the chief saw all of it.

I wanted him to know something before I told him about the luggage.

Something. *Hell, anything.*

# Not All Juries Are Grand

When Sergeant Crowder called us all in for muster, we almost immediately began to think he'd been watching too much television. In large metropolitan areas, the muster, or pre-shift pep talk, frequently amounted to heads-ups about "be on the lookout for" and a list of individuals would be furnished, usually based on criminal events during the previous shift, or perhaps on newly-acquired informant data.

What we usually got was a basic reminder that we were cops and were paid to do what cops do, so we should do it. There were rarely unsolved crimes to be concerned about.

Today was different, though I had no idea. Crowder, known affectionately but privately as "Chowder head," heaved himself up to his full 5'3" height—his girth was the reason for the 'heave'—and told us how busy today would be, as it would involve Edwina Griffin's wake as well as the beginning of the Grand Jury session at the County Seat.

Somehow, perhaps because nothing serious happens in Hamlet, it would have been fair to say that we already knew all of that. Crowder did take a moment to remind me that I might be called at any time, but if I were called, I was to return to the headquarters and take my own vehicle, as all of the municipal police cars were going to be needed on the streets as well as in Vychon's neighborhood today.

He also made the same notation about Gino Franzetti, another one of the blues on my shift, who might also be called by the Grand Jury. Neither of us had ever testified before in such a proceeding, but testimony is testimony, and there are no challenges. You sit in front of twenty-three "jurors." You are asked to tell what you observed, your report is put into the record after you authenticate it as your report and for its contents, and then you're outta there. There is no cross-examination. *Why cloud guilt with controversy?*

So on this day, "muster" was something just slightly more than bagels and coffee. Not much more, but in Hamlet, a vandalized mail box, a non-curbed dog, or a kid's motorized scooter on the street could be big news. Parking in a handicapped zone without the appropriate sticker or license plate could mean the gulag.

As we left, I was telling Franzetti not to sweat the Grand Jury if he got called, and I caught a look at the senior officer to whom I'd given the bottle Vychon had handed me. The lieutenant gave me an ever-so-subtle look that said, "We're on it."

For the briefest of moments, I wondered if it had been handed to me intentionally, as some kind of false flag. People like Vychon did not attain their current level of status without maintaining some manner of anonymity, so why would he so willingly surrender his? Was it a plea bargain? Was he willing to trade himself for his son?

Anything was possible. But the one certainty was that he had not handed me that bottle because he thought I was thirsty.

The morning hours of the tour were largely unremarkable, except when we learned that a caravan of over 200 New York vehicles was driving around the Courthouse, raising all kinds of hell and possibly causing the postponement of the Grand Jury for that day. The rumor mill had it that the County cops wanted to break it up, but there's nothing illegal about driving around in circles, as long as you obey traffic laws.

Stopping is another matter, which is why when individuals or groups decide to set up a picket line, everyone involved is required to be moving.

Was this payback for the caravan of townies that had circled Hamlet's P.D., and later sprayed Vychon's property with liquor bottles? Did Hamlet have that many drinkers who kept empties around, or did the affluent simply buy a few potables and empty them just to throw them at randon targets?

Ordinarily, I'd have stopped somewhere near noon at the local Slurp and Burp for the lunchtime special, "Extra Grease," but out of deference to Edwina Griffin, I went to the more up-scale bagel establishment and had a respectable sandwich and a ginger ale. I even used a napkin for a bib, as I wanted a clean uniform for the Wake, and not the remnants of what could have appeared like a food fight. I also chose Carlo's Bagels because the menu at the Slurp and Burp included "gas" as a freebie. Gas in a one-man prowler is not a crisis. But at a crowded wake....

The wake was scheduled for two to four p.m., so I decided to split the difference and arrive at three. I took a ride past the mortuary at one, and the parking lot was already full, so I pushed my time-table up to 2:30, as I assumed time would be necessary once inside.

And part of me was dreading the moment. This was not just the local cop paying respects to be politically correct. This was the Man who was once the Boy who would have known and loved an elegant woman from Hamlet; as a cop, I also carried the anger that a handful of drunken little rich bastards could have killed her, although I did remind myself that all things considered, the little thugs probably did Edwina a favor.

Still, none of them were going to be nominated for any Jack Kevorkian awards.

At 1:10, I had to pull over a speeder, and I basically just wanted to tell him that a lot of local folks were out today, and to please slow down. But, as things happen, he got stupid and told me he'd bet my blue suit made me feel like a real man, so I asked him for his license, vehicle registration, and insurance card. I ran the plate through the state data bank, and it, and the driver, were clean.

But I could hear him bitching the whole time. "Gimme back my damn papers, dickhead..."

"Dickhead" was pretty much the last straw, so when I returned to his vehicle, I was very pleasant in saying that I was not going to write a citation, and he answered that I damn well shouldn't. But, as things happen, as I went to hand him his papers, I hit the lip of the driver's side window, and the papers slid down the window to the door-frame and disappeared inside the driver's door. Oh, gee, my bad.

He was enraged. I did say I was sorry, and that an auto body would probably be able to retrieve it. For a few bucks.

He suggested I have sex alone—well, that was not exactly how he phrased it—and then drove off in haste. I got on the radio and told another officer a mile down the road to be on the lookout for the car and to toss him, and when he had no documents, to take him in.

It's not nice to fool Mother Nature.

Not wanting to be on the streets when that gentleman regained his freedom, I headed to Edwina's service earlier than planned, arriving at just past 1:30 and joined the line already formed outside the door. A number of people tried to engage me in conversation related to Edwina's murder by vehicle, but I simply told everyone that I shared their sympathy for the deceased, but that I could not discuss the investigation, lest it jeopardize the chances for conviction.

It was almost an hour before I reached the family, which consisted of Edwina's daughter, with whom she had lived, and her son, mid-50s, salt and pepper hair, medium height and build but wearing an ill-fitting suit. He clearly was not prepared for this either, although sobbing at a wake for an Alzheimer's victim—well, it wasn't as if the loss was sudden or unanticipated. But the sobbing told me he was not the full-time caretaker, because that burden would have been lifted.

There was a woman alongside him who could have been another daughter or the son's wife, three 'children' in their twenties—the grandchildren, and one older gentleman who, for all I knew, could have been an ex-husband of

Edwina. Her husband had died in 1980, but there could well have been one or two before that.

I shared my condolences quickly, as the line was growing, and the son, who introduced himself as Sam Griffin, asked me how the investigation was going. I repeated the "party line" and also told him I was working on the disappearance of another local man named Peter Rizzoli.

"That no-good bastard?" the son said, somewhat harshly for a person, clearly grieving, in a greeting line at his mother's Wake.

"So, you knew him..."

"Yeah. A couple of years back—well, it could have been as many as seven years back, I had to sell my collection of baseball cards, and they wound up going to Rizzoli. One other guy came to see them, but Rizzoli spoke much better English."

At that moment, my attendance at the Wake suddenly ended. I had not had the chance to kneel before the closed coffin to pay my respects, because a four-second blast of a siren alerted me to the possibility that my presence was sought outside. Beyond that, the siren scared the living hell out of most of the people inside, and considering this was a life meets death event, maybe that was a good thing.

I worked my way through the crowd, apologizing for my haste as I went. As I cleared the door, there was a Melrose police vehicle sitting right in front of the bottom step. It was Arty Swanson.

"This has to be important," I said.

"Well, we do not know quite what it means, and we figured you'd want to join us in the dark," Arty responded.

"And?"

"Rizzoli's credit card was used. Saturday, two days after he got the phone call and left."

"And?"

"Deck, I'm sorry. I'm trying to sort it out. Luckily, there was a receipt. The card, a VISA platinum, was used at a Westchester highway rest stop, for gasoline. But it was not Rizzoli's truck. The plate number written on the receipt tracked back to a new-model black town car, registered to an address in the 600 block of West 93rd Street in Manhattan. Mean anything?"

"Not right off, except that Rizzoli might have gone to New York City and then traveled with a friend or bodyguard. Or, he and somebody went to the storage locker in that vehicle.

Or someone, without Rizzoli, went to that storage locker, and if the person or persons had Rizzoli's platinum Visa, they may well have had access to the storage locker."

Arty thought for a minute. "Yeah, I know. Maybe the stakes were really high this time, value-wise. Could have been anyone in that car—Rizzoli, his surrogate, or someone who'd already taken Rizzoli off."

"The smart money tells me it wasn't Rizzoli. If he had pulled a deal that big, the whole world would know about it."

"Absolutely; sure, that was his style," Arty said. "Well, I just wanted you to know."

"Thanks, Arty, I appreciate—wait a minute. You said the 600 block of West 93rd in Manhattan?"

"Yeah. Mean anything? You got any rich friends there?"

"I don't have any rich friends anywhere," I told Arty. "But that is the location of the Russian Consulate. Not the Embassy or the so-called Diplomatic Residence. The Consulate, where you would go for a visa if you had lost enough of your marbles to want to visit Mother Russia."

"Are you thinking--?"

"Yeah. And Sam Griffin—Edwina Griffin's son--just told me he sold his baseball card collection to Rizzoli. I'm guessing he did it for Edwina's care, but he said something that didn't register at the time. He said he sold his collection to Rizzoli, whom he had no love for, but he did it because, and I'm quoting, 'Rizzoli spoke much better English...'"

"Better English than who?" Arty asked.

We both answered the question at the same instant.

*"Billy Vychon."*

Arty and I had come to the beginning of a meeting of the minds. Now it was a matter of brainstorming all imaginable concepts until a reasonable hypothesis emerged.

"What are you thinking, Arty?"

Swanson hesitated. Then: "It is becoming a very clear possibility that the Hamlet case—a drunken driving affair—and the Melrose case, the disappearance of a very wealthy individual, have a serious overlap."

"It's more than clear, Arty. It's fact." I told him what I had been kicking around, and he listened without interrupting, which I took to mean he was not finding any problems with it.

Not any major ones at least. Finally, when I shut up, he nodded his head a couple of times as if he were having an internal debate, and then said, "I gotta go to Porterfield with this. But most of it is yours, Deck. Can you come along?"

I was not sure that I could, so I asked him to get his prowler out to the street, where I'd meet him with my vehicle, and have him contact the Melrose chief and ask that I be included.

He called in, and Porterfield told him to bring me along and he'd clear it with Hamlet's Imbecile-in-Chief. "After today's Grand Jury fiasco," Porterfield had told Arty, "the County is going to need a task force. I'll start picking the Melrose 'volunteers' and you two get up here."

We let the Melrose chief know we were on the way, although I knew from my own instructions that I'd have to stop at the Hamlet P.D. and exchange my prowler for my own car.

I didn't know how long I'd be on loan to Porterfield, and at this point, I wasn't concerned about what car I'd be driving, how much fast food I'd be eating, or whether or not the newspapers would stack up in my driveway. Now, more than halfway through Thursday, it looked like a long weekend ahead, but there was an answer to be had, and I felt like we were closing in.

# Bad Moon Rising

After changing vehicles somewhat surreptitiously, without entering the Hamlet Police Headquarters, a large number of concerns filled my head as I drove north to Melrose.

Not the least of them was what the Chief would be quoted as saying about me in my obituary, to be published on Monday, if I was wrong about my numerous surmises.

Could Vychon just be another well-heeled parvenu Slavic entrepreneur who was, for the most part, basically legitimate?

I doubted it.

Did he have the clout to save his son and the son's friends from serious jail time?

I doubted that, too, but I'd been aware of way too many crimes where on one hand, some minimum-wage flunky had stolen the tip money at some diner and gotten three years in jail, while five miles away, some slick accountant embezzled millions and got probation, with the promise that he'd pay the money back.

When pigs were cleared for takeoffs and landings, no doubt.

And what of Rizzoli? He was either a miserable husband who skipped out with enough untraceable cash and rare collectibles to start a new life with exotic starlets, or he was a rotting corpse.

That thought did not work perfectly, because Rizzoli had always reminded me of a rotting corpse when he was alive. Geez, I'm using the past-perfect tense. In that case, he must be dead.

And finally, was Vychon in any way implicated in what may or may not have happened to Rizzoli? Well, if nothing foul had happened to Pete Perfect, Vychon wasn't implicated, but that seemed to me, at least, the only way he could *not* be implicated.

Something was really nagging at me about a mile south of Melrose, but I couldn't separate whatever it was from everything else spinning through my head. I felt, deep down, that I had made enough linkages—well, common sense leaps, perhaps, to state a case.

But there was an anomaly that continued to bounce off my perceptions and I could not retrieve it.

I just missed the traffic light at the southern border of Melrose. Given that I was in uniform, I could have slid through, and, as always happens in those situations, the car behind me probably would have made it through also. But, I was a "law enforcement officer," so I had to sit, ruminating, at the intersection of the main north-south thoroughfare and the exit from a shopping plaza. I took a quick look around and the anomaly hit me right between the eyes.

It was the sign that read, "Fine Wines and Liquors," and there were undoubtedly hundreds of them in locations that dealt in spirits. But that was the anomaly. *Why had Vychon, a man about whom nothing was known prior to the year, what was it, 1984—1985?-- given me the bottle of liquor that would have contained his fingerprints?*

*Did he want me to find out who and what he was? If so, had I walked into a trap?*

The word "trap" was embedded in my mind as I pulled into the Melrose P.D. and parked in the lot for non-police vehicles, noticing in the process that most of the cars were much newer and more expensive than mine.

Maybe I should listen the next time Porterfield makes an offer.

Since I was still in uniform, I was pretty much expected, and the middle-aged female desk sergeant just nodded her head in the direction of the conference room.

Within, I found the usual suspects, Porterfield, Detective Banta, who undoubtedly had a first name, but damned if I could remember it at that moment, plus Arty, and four men in suits. Two were other Melrose detectives that I'd seen one time or another and they simply nodded in a friendly manner, although I'm sure they viewed me as an outsider/intruder.

As I headed for an empty seat, Porterfield announced me to the other two, who were FBI agents, but the federal agent—Longwell?—from earlier in the week was nowhere to be found. Porterfield did have the courtesy to tell them who I was, and also to tell me who they were, but my mind was so busy sorting things out that they could have been Special Agents Abbott and Costello and I would not have registered the names.

Once that was all seen to, everyone was seated and Porterfield, coat off and tie loosened, took charge.

"Here is what we know. First, Melrose. Peter Rizzoli, a well-known dealer in sports memorabilia, received a phone call a week ago today, made his wife aware that he had some "big money business" to attend to, and left in what we now know was a custom-made truck—a reasonably expensive truck 'aged,' if you will, to make it appear older. Since that phone call, and to the best of our knowledge in law enforcement, he has not been seen or heard from."

A pause. "And we all know that when someone goes missing, the magic number is usually forty-eight hours, although since no ransom calls were made that we know of—and I say that because the Federal Bureau of Investigation did not intercept and record his phone calls until this past Monday—the magic forty-eight hours might be somehow negotiable.

"Still, it's been over a week, and nothing, and that does not bode well for Mr. Rizzoli. Let me turn over the follow-up to Agent Magnuson."

So, "Abbott" was Magnuson. If I'd had to describe him, I'd simply say "stud" and move on. He was big boned, well built although height and weight are difficult to compute on a seated person, and had perfectly combed auburn hair set over high cheek-bones and perfect teeth. I'm not the jealous type, but in Magnuson's case, I'd make an exception. He was also wearing garments, starting with a spotless cashmere sport jacket, that probably cost a week of my salary. Either he was living well off an inheritance, or I was underpaid. *Both were possibilities.*

Magnuson stood up to speak, easily six-feet in his socks, "The Bureau has nothing to report regarding Rizzoli's home telephone—no calls of any import. We are still trying to trace the call to the 'suitcase phone' that launched this event. We have checked with the State Department, which has jurisdiction regarding overseas travel, and there is no suggestion that Rizzoli's passport was used at any place from which he could have left the United States. That does not guarantee, categorically, that it was not used, but that is our information at this time.

"We have checked hospitals and police morgues for a 100-mile radius and there is no trace of any 'Rizzoli' or any John Doe's that fit the perhaps inexact description we have of him. It is the Bureau's belief in matters such as this, that we would be aware of any hospital care he had received or was receiving. As for unknowns in morgues, there are several, but it is March, and these are for the most part disheveled, homeless types. Four men and two females."

I wanted to interrupt to say that Rizzoli could have resembled any of those four, but, uncharacteristically, I did not.

"The only result we have so far is that his credit card, or perhaps I should say one of his credit cards, was used in Westchester, on Saturday, 7 March, for a gasoline purchase. The agents who visited the facility could not find anyone who recalled that card being used, so that was a dead-end, so to speak." *Poor choice of words,* I thought.

Porterfield again: "Does anyone have any questions for Special Agent Magnuson?"

Naturally, I did, and Porterfield recognized me.

"A credit card receipt contains information on the vehicle that bought the gas. Was that checked and what did it reveal?"

"Yes. I should have included that. The car had plates that suggested it was a rented town-car, and it was rented to an address in the 600 block of East 93rd Street in New York City."

"Who or what exactly is at that address?" I asked, trying very hard to be obnoxious, since it seemed clear we were only being told part of the story.

"The address is the Russian Consulate." I was surprised by the brevity of that, with no editorializing.

"Were they diplomatic plates?"

"No." *Magnuson–the master of prolixity.*

Sensing this, Porterfield asked if anything could be inferred from that data.

"Not necessarily," Magnuson replied. "It is our understanding that Mr. Rizzoli had a rather broad-based, or cosmopolitan, if you will, clientele for his high-priced memorabilia, and therefore it is not possible immediately to put up a red flag."

It was a huge temptation to ask if the Bureau had any data on baseball card collectors in Moscow and its environs, but they would not have had any such information, and Russia was quickly becoming a "1% society" where the wealth was for the most part in a very limited number of hands. The borscht-belters could have, I assumed, hedged currency in rare collectibles.

Maybe. But to whom would they sell them? It seemed unlikely that Sandy Koufax or Ernie Banks had fan clubs in places where housing projects constituted "good living."

Porterfield cupped his hands behind his head and leaned back in his chair, and continued the general questioning. "So, nothing else, Melrose related. Have search warrants been obtained regarding the three storage lockers?"

It was the turn of the non-stud FBI agent to talk.

"It is the understanding of the Bureau that Melrose would seek a local warrant for the storage locker here in New Jersey. The Bureau will have warrants for the other two locations—Rye, New York, and Brighton Beach, tomorrow, and the searches will commence as soon as the warrants are obtained. You will be immediately informed, Chief Porterfield."

"Thank you, Agent Tyler. Questions?"

Again, it was I who spoke up. "I listened carefully to Agent Magnuson's caution regarding linkage between a Russian Consulate vehicle and Rizzoli. But considering that the Russian vehicle—clearly not a vehicle owned by Rizzoli—was in proximity to the Rye location, and considering that the other location, Brighton Beach, is a virtual Russian enclave, would you allow for the suspicion that such overlaps increase the chance that there is a linkage of some sort in operation here?"

Magnuson, not Tyler, spoke up. "It certainly is possible, Officer, uh, Decker, but it is still a surmise until there is something more than geographical coincidence to base it on." *I suppose it's always better to be put down by a stud than a dork.*

"Thank you," I said, much in the tone I use when Jehovah's Witnesses leave me pamphlets.

Porterfield then re-focused events: "Story-line part two: Hamlet. And let's be very clear on this. The Hamlet events are Russian Federation-related from top to bottom. Agent Magnuson?"

Stud again stood to make his report: "We have learned from the Hamlet P.D., particularly the detailed report of Officer Decker, that a vehicle belonging to "Billy Vychon" was involved in a drunken driving accident on Monday, 9 March. It was suspected at the time, and since confirmed by the Bureau's Laboratory facilities, that the blood alcohol levels in the youths involved made them all well past the level of inebriation. We have also been able to confirm that the fatality, Edwina Griffith—"

"Griffin," I interjected.

"Edwina Griffin, thank you, was hit and killed by the vehicle, a Yellow Camaro. Examination of the right rear fender contained enough forensic evidence to eliminate any doubt that the decedent, Ms. Griffin, was struck by the car, at a point approximately midway along the right-rear fender. It cannot be ascertained if the collision of the car and pedestrian was accidental or intentional, but the placement of the damage on the right rear fender at least suggests accidental. The Bureau also found a number of bottles that contained, or were broken and had contained, alcoholic beverages, and we are running the fingerprints on them as I speak."

He then went over the fingerprints on the bottles, etc.

I stuck my nose in again. "Was there any overlap between the bottles found in the Camaro and the bottles found in the truck that had been hastily tagged with red, white, and light blue paint, the colors of the Russian Federation?"

"I can only say, Officer Decker, that at this point, liquor is liquor, and we cannot make any matches without fingerprint confirmation."

"And 'Bolzov' Vodka?" I asked.

Agent Tyler leaned forward as Agent Magnuson sat down. He seemed to be searching for words, as if he was about to reveal some long-hidden, TOP SECRET fact to all of us. Eventually, he spoke quietly: "We have this from CIA. 'Bolzov' Vodka was, well, it was—years ago—like some of the micro-brew beers here in the United States. Apparently a small group of well-to-do Russians had very high quality Russian wheat turned into high-quality Vodka, and the name 'Bolzov' was a joke to reflect the then failings of the Soviet economy in the late 1980s. It was said that the vodka had to be consumed at a near-freezing temperature, reflecting the heating crisis in some cities, to be enjoyed. So, the story went, you had to 'freeze your Bolzov.'"

Nobody laughed. Tyler sat back, seemingly exhausted from storytelling. I could only wonder what other crisis-related data the CIA had locked securely in its vaults.

"There was a driver's license found in the vehicle. Boris Petrov, if I recall correctly."

Magnuson spoke up. "Your recollection is excellent, Officer Decker. We were able to lift prints from the plastic holder that the license was in, and they got a hit almost immediately. The subject, Boris Petrov, was a rich Soviet banker before the USSR went belly up. Thereafter, his wife, Elena Ivanayevna Petrova, became a Soviet street whore and we suspect, but cannot yet prove to a certainty that she wound up a subject in Billy Vychon's films."

"I'd be happy to study them if it would help," I suggested. "In the meantime, what about the liquor bottle that Vychon handed to me that would have undoubtedly contained his fingerprints?"

Tyler again, and again, leaning forward in quiet tones. "We have over 500 million sets of fingerprints in the Bureau's files, but we could not match any to the bottle you submitted for testing. We have, and I would say grudgingly, turned it over to Interpol. The hour is late, but they work around the clock, so if there is anything to be learned, we should have that answer within a few hours, and, again, the results will immediately be made known to Chief Porterfield as well as to your department."

"Okay, thanks." I wanted to ask how many of the owners of the 500 million prints in Bureau files were still alive, because some of those prints went back way too far for all of the owners to still be breathing. I also repeated my willingness to comb through Vychon's film library if it would help the investigation any.

"I do not believe that would aid the investigation, Officer Decker. Right now, as we have stated, there is a very clear *possible* linkage between the two events, but there is not yet sufficient proof to do anything about it. We need to find out exactly who Vychon is, what he's been doing all his life, and then tear apart his financial, credit, travel, and all other pertinent histories. If Interpol can help with the fingerprints, we'll have what we need. We also have to secure the warrants for the storage lockers and hope they point us in some direction that furthers the investigation. That part, at least, is thankfully a mystery that can be solved tomorrow. Agents will be standing by at the locations once the warrants are signed."

*FBI- speak for a wing and a prayer.*

Porterfield, looking weary in the shoulders but still with fire in his eyes, tried to recapitulate and add the Grand Jury events of the day. "I can only add, gentlemen, that today's Grand Jury schedule was badly disrupted, and this may be another linkage. The officers from Hamlet who were on the scene of the automobile accident were to give depositions today, but the entire County Court system was disrupted by well over 200 vehicles, believed to be from the Brighton Beach enclave of "Little Odessa" which circled the courthouse for several hours, denying admission to all other vehicular traffic.

"The Hamlet officers on the scene were able to get photographs of approximately 60 of the drivers of the vehicles—who, I add, were not happy about being photographed, and said so. As soon as those photos are developed and enlarged, we will make them available to the Bureau."

At that point, Porterfield looked at Magnuson and Tyler, both of whom nodded like bobble-head dolls; definitely non-collectible.

Porterfield concluded, "I have also been informed by Sergeant Crowder, in Hamlet, that the Hamlet Police Department, and the Borough Attorney have been warned, in what was termed 'stern diplomatic language,' from the Russian Federation Embassy in Washington that there would be repercussions if any prosecution was attempted against any of the five juveniles. Personally, I find that the oddest element of all—well, putting aside the disappearance of a multi-millionaire local resident."

I had not been aware of that development and it shocked the hell out of me.

"It's almost dinner time. Shall we adjourn for a meal or have something delivered to us, either by a local restaurant or a Melrose prowler?"

I had very little appetite, which is unusual for me. I still felt I knew what had happened, but I also was getting the gut feeling that all was not going to end well.

A bunch of drunken kids hit a pole. Could that have been a distraction for something that the parents of those kids had been up to that had far more serious consequences than a damaged light pole?

Could Vychon have been pulling a bait and switch, getting the cops to look at a traffic accident while a multi-million dollar theft, possibly involving the deep-sixing of the victim, was going down?

It was possible. Somehow they had not planned that Edwina Griffin would be involved.

Or that two baseball card collectors were wearing blue uniforms in the respective towns.

# Will You Still Love Me Tomorrow?

There seemed to be a collective sigh when Melrose Chief Porterfield suggested the dinner break, but it was unclear exactly what it was going to be a break from.

*A litany of FBI Bureau-speak was one possibility.*

As Porterfield rose, stretched, and walked to the window to have a look around, I asked Arty, "A break from what?"

Arty told me that in serious cases—although they had not had many—it was customary to 'brainstorm' possibilities.

That opportunity was seriously enhanced when the two feds stood to leave, citing an auto-theft ring they were also working on. The two as-yet-silent Melrose detectives also indicated they were leaving, and my suspicion was they were on the clock and otherwise bored.

They did pass along some compliments to Arty and me for having dug as deeply as we did, but suggested, "You baseball card guys must really stick together."

*Yeah, as if I gave a rat's ass as to which shark in mid-ocean had had Rizzoli for a snack.*

"Any ideas for a dinner, or does everyone want to get home and try to be back here an hour or two earlier than usual in the morning."

"Deck and I are in, Chief," Arty told him. "We'll go pick up some take-out. Chinese or Japanese?"

Porterfield and Banta both opted for Japanese, making the choice unanimous, but when Arty and I stood to volunteer to collect it, Porterfield pulled out a wad of money and tossed a couple of fifties across the table.

"It's just food, Chief. We're not buying the island of Honshu."

"Get some good wine to go with it. I don't know what would go best, but they'll be able to tell you. They do have liquor, don't they?"

Arty assured them that such was the case, and we set off after calling the order in. There had been one serious auto wreck in Melrose that day, so the 8 to 4 shift was just coming in as we were leaving, and twilight made it clear it was well past 6 p.m.

"Stay off Standish Rise Hill as much as possible," one of the cops told Arty. "It's a mess."

When we got into the nearest available Melrose prowler, I couldn't resist asking Arty about Porterfield's gesture in tossing big bills out of a wad of currency.

"Old money, Deck. Old New England money. His family owns one-third of all the worthwhile real estate that borders the ocean, and they've got nice holdings in St. Barts and elsewhere. He doesn't need to work. He just loves the job. Dresses up–"

"Yeah," I cut in. "I couldn't pronounce the brand of shoes he was wearing and I know I damn well couldn't afford them."

"The suits he wears—which never got near the rack, mind you, and the shoes would cost more than a decent set of 1953s."

"I don't doubt it. Hey, rich or poor, it's nice to have money," I added, more wishfully than wistfully.

"He's the last of his line, Deck, no kids, no family to inherit, and the scuttlebutt is that his wealth will go to Melrose to give it the finest P.D. on the face of the earth."

I should seriously reconsider the offer Porterfield had made to me. In Hamlet, Chief Shit-fer-brains tells duty officers to buy him cough drops and he'll pay them back. And they're still waiting.

We pulled into the shopping area that housed the Japanese restaurant, but we knew we had arrived early, even with the lingering traffic snafus from the earlier vehicle smackdown. Arty shut off the car and turned to me. "I'm curious about one thing, Deck. You cringed visibly when the feds said they had 500 million fingerprints on file. What's the skinny on that?"

"It's a typical fraudulent statistic maintained by the feds," I told him. "They hammer you with statistics that are usually empty and meaningless. Did you get into any of the FBI's history when you went to the state police academy?"

"No. Didn't go. Didn't have to. Porterfield knew I had cop experience when I was an MP in 'Nam, so he waived it. Did I miss anything good?"

"Hell, yes. They spend the better part of a day or two kissing the FBI's tush, because they know they'll need favors from time to time. And they'd recite the same fingerprint rubbish. At the end of the day, it's all smoke. The 'Bureau of Investigation,' before it was the Federal Bureau of Investigation was founded in 1908 by Charles Buonaparte, a grand-nephew of Napoleon...."

"No shit..."

"Yeah. The irony, of course, is that Hoover ran the show for 48 years, from 1924 to 1972, and he, more than any other great patriotic American, was the archetype 'Napoleonic complex.' He didn't ever think he was God. He woke up every day knowing it.

"Hoover," I continued, "had worked as a kid in the Library of Congress, cataloging whatever new stuff came in. It became a mania for him, so once the Bertillon system was discarded, he started a fingerprint collection like an eight-year old obsessed with stamps and coins."

"Or baseball cards," Arty reminded me.

"Well, of course baseball cards. But the feds have tens of millions of prints of people long dead, and they have tens of millions of prints of American kids under the age of 14, so their real data base is a helluva lot smaller than what they brag about, and it makes you wonder if their experts have to compare the prints we got against the dead folks and the kids, or only against real possibilities."

"Never thought of that. And what was Bertillon?"

"Damn, Arty, you really did miss the police academy. Let's see if the food's ready."

We got out, marched in, carefully, but not obnoxiously, hitching up the gun belts as if we were looking for a handout, and the first employee who saw me said, "I know you. Hamret."

*Hamret. Yup.*

"About 15 minutes. You want to sit?"

"No, that's not necessary." *He was afraid we were going to scare off customers.*

"Bertillon?" Arty reminded me.

"Oh, yeah. Well, fingerprints only really got started in the early 1900s. Guys who studied police work began to suspect that those markings on the underside of fingers were unique, but selling that concept—that the 2 billion people on the planet at that point in time had a total of 20 billion totally unique markings was a tough sell. The Bertillon system was named after a Frenchman who came up with a system of measurements that involved virtually every body part or anomaly, so when hair color and style, if applicable, eye color, jaw bone, shoulder girdle, height, spine curvature, scars, ethnicity, and all manner of other things were factored in, an individual got a Bertillon reference number that was longer than a bar code would be today. I don't recall exactly, but 16 or 20 digits, and the near-impossibility of two of them being identical convinced law enforcement that it was the way to go.

"And then Will West was taken to Leavenworth, in Kansas," I concluded, as a tease.

"Who's Will West?"

I laughed. "A crook responsible for fingerprinting science as it exists today. When he was taken into Leavenworth in a horse-drawn paddy-wagon, and he was African-American, not a paddy, the guards said, 'Hey, back again, eh?' But West insisted he'd never been in Leavenworth before. The guards treated it like every inmate who insists he's not guilty.

"But West persisted, and of course, they did the Bertillon on him, and it matched 'William West.' Confusion reigned until one day, one guard saw both men—Will West and William West—in different parts of the prison. They were brought together, and they were, literally, identical strangers. No relation. Never seen each other. Came from different parts of the country. But down to the smallest Bertillon measurement, they were identical.

"That made news and killed Bertillon and it opened the door for the people who had been preaching fingerprints."

Arty was about to say something when he was handed the food. "Have a good day, officers."

"We're paying for this. How much?"

"Is okay. No worry."

"We'll have a bottle of Sake, and some plum wine." Arty forked over the $100 and told the manager that should cover it. I had no doubt that it did, and I had even less doubt that Porterfield, now that I knew his pedigree, was going to ask for change.

The ride back gave us another chance to see the collateral damage from the mid-afternoon wreck, probably a result of some lingering black ice. One yard would clearly need to be re-landscaped, as the shrubs and one sizable tree would never be the same.

I had wanted to detour slightly to pass Vychon's property on the way back, but my stomach, suddenly having discovered an appetite, won out over my police curiosity. When we walked into the Melrose P.D. entrance, me with the food and Arty with the booze, he immediately saw Banta and said, "Know who Will West is, Jack?"

"You've been talking to Decker, haven't you? That's an old academy story, but it's true."

"*Jack* Banta?" I asked him. "1950 Dodgers?"

Banta looked at Arty and asked what I was talking about. Arty gave him kind of a blank look.

"Jack Banta pitched for the Dodgers in 1950, or at least there is a baseball card of him. Looked a lot like Billy Loes."

"Who's Billy Loes?" Banta asked.

"Another Dodger. But he has the dubious distinction of being the only player to claim he lost a grounder in the sun, and he did that in the World Series. And as a Dodger, he was asked about the 1953 series, and he picked the Yankees in six games."

"No wonder they have the two of you on Rizzoli. Let's eat the goddam goodies."

Upon entering the conference room, it was clear that the Melrose P.D. was in the habit for sending out for meals, an event relatively unknown, at least at the dinner hour, in Hamlet.

The conference table was covered with a gentle, print design tablecloth, although upon inspection, it was paper. There was a stack of dinner plates as well as snack plates, plus silver, which seemed extravagant for just the four of us.

Then I noticed the inlaid "P" impress on the china and the flatware and suspected it was excess from the Porterfield cutlery cabinet. *What a concept: a police chief who knows how to show respect for his officers.*

When we opened the package, it seemed as if they'd cooked for eight, although Arty had ordered for four. A bribe is a bribe is a bribe....

I helped myself to the chicken, shrimp, rice, noodles, and vegetables that had been cooked hibachi-style. When it reached my palate, I knew my appetite had been restored, and discussion of recent events would have to be held in abeyance.

Porterfield commented on the quality and asked Arty where it came from. I desperately wanted to say something foolish like "a farm and an ocean," but Arty quickly answered that it was from the Japanese restaurant right there in Melrose.

Porterfield acknowledge his gaffe in not knowing, adding that he should have had an in-depth awareness of every business in Melrose, or "On his watch," as he put it. "But, well, my uncle—my mother's brother—was killed at Pearl Harbor when he was twenty-six, and the Porterfields have since avoided proximity to what were always referred to as 'Japs.' I'm sure that would rankle a lot of sensitivities, but that was the way it was. This meal is delicious, and as Chief of Police, I will have to revise my prejudices and check this establishment out."

When everyone had finished, Porterfield excused himself briefly, and Jack Banta used the opportunity to ask Arty and me how well we knew Rizzoli. It sounded to me like he wanted to verify that, in fact, we did know him.

"We both go back with him a long way," Arty said. "Deck first met him in 1977 or so, before he hit the baseball card lottery. It didn't take him long before effete snobbery set in, but he was just Joe Blow when Deck met him, and we ran into him together at collector's shows for a few years after that. Then he became too famous to appear at such events."

Banta looked at me as I put my two cents in. "Yeah, the man has—or perhaps I should say *'had'*—a really bad case of "I" strain."

"You really think he's bought it?" Banta said, quickly adding, "From the one time I met him—a neighborhood complaint that kids were hanging around too often to try for free baseball cards—he seemed like an okay guy. But I wouldn't want my daughter to marry him."

"Jack," Arty said, "Your daughter is seven and Rizzoli's in his 50s..."

"Well that's a relief," Banta said, laughing.

Porterfield returned. "Rizzoli?" he asked.

"We were just sharing memories," Arty said.

"You think he's gone for good....and I agree with you. It's been a week. If he's alive, he's gone somewhere to start over, and he'll never grace Melrose with his presence. If he was kidnapped, nobody could have ever tolerated his egotistic bullshit this long, so he would definitely be fish food."

"Oh, you know him?" I asked.

"Everyone knows him," Porterfield said, almost casually, "but not everybody likes to talk about knowing him. He's been generous to Melrose on occasion, but that generosity came from a career of cut-throat greed, and that sours the whole process."

The room fell briefly silent. Then Porterfield, after creasing still-neat trousers, put a leg up on the corner of the table and asked me what I thought. I wasn't immediately sure of his meaning, but he added, "Rizzoli—dead or alive?"

"Dead."

"Taken for a bundle?"

"A serious bundle," I answered. Once again, I'd almost said it was more than we could imagine, but based on what I knew about Porterfield, I felt strongly he could imagine it.

"Anybody think the Russian is somehow involved?"

Arty and I both put up a hand just enough to be noticed, but Banta held his hand out level and rotated it to both sides, as if he was uncertain.

That at least meant he was leaning toward the possibility.

"Why, Officer Decker?"

"Chief, it just seems like a huge coincidence that at the very moment his son gets the family on page one of all the newspapers, Vychon decides to exit the adult film industry and become respectable with antiques and collectibles. Sure, he's got the money to set himself up in that business, and more than enough if he could sell off his movie holdings, but it's still too much of a coincidence.

"And look at the overlap. The kids go out and wreck a car that Vychon owns—not one of the other children's cars, but Vychon's. Rizzoli's truck winds up in the one New York borough where Russians abound, and the truck is amateurishly splashed with red, white, and light blue paint—the colors of the 'new' Russian Federation. Maybe it was amateurish by design... And that truck, like the Camaro that the kids were driving, contained the remains of a vanity-label brand of Russian vodka.

"Rizzoli's credit card is used by a Russian-related vehicle in proximity to one of his three storage lockers, where I believe it is safe to assume that he did not store Granny's old night tables. And Rizzoli had a storage locker in Brighton Beach, suggesting at least the possibility that he and Vychon had prior knowledge of each other and were headed into some joint venture—but then Vychon wanted it all.

"But there is still one more anomaly, and that has been gnawing at me since I came up here after talking with Arty outside Edwina Griffin's wake. I can't understand why Vychon handed me that liquor bottle that had his fingerprints on them. Does he think, if he took down Rizzoli, that he can just do it and get away with it? I can't buy that."

Porterfield regarded me with an intense gaze before speaking. "Are you really convinced that it was Vychon who took Rizzoli down?"

"Yes, but it may well be that he was only the mastermind of the operation. I strongly doubt that he made the call—the Thursday call last week to the 'suitcase phone'—himself, but he could have had someone do that from an untraceable number. Vychon had a very good alibi—most likely the party that we visited following the accident with the Camaro. They could have grabbed Rizzoli on the first day, but when his ego outran his common sense, they knew they had to deep-six him, and that soiree at Vychon's was the perfect alibi. The beautiful people danced and partied, while Vychon's boys put terminal punctuation on Pete Perfect."

Porterfield put his left hand on his chin and looked past me as slowly drew his left index finger across his chin: "So if Rizzoli—well, if Rizzoli's remains were to be found, a medical examiner would put the time of death at mid-evening of Monday, March 9—assuming, of course, that a time of death could be arrived at. Water can prevent such determinations..."

"I believe that is how it would happen, and when considered that way, it seems equally reasonable to rule out a death by deep-water drowning, because precision would be necessary to overlap the alibi. The body would have to be found, and found in such a way that the time of death could be ascertained, even days later. Unless it was in the water, or on land, but only found long after the fact. And who could prove where Vychon's 'employees' were at that time? So what are the other choices?"

"Like in a storage locker," Banta said.

Silence– like the silence of Pharaoh's Tomb.

Arty noted that a storage locker might not present the kind of ambient temperature for a medical examiner to determine precise time of death, and that point was well taken—and somewhat meaningless unless Rizzoli was actually found within one of his lockers. And, of course, it was still winter.

We all looked at each other before Porterfield spoke: "Well, that possibility will be dealt with in a few hours, but even if that is the case and it validates what has been said here, the fact that an M.E. can put the time of death to coincide with an alibi—an ironclad alibi ratified by the angry citizens of Hamlet—that doesn't prove anything except that we are a bunch of bright guys and Vychon would be home free…"

"But without his son," Arty noted.

"Yeah," Porterfield said, still musing. "That seems like way too much of a loose end not to be considered in any plan."

Banta jumped in: "The elderly woman being killed was not counted on as a variable."

Porterfield took Banta's bishop with a pawn, which Banta's knight then took: "But the son would have been in trouble even without the accident that seems to have been the cause of death of the woman. Maybe—here's a thought—maybe Vychon figured that an incident involving his son and some friends would raise enough emotional angst, locally and state-wide even, to get him and his family deported, and that would be the perfect getaway."

"The perfect crime," Arty and Banta both said.

"Except for Edwina," I added.

"Still," Porterfield thought aloud. "If it played that way, it's brilliant." Almost as an afterthought, he spoke to me: "Could the so-called 'Russian mafia,' an emerging crime element, have had a hand in this?"

I waited to see if anyone else would speak, but the two Melrose cops had gone silent. "Absolutely," I finally said. "The so-called 'Russian mafia' is a network, more tightly knit than our own, home-grown organized crime. Here in the States, we have 'crime families,' but we've seen enough mob-insider murders on page one of the newspapers to know that those different crime families can wage holy wars to extend their turf or protect their flanks. From what little I've been able to gather about this Russian crew—and my knowledge is admittedly thin—they are more tightly knit, they are more of a network than a family, and they are doing whatever it is they're doing to lift Mother Russia off the world's carpet—which is where the Soviet Union wound up when they went bankrupt. Hell, they were so economically destroyed that when the bankruptcy and break-up did occur, they had a cosmonaut in orbit, and they did not even have the resources to bring the poor bastard down for several months. Since his eventual return, he has been a full-tilt cripple from too much exposure to weightlessness.

"That is how bad it was, and that's what the emerging Russian crime syndicate is out to correct. They'd kill an outsider for a few bucks and think nothing of it. Vychon's 'adult film' industry was a good cover for a whole lot of dirty shit. And forgive my frankness, Chief, but it's not a good thing to fuck with the Russian mafia."

Porterfield just said "Huh." *The man was speaking my language.*

"Well, gentlemen," Porterfield responded, "they are putting special measures in place at the County Seat so that the Grand Jury will meet tomorrow, whether Brighton Beach cars arrive to disrupt things or not. We should also know what is in those storage lockers. If Rizzoli is among the contents, I'm going to ask the District Attorney for the authority to have Mr. Vychon taken into custody as a material witness. At least we'll know where he is."

"And if Interpol or Scotland Yard come through with a fingerprint identification, we'll also know *who* Vychon is..."

"And that could be critical," Porterfield noted.

"And that would be critical," I replied.

The mental energy had been spent. The words had been said. The ideas had been delineated. They could all be wrong, but nobody in that room thought so at that moment.

We adjourned, with the plan to be back in the Melrose P.D. Conference Room at 07:30, so that as the morning broke, we—and by 'we' it meant Porterfield's *ad hoc* task force, plus his entire department and such federal help as his influence could bring muscle to bear upon—would be ready for anything.

Or so we thought. As we walked outside, there was the lingering coronal remainder of a bright red sunset that had happened hours earlier.

*Red sky at night, sailor's delight. Red sky at morning, sailor take warning.*

We knew that Friday, March 13th—the proverbial Friday the 13th—would bring news.

But none of us could have known that the beauty of that sun-reflected image was merely the gentle calm before the tempestuous storm. It was hardly a sailor's delight, and but an understatement for all of us to "take warning."

# The Beginning of the End

In the foggy haze of my mind that was attempting to pass as a dream, I was hearing a phone ringing. Somehow, while still asleep, my brain sent itself a memo saying that phones don't ring in dreams.

The phone really was ringing, and although I knew I had multiple extensions in the house, the location of any of them was shrouded in mystery, even as I regained consciousness.

Finally, I put a light on in the kitchen and sure enough, the phone was still ringing, and I was awake. "Yeah?"

"Get up to Melrose now and report to Porterfield. Then pray that you still have a job in Hamlet when this is all over."

"Who is this and what are you selling? I already have life insurance."

"You're going to need all the life insurance you have and then some, if you are not in Melrose in ten minutes," I heard Chief Shit-fer-brains say.

"Good morning, Chief. How was your 'nap'?"

"Did you hear me, Decker? Get your ass up to Melrose. Porterfield is waiting for you. Ten minutes."

"Have a nice day, Chief."

I looked at the digital LED clock on the counter: "4:09." *She's real fine my 409....* Then it changed to 4:10 and the beauty of the Beach Boys' hot rod was lost. *And I had between eight and nine minutes to get my shaggy butt to Melrose.*

I splashed water on my face, found and quickly donned the last of the clean uniforms, and was in the car in about three minutes. In the pre-dawn darkness of a Friday I could make it to Melrose in five minutes.

And what did Shit-fer-brains mean about still having a job in Hamlet when this was over?

I blew the rust out of the old six-cylinder Firebird and arrived at the Melrose P.D. within one minute of the mandated goal and told myself I needn't worry about those particular sixty seconds. Porterfield was standing alone, just in front of the entrance, as if he were waiting for the posse to arrive.

Damn. The man was dressed in jeans, boots, and a bomber jacket, and I was reminded that this was one police chief who knew how to dress for any or all occasions.

"Batting leadoff, Decker."

I didn't have the intellectual stamina at that moment to respond, so Porterfield translated: "You're the first of the cavalry to arrive. Banta and Swanson are no doubt getting lectures from their wives about being careful today, and the other two detectives…."

"Are you saying today is going to be a day when additional care will be necessary?"

"That's exactly what my concern is," he said, and I told him it was suggested to me that I be concerned about my employment status in Hamlet.

"I've got your back, Decker. I called your boss to get you here. Do the men and women in your department know that the Chief of Police in Hamlet has a cashew for a brain?"

"We never actually gave him that much credit."

"Well, don't worry. I suspect the man is closer to retirement than he realizes, and the one person in Hamlet who is going to come out of this looking good is you. I've got friends in the media, Decker."

"Fair enough. What have we learned to move up the scheduled time of this get-together?"

"I'll tell you inside." With that, Porterfield turned and we got about ten feet before a catering truck pulled in. *If I worked for Porterfield, I'd never have to cook. The man had called in breakfast before he called in the posse. Class is as class does. Only my waistline may have had regrets.*

The conference table was reasonably arranged, but Porterfield walked to the far corner of the room. I suspected he didn't want the boys from the bakery to overhear what could be important commentary.

"The two detectives you met yesterday…I sent them home for some sleep and then they were on the midnight to eight, so they would be available when we got the warrant for the local storage area Rizzoli had.

"The warrant was issued because I got a very pissed-off magistrate out of bed, and then the two suits had to get the owner of the locker facility out of bed. The feds had run down his identity. We could have gone to Mrs. Rizzoli, but that would have been a helluva wake up call in the middle of the night."

"And?" I asked.

"The place was virtually empty. No boxes, no nothing. Not even a gum wrapper."

"You said 'virtually.'"

"Yeah. That's why I'm glad you're here. I'm sure you've seen a good number of the advertisements Rizzoli ran in sports publications. A caricature of himself—small body, huge head, and wads of cash."

"Sure. It was his logo, ferchrissake."

"The boys are coming in soon, after they've dusted critical areas for prints. It's damn tough to dust something when there's nothing to dust. All that was in that storage area was a good number—one of the detectives said 'a shitload' of those caricatures, taped to the walls, everywhere."

"That was Rizzoli's ego, writ large," I said again, stating the obvious.

"Probably," Porterfield pronounced, syllable by syllable. "But the ads you would have seen were in English. These were all in Russian, and we're going to get a translator from the New York office of the Bureau to try to make sense of them."

"I know a little Russian," I offered, but to break the tension, I added, "but I always collected baseball cards in English. Made more sense."

"Yeah, that does have a certain logic on its side," and with that, Porterfield chuckled. Seemed like a man who needed a laugh at that moment.

In virtually the same moment, a vehicle could be heard outside, careening into the all-but-empty parking lot, since the majority of municipal employees would not arrive until at least some point after sunrise.

Or so I thought. Porterfield would soon make mention that all critical posts would be manned by 04:45 a.m. I doubted that meant the tax collector, the truant officer, or the dog-catcher.

The car was carrying Arty and Banta, as they only lived about four blocks apart. No sooner had bagels hit the table than each grabbed one, plus a plastic knife and a couple slabs of cream cheese.

Porterfield quickly made them aware of the news regarding the local storage locker, then added, for the benefit of all, "AND….and the local FBI residence office got a call—get this—at 03:45, just before you were all called in—from the White House…that's the big, expensive building in the middle of Washington, D.C….and the feds were told to gather all of us together and, and I quote, 'await developments.' Anybody want to guess what that could mean?"

I couldn't resist. The tension needed breaking. "Maybe the President is going to appoint you as the new Ambassador to Iceland…"

Porterfield chuckled again. "You know Decker, there are times when you can be very funny." And after a pause, "And then there's now."

I got the message.

That drove the breakfast dynamic to virtual silence, punctuated only by the need to pass items.That silence was interrupted by the wail of a siren that seemed to be headed directly for the conference room. Moments later, a breathless, way-too-skinny and slightly balding detective came running in with a handful of papers. *The Rizzoli broadsides, in Russian.*

Porterfield immediately told me to have a look at them, but I listened carefully as he began to question the still-huffing Detective Caldwell. At least I'd learned one name. And reminded myself to stay in better shape.

Porterfield's first comment was not evidence-based. He asked Caldwell if these were all of the papers, because he did not want Rizzoli's widow—and he paused briefly after he said "widow" and corrected himself to say 'Mrs. Rizzoli' to see what seemed to him to be "Wanted, Dead or Alive" posters.

Caldwell said he would call out to Lester, but that didn't help me to learn if it was Detective Lester or Detective Lester ... something.

"And be cautious what you say. As always, anyone can hear what is on police radio."

I jumped in. "Did anyone ask when Rizzoli was at that storage area last?"

"Good point. Caldwell?"

"Yeah. We saw the records. Lester has them. The last time Rizzoli was there was 2:41 p.m. on Thursday, 5 March. That was the time he checked in. No record of when he left."

"The day of the phone call," Banta said.

"Yes. But he had been at that locker for either eight or nine consecutive days, up until that Thursday."

*March 5, Boston Massacre Day,* I thought. *How fitting a choice of calendar dates for someone to go after Rizzoli.* "All right. You tell Lester to bring in all of the, uh, hmm; 'placards' sounds innocent enough, and also the time sheets of the visits. Word it in such a way that a stranger won't make sense of it. Also, have Lester shake down the locker guy for additional information—was Rizzoli alone, or with someone, and if so, who? The rest of us will have to dig in one big-ass hurry through phone records. Caldwell...go."

The mention of phone records seemed to point directly at both Rizzoli—at least in terms of his home phone and business line, but it was still a stone wall with respect to his special phone—and to Vychon, but that was a thin prospect because we already had a consensus that this was not a deal of his exclusive doing.

I looked at the clock surrounded by aging photos of past Melrose mayors. 5:17. It was going to be a long day, and that did not take into account the fact that we were "awaiting developments" from the White House.

And where were the feds?

"Can you make anything out of those posters, or whatever the hell they are, Decker?"

"A little, I think." I spread out the first few, and eliminated duplicates, leaving about seven different formats.

Before I said anything, Porterfield told Arty to go out to the desk and have a uniformed officer maintain a presence at the storage locker. "He stays until he's relieved," Porterfield insisted. "Decker?"

"I can't make much sense out of any of this, and that in itself is a red flag—no pun intended. Rizzoli was always pretty much in-your-face with his self-advertising. 'I want your cards, you want my cash.' In even the most primitive Russian, that would be, and I'm doing this in phonics, 'Ya ho-chu…the word for cards,' and 'tee hochu mne ruble.' That's primitive, but there's nothing of that here, and all of this seems to be some kind of bastardized language. Appearance, too, because there is print and script in some of these words. I'm sorry, Chief, but from what I've seen, I can't help you. And just for shits and grins, I'll bet the fed they send to translate has a problem as well."

"You think?"

"I'm too tired to think, but this is some dialect, and not a very close relative of Russian."

"So it's not Russian?"

"Not any Russian that I'd recognize, but it's not really for me to say. See what the feds think."

Caldwell walked back into the conference room. "I told Lester not to leave anything so much as dust behind, and as soon as the uniform gets there, Lester will bring in the locker guy as well. To hear Lester talk, that guy already needs to change his underwear, so he'll cooperate."

"Okay, then, we wait. In the meantime, I need to rattle some federal cages."

Before Porterfield got five feet, the door to the conference room opened and a civilian, manning the desk, told him there was a call for him. When asked if he wanted it in his office or in the conference room, Porterfield said he'd take it right where he was.

In a way, that was a huge statement of trust in us.

Of course, we could only hear one side of the conversation. "Yeah, Porterfield. Yes, an early good morning, your Honor. Uh huh. Uh huh. Who? He didn't leave his name? Okay. What diplomat? From *where?* Uh huh. He 'demanded'? Uh huh. So what is the White House saying? Yes. Okay. I see. I trust you'll call me back when they fill in the missing pieces. Yes, your Honor. I've got the right people in place and we'll wake up the boys in Hamlet if necessary. But I don't think we'll need to roust them. They'll be on duty in two hours."

The clock now read 5:40. Two hours to 'muster' in Hamlet. Crowder would be giving marching orders. What a pity that I had to miss it.

Porterfield sat down—well, he actually slumped down in his chair, shoulders somewhat hunched as if affecting defensive body language. He wanted to speak, but clearly, he was collecting his thoughts. Shit-fer-brains in Hamlet could collect his thoughts with a lint roller.

"You're not going to believe this," he began.

The reality was, we were going to have to believe it.

# The Middle of The End

Sunrise. It seems to be one of the few times of day about which just about everyone has an opinion. Some people love to be awake to see the sunrise, although I do not count myself among them. Others enjoy seeing the sunrise as they are coming in after a long night. I would probably fall into that category, if I had long nights. Another story for another time, perhaps.

Still, nobody talks about the beauty of 'noon' or 'midnight' or anything similar, so sunrise remained the benchmark, and it was something to be appreciated when one found oneself in the dark, both mentally and meteorologically. At least as I viewed it, it seemed to have lowered the chance of precipitation from 40% to zero.

Clearly, Chief Porterfield had a working knowledge of what he'd just been told, but there was uncertainty about the proverbial 'big picture,' and he was straining to find a way to share the knowledge without being overly obvious in manifesting the uncertainty.

"That," he began slowly, "was the mayor, and we can add him to the growing list of people who are not happy about having their regular sleep habits interrupted. He's not now or ever to be confused with law enforcement, as his grasp of details is not as finely honed as we have to be in our business. He apparently got a call from 'someone' in the White House, and that unstated someone alerted him to the fact that a long black limousine, flying fender flags not immediately recognized, had demanded entrance at the White House gate. The purpose of the visit was to let the people in the White House know that there would be an ugly mess—that's exactly how the mayor phrased it, but I doubt it's an exact quote—but there would be an ugly mess if anyone tried to interfere with the seemingly placid day-to-day existence of Billy Vychon. I—make that *we*—are waiting for more details, but in the meantime, I really don't like the smell of it."

Banta jumped in, "Who the hell is behind this? Forgive my anger, Chief. But where is it written that Vychon's shit doesn't stink?"

"I don't know, Jack, and this would be an inappropriate time to speculate."

When Porterfield mentioned 'time,' I again looked at the clock. It read 6:17, which meant less than an hour and a half until muster in Hamlet. The dead mayors in the picture frames looked more tired than they had only an hour ago. *Maybe when one mayor is awakened in a crisis, the ghosts of mayors past all awaken. Note to self: get a grip, Decker.*

With only our private thoughts to deal with—meaning no full understanding of the mayor's message, no full understanding of whatever the hell the Rizzoli posters said, and no understanding of why Rizzoli would have visited that local storage locker several days in a row, there remained too many open questions. We also now had more questions—why would someone go to so much trouble to protect Vychon, even before he was officially cited as being in trouble? Did Rizzoli make trips to all three storage facilities? And on that note, we'd have to dig deeper into credit card purchases for gasoline as far back as late February to discover the kind of mileage Rizzoli was piling up. New Jersey Motor Vehicles might be of some help, if Rizzoli had any vehicles inspected in the last ninety days, but it was a thin hope when I realized that Rizzoli only drove new sports cars, and new cars did not immediately go through the inspection process.

We also needed someone with forensic ability to have a look at the Russian posters and try to make a connection to a printing company, if that were possible, as they could well have been computer generated. Still, that would have taken some expertise.

Only one other real question was on the table at that moment: What the hell was going on?

Given many questions that would not be solved by uninformed brainstorming, the five of us—now including Caldwell full-time, and early-arriving municipal workers now and then, continued to pick at the breakfast. The next to last piece of pineapple, half of that chocolate chip cookie, and absolutely that one salty end of that penultimate bagel. Another can of caffeinated Coke for me, giving rise to two possible wagering pools: How many would I consume today, and who would be the first to ask, "What's for lunch?"

Those mental meanderings were, like earlier ones, interrupted by a new arrival, Detective Lester and a somewhat disheveled individual who we suspected was the keeper of the lockers. He had a four-syllable Italian last name, suggesting Corsica or Sardinia, rather than Italy, to me, but that wasn't important. We kept it to "Johnny," and Porterfield put a uniform on the door to keep the civilians out while we chatted with Johnny.

On previous occasions, the conference room door had simply been locked. By actually putting an officer on the door, it suggested that we'd be seeing a surge in traffic on this day.

Beyond that marginal detail, we definitely needed to get a broad cross-section of information from Mr. Johnny. Did he know Rizzoli well enough to recognize him on sight? Did he recall the multiple visits prior to March 5? Could he recall if Rizzoli was alone or not? Could he recall the vehicle that Rizzoli arrived and departed in, assuming they were the same? Did he have any recollection of whether or not anything was removed from the locker during those visits?

He told us, almost with a sense of pride in his work, that of course he knew Rizzoli by sight. He was good for a bottle of liquor every Christmas. *Don't count on it this year, Johnny.*

As for the rest, he was somewhat fuzzy, a polite cop euphemism for "intentionally stupid." The one thing he was sure of was that Rizzoli did not take anything out of the storage locker in any of the five, six, or eight visits. He based his certainty on a review of the "security camera," which, when translated into "fuzzy," meant there was no auto visible and, accordingly, no license plate or vital data.

For Porterfield, that was absolutely the last straw—or perhaps the first of several last straws. He stood, turned his back on the group, walked to the window, looked out and then came back, leaned on the conference table just next to his chair, and quietly said—the temper having passed, "Lester, read 'Johnny' his rights and book him on charges of accessory to murder."

Johnny screamed and possibly crapped his pants in the same second, pleading innocence. Yes, he knew Rizzoli, yes, there were multiple visits, and no, nothing was taken out. He didn't spy on every customer and he had almost 200 units to take care of.

Porterfield walked around the table, and got right alongside the hapless vendor. "That storage locker was empty except for dust when we met *you* there a few hours ago. Do you really want us to believe that Rizzoli visited it eight or nine days in a row, and that he was visiting an empty locker? You know, Johnny, it doesn't play that way."

Then, far louder, and in Johnny's right ear. "Rizzoli is dead. Killed by the people he went in there with, if he went in there with someone. You don't know or will not tell us. You're hiding something—a whole lot, and maybe the prospect of 7,305 days in prison—that's twenty years, with five of them leap years. Lester, get this lying sack of shit out of here before I save the state the cost of feeding the bastard."

"Wait. Let me think." The standard comeback to a perceived threat. "I think maybe one day, maybe two—like I said, I don't watch every moment, as I have 200 storage units. But once or maybe twice, he arrived as a passenger in a big black car—limo, maybe. And he was not driving, so I guess he had to be with someone."

"Your sudden recall amazes me," Porterfield said. Nobody else, of course, was going to ask questions. One suspect, one interrogator. It might have been good theater for the other cops to just walk out and leave it to the chief, but my sense was that he when he was done with Johnny, he'd want our perceptions—collectively—so we stayed.

"Now, you say it was a large, black vehicle, limo, maybe. Johnny, those are perceptions that we call 'absolute.' You're not saying, 'Maybe it was black, and maybe it was big.' Anything unusual about the front of the car?"

"No, not that I saw."

"Were there flags on the fenders?"

"Oh, no. No. I would have remembered that."

"But you were suddenly able to recall that Rizzoli wasn't driving. Are you able to recall a description of the driver or other possible occupants?"

"No. The windows were, I guess you would say 'cloudy.' And see, Rizzoli liked to be waited on. He'd drive the truck and stop, make me come out and then he would tell me to check him in. But in the black car, he already had the window down and the car didn't even come to a full stop. Just 'check me in.'"

"Do you remember Rizzoli's locker number?" Porterfield asked. It was clearly a control question, as it had to already be known to the Melrose Police in order for them to have searched it.

"Yes. Fifty-two. Storage unit number fifty-two. The twelfth unit from the back in the second row…there are forty in each row."

*Fifty-two. Arty and I looked at each other and silently mouthed the word "Mantle."*

"And that's all you can remember?"

"Yes, I swear."

"Well," Porterfield continued, "you have been slightly helpful after all. But you're going to be our guest for a little while longer. Is there anyone you need to contact in order to run the storage unit area today or for the next few days?"

Johnny was broken, but Porterfield was not bending. And Johnny had said the magic words: Large black vehicle. Like the one that visited the White House hours earlier. Similar, perhaps to the vehicle that had used Rizzoli's credit card in Westchester.

The pieces were falling together. The puzzle was extremely unpleasant, but at least it was coming together.

Johnny was taken away, as he had to be kept under wraps at least until someone could spring him on a *habeus corpus* writ, because he'd been told Rizzoli was dead. We had to consider the possibility that he knew someone who could profit from that knowledge.

He wouldn't even get his one phone call, or if he did, the operator at the desk would take whatever number Johnny wanted called and then dial the weather bureau. An ugly procedure, but sometimes it had to be that way. Sometimes, they would dial the phone company's "busy number." In any exchange, if you dialed the local exchange and then 9970, you got the busy tone. It was the phone company's way of knowing that the system was working. It was the police way of keeping a suspect from the outside world.

Porterfield had returned to his seat and put his hands behind his head and leaned back. "Is anyone *not* thinking what I am?

No answer was necessary.

When Lester came back, he made it known that he'd taken the locker storage guy to the toilet, where custodial service was probably now needed, and then to the temporary, in-house lock-up, where custodial service would be needed when Mr. Johnny was released.

"A couple hours in there should jog his memory," Porterfield concluded. Thereafter, we briefly sat like a collection of relatives awaiting word regarding a long-overdue airline arrival.

We knew the bottom line, but we were starved for the details. At least we *thought* we knew the bottom line.

Porterfield, clearly bored with the slow pace of events, put a call in to the FBI residence number that had received the initial, middle-of-the night notification about events in Washington.

"Porterfield, here in Melrose. Yeah, I know you were awakened during the night, but it's not night anymore. What is going on with the searches of the storage lockers in Rye and Brighton Beach? Uh huh. Well, if you don't know, call someone who would know and have them call me at the P.D. in Melrose. Preferably in the next ten minutes. What's going on here is growing exponentially, and we cannot wait any longer for the answers we need. And have somebody get us the results of the fingerprint inquiry. Preferably in the next *nine* minutes, since one of the original ten is gone. Yes, I know you'll do everything you can. Make sure it's enough."

He put the phone down without waiting for an answer. He did not do so with anger, causing me to suspect that his sudden outburst at Locker Johnny was creative staging, a necessary talent in our profession.

"They claim no results yet, but I know better. Hell, if we can have one entire scenario wrapped up, who is going to believe that the FBI, with all their friggin' manpower, can't handle two? And I have to believe they have the print results. Does anyone besides me think they're trying to muscle us?"

"It is inter-state," Banta said.

"Yeah, technically it is," Porterfield answered him, "but professional courtesy does not stop at a 'Welcome To' sign at a state border. Damn."

The mayors on the wall were not aging, but the clock had now reached 6:59, and Porterfield got the return call from the resident agent, alerting him to the imminent receipt of two phone calls, one from Rye, and one from Brighton Beach. Although the agent making the call claimed to have no details, Porterfield thanked him politely and told him he would say nice things in the final case report.

Personally, I doubted that, but a kind word never hurt during an investigation; afterwards, it didn't much matter what was said. Only the results mattered, and if they were good, you were just fine; if they were not good, you wouldn't be either.

I think everyone present wanted to find some gentle words of respectful praise to say to the Melrose chief for kicking some federal butt; however, the feds still had the clout—and the evidence—and we still had the right to say "please."

The phone rang again, but before picking it up, Porterfield grabbed a pad of legal paper from a sideboard and pulled a somewhat elegant pen out of a shirt pocket.

"This is Police Chief Porterfield of the Melrose, New Jersey, Police Department. To whom am I speaking? ... Yes, good morning, agent. Please make your report. It's 7:03 and I'm writing. Okay, Rye, New York. Uh huh, yes, that's interesting. That was all? Are you bringing the storage locker manager here for us to talk to him? Oh? ... Let me see if I understood what you just said. 'Because it is an interstate matter, the FBI is taking jurisdiction regarding Rye, New York.' Did I hear that correctly? ... And what crime, exactly, are you investigating, if any?"

Porterfield was no stranger to sarcasm.

"Disappearance and possible kidnapping. Well, yes, that would be FBI jurisdiction if it happened, but we are the office of origin, and we're trying to figure out *if* it happened. Is there any way, at least as a courtesy, that you could put the questioning of the individual on a conference call line?"

A long pause allowed Porterfield to look at each of us and display annoyance that we were being treated like children at the moment. "I see. Thank you. Uh huh. Yes, I'll be sure your superior gets a full and complete copy of my report."

Porterfield put down the phone, gently again, proving if nothing else that either phone repair was expensive in Melrose, or that he had amazing self-control.

The legal pad was hardly used to this point, but Porterfield spoke as he wrote. "As you all heard, that was Rye, New York, checking in. The storage locker there was also devoid of anything for which one would rent such space, but they did find, approximately two and one-half inches from the far right-hand back corner, quote, a paper clip. Apparently, there were no prints. They have the records of when Rizzoli was there, but they're not sharing just yet, and they obviously needed the manager to get access, but his memory's not good, they said."

"Fair to suspect we'll get the same treatment from Brighton Beach," Caldwell said.

"It's a guarantee we'll get the same treatment at Brighton Beach." Porterfield paused, and then vented, for the first time. "If any FBI agent shows up here, he damn well better have a subpoena and something to do to keep himself busy while we 'eagerly' search for whatever it is he's after. Have him sit in the waiting room. And they get nothing without my presence and approval. And I may not be able to be found at all times..."

We got his drift. Clearly, he had some kind of combat experience, whether it was as a boxer in college or a Vietnam grunt or pilot—although I doubted anybody with old money went to Vietnam.

But he'd been in a helluva fight somewhere.

And now, he remembered how.

Where didn't matter. He was home, in Melrose.

His turf.

# The End of The End

Daylight. A conference room, containing a chief of police, three local detectives, two local officers, and one visiting officer—me. *And no feds, despite the 'interstate' caveat.*

It seemed at that moment as if it were the seven of us against the world. To our left, politically and geographically it seemed, was a Russian with either enough money or enough clout—or both—to thumb his nose at us, even after his son had been involved in a vehicular homicide.

To our right, again politically at least, was the FBI, who were padding their statistics with an investigation that was ours, but one that had "international overtones" and they would remind Congress of that at budget-hearing time. We only had the voters of Melrose, and I wasn't even officially one of that "we." *I felt like getting a name tag, writing "Tonto" on it, and slapping it on my shirt.*

But who took up the middle? The only choice seemed to be Rizzoli, and at this point, he seemed like a place-holder, because his existence anywhere, even on a grid created for brainstorming, still seemed very temporary.

Ten minutes passed, then another five. It was 7:20 and we'd heard nothing from Brighton Beach or from any FBI source regarding the fingerprints. After additional small-talk about the suddenly-discovered enormous value of baseball cards, of all things, Porterfield changed direction and suggested that the prints turned up either an American or some international scenario in which Vychon was wanted for some serious crime, and the FBI was putting together their SWAT team as we were sitting there. At least, we reasoned, that might either get Vychon talking or at least out of the picture. "They could swoop down on him and we'd never know about it until it was over," Porterfield concluded.

I gently reminded him that Hamlet had his house under protective custody, so to speak, and it would be that way for at least another day or two, as Edwina Griffin was being buried today, and there would still be anger coursing through the local Hamletites. Hamletians?

The room lapsed back into silence briefly, although Porterfield was showing signs of the 'caged tiger' syndrome. Not long after my comment, he stood, adjusted his clothing briefly, and headed for the far door. Before he got to it, the female desk sergeant opened the door into the conference room, and her look gave us a hint that perhaps Charles Manson and his "family" were overrunning the Melrose P.D. It was way beyond the deer-caught-in-the-headlights apparition.

"Ch-chief, Mrs. Rizzoli is here. I made her comfortable in your office." Porterfield thanked the sergeant, asked her to close the door, and put it to us if he should see her alone, or if she should meet "the task force."

Lester suggested that whatever we do, we do it quickly, as she might have information. That reminded us that the only outside link she had to law enforcement was, once again, the FBI.

"Sergeant," Porterfield called, through the now slightly ajar door. When the sergeant returned, Porterfield instructed her to bring Mrs. Rizzoli into the conference room, and be certain to ask if she needed coffee, tea, or anything along those lines.

Porterfield stayed near the door to greet the visitor.

A moment or two later, Mrs. Rizzoli was led through the door. She appeared to have visibly aged since—what was it, three days ago? She was sobbing, with a handkerchief in her hand, and her outfit did not appear to have been carefully chosen. Makeup was totally absent, although it could have briefly existed before being washed away by a flood of tears.

Porterfield led her to a chair opposite Arty and me, perhaps thinking that to put her at the end of the table would be too much of an on-the-spot seating arrangement. As it was, although I admired Porterfield's tact, she was sitting in the chair so recently occupied by Storage Johnny, and I wondered if she picked up any odors.

She came right to the point. "I know he's—he's dead, isn't he?"

Porterfield had stayed at her side as she got settled, and he now knelt a bit to speak to her. "Mrs. Rizzoli, if you are asking us, it means you do not really know. Isn't that correct?"

"I guess, yes. But it has been over a week and—"

"We are doing everything we can, Mrs. Rizzoli. And because your husband maintains storage lockers in the state of New York, the FBI has also been investigating these events."

I gave Porterfield credit for honesty in not saying that the FBI was "helping." He did append, "These gentlemen, and you've met some of them already, have been here most of the night, and they're not about to leave."

For the first time since she sat down, she looked around at the group of us, but did not seem to recognize anyone. Perhaps she was still under some form of sedation, and if she was not, she probably needed to be.

"Do you have any information for us, Mrs. Rizzoli?" Jack Banta asked.

"No. I have not slept. I thought I'd come for the materials I left here, you know, before there was traffic."

"Is there anything else?" Porterfield asked.

"No. Just...please...accept my thanks and do anything that can be done. Please." The sobbing understandably returned.

Porterfield gave orders that the materials in the safe—Rizzoli's coveted inventory, which we now considered inoperative—be returned to her, and he asked Banta to take her to his office, stay with her, and then have a uniformed officer drive her home in an unmarked vehicle, and to have another uniform drive her car home as well. "The 8 to 4 will be arriving any minute, but stay with her."

The 8 to 4 shift. 'Muster' time in Hamlet, and I was missing it.

Billy Vychon, however, was not missing it. The desk sergeant appeared again and told Porterfield there was an urgent call from Hamlet.

"Yes, Porterfield here. Yes, good morning, Chief. Yes, he's here, and he's been an invaluable help to us. WHAT?" After a pause, "WHEN? What are you doing about it? Have any be-on-the-lookout orders been sent out? Do you have plate numbers? What, say again! What about descriptions? They were all black? What can we do? Yes. Okay. Certainly. Keep us posted please."

Porterfield sat down and reached for his pad. "I'm glad Mrs. Rizzoli was not here for that call."

I suspect that the rest of us were thinking the body had been found. I didn't take a survey, but I know that's what I was thinking.

"According to the chief in Hamlet—your boss," he added, looking at me, "at 7:41, literally the moment of the shift change, five of Vychon's garage doors opened, and five black vehicles emerged, and headed for the street, seemingly unconcerned about the speed they were making. When they reached the street, some went left and some went right. The Hamlet officers gave chase, but at the first opportunity, the cars that went left split up and the cars that went right split up. So now there are five cars, ostensibly carrying some manner of Russians—presumably Russians, going in five different directions. The Hamlet chief did not say so, but it sounds like some kind of diversion.

"But here's the kickers, plural. The cars were all black, fitting a pattern that is becoming all too common, and...."

Porterfield paused as if he almost could not say what came next, "and at least the two cars that the Hamlet officers followed had diplomatic license plates."

"They're essentially untouchable," Caldwell said.

"Yes they are, and that could explain why we are awaiting word from the White House. This is fucking crazy…forgive my French."

I suggested that Hamlet cops hit the house on some ruse as if they want to know if everyone is okay, or if there was a telephone threat, but really to see who, if anyone, was left behind.

Porterfield saw the wisdom of the idea and immediately called Hamlet. Predictably, Shit-fer-brains told him they would do that right after the morning muster. Porterfield gently suggested, "Do it NOW!" and put the phone down hard.

The three-word epithet reminded me that I'd been in need of a visit the men's room for over an hour, and I'd better 'do it now.' I found my way to the facilities, passing Storage Johnny still uncomfortable in the temporary lock-up, and wondering to myself, whimsically, if there would soon be a rapper band named "Storage Johnny."

After seeing to immediate needs, I gave my hands and face the good scrubbing that had been forfeited hours earlier, and I also took a moment to carefully remove a spatter of cream cheese that had not quite made it to my digestive system.

In my absence, the call had come from Brighton Beach. Porterfield briefed me on my return, just as Arty was intent on tracing my steps to the men's room. "The Brighton Beach locker was not empty as the others were, although there was no, uh, merchandise—no sports memorabilia—there. What was there seemed to be an of-necessity small makeshift workbench area, and there were documents—scattered papers and some arithmetic—suggesting that the owner of the storage locker was considering going into the sports memorabilia business in other countries. Beyond that, they will 'probably' inform us when they run fingerprints, and they are currently questioning the proprietor of that locker facility. Another FBI-induced dead end."

"That makes no sense," I protested. "Why would there be any market for sports memorabilia—baseball cards—outside the United States? Rizzoli was paying some taxes, so it's not a dodge, and it's a helluva stretch to think someone would buy rare cards, as they buy rare stamps or coins, as a hedge against inflation. I was in London in 1988, and there were a couple of shops that sold ephemera—old papers, autographs, *belles lettres,* and they had a handful of scratch-common baseball cards—from 1988. I cannot imagine any business there."

Caldwell picked up my thought: "Why would Rizzoli even need that market if he was so prosperous here in the States? Was he planning to advertise himself as the worldwide pasteboard mogul?"

"That would be the only reason, and it still makes no sense," I answered. "But it almost seems like the FBI fed us trivia so we would miss the larger picture, which is that Peter Rizzoli, aka 'Pete Perfect,' had three storage lockers rented in order to do business, and perhaps by extension lessen the threat of a burglary to his residence.

"But," I continued, "what was in the lockers? No cards whatsoever, and not a hint that any cards had ever been there. No cabinets, no traditional card-protection features, no proof that the lockers had ever been climate-controlled. It sounds to me like those three sites have been seriously sanitized."

Lester, less aware of Rizzoli and his reputation, asked, "Is it even remotely possible that Rizzoli really did not have any so-called baseball card empire?"

Arty Swanson was just coming through the door when that question was asked, and just as quickly answered it: "No f-ing way, Lester. Deck and I go way back with Rizzoli, and when he even had one batch of cards spread out at a high-end baseball card show, what he put on the table was dazzling. And he never gave a shit if he sold anything or not, because he always had private buyers—people who did not want it known that they had unaccounted-for cash that they could spend on high-end collectibles. His card show displays were at the very least bragging rights to show his little boy was bigger than anyone else's. That was his way. Deck?"

"Absolutely," was all I said.

"Okay. Where are we?" Porterfield asked, and then began answering his own question. "Rizzoli gets a call, ostensibly for some big money. We don't know who called him, but it set his wheels in motion. That was eight days ago, on 5 March. He has not been seen since." Porterfield paused a moment, then: "Is it possible that Rizzoli and Vychon were somehow working together, and Vychon was the 'unknown' insider who had access to Rizzoli's briefcase—or suitcase phone?"

"We'll know the answer to that when the phone company wakes up," Banta said, "but if the FBI, plus the White House, plus diplomatic license plates are stacked against us, the phone company will simply ignore us and the whole investigation."

Porterfield spoke again, coming forward out of the chair he was in to be in contact with the conference table, for emphasis. "Stop me if I misspeak. Next thing we know, Mrs. Rizzoli comes in here to report his disappearance on 9 March, coincidental—or perhaps more than that—with an accident involving the son of a Russian who was in the adult film business but admitted he was stepping aside to go into antiques."

"And collectibles," I added.

"Yes, absolutely. So then we dug just about everywhere we could, and discovered nothing other than one clearly empty storage locker here in New Jersey. The feds have such phone records as existed, and they have everything from the other two lockers."

"And Vychon's fingerprints, from the bottle he handed me," I said, out of the necessity to get some kind of venting against the FBI.

Porterfield returned to his summarizing. "And that, but they're not talking. An elderly woman will be laid to rest in a couple of hours and we do not know how, or if, that relates in any way to the disappearance of Pete Rizzoli.

"Then, less than thirty minutes ago, five black vehicles—not necessarily new items on the evidentiary chain—go sailing right out of Vychon's garage, headed for who-knows-where, and the two that could be followed were bearing diplomatic license plates. The worst-case scenario. So, realistically, where are we?"

Nobody said anything, probably because nobody wanted to tell the Chief of Police that he was right about thinking we were basically nowhere.

"The only thing left to focus on is Rizzoli. Is he alive or dead? Could he have been in one of those five cars? If so, was his presence voluntary or involuntary? Again, we don't know."

Porterfield paused again, but he was seemingly having some form of epiphany. "All right. You men have been up most or all of the night. We're not going to get anything more right now, except possibly the identities of any stragglers left in Vychon's house, if that is even possible.

"Everybody: go home, get some rest," and looking at me, "get the breakfast leftovers off your shirts, and let's be back here at 17:00. That's 5:00 p.m. in Hamlet. ... I'm just busting your hump, Decker."

As we stood to leave, calculating that we'd arrive home at 8:30 or 8:40, the desk sergeant opened the door and handed a sheet of paper to Porterfield. "This just arrived by fax. I think you need to read it."

Apparently, the print on the item was either small, or grainy from the fax machine, so Porterfield produced a pair of glasses and read the document. Then he laid it face down, took off his glasses and looked at each of us.

After a brief moment, he picked up the document, put his glasses back on, and read aloud:

"Fingerprints developed by the Federal Bureau of Investigation reveal that Billy Vychon, real name blah, blah, is an accredited diplomat with the Embassy of Kazakhstan, a former republic of the Union of Soviet Socialist Republics, and, accordingly, must be accorded the courtesy of diplomatic immunity at all times.

His eldest son, Mikhail Olegovich Vychon is also accredited as a junior cultural attaché with the Embassy of Kazakhstan, and is equally afforded the international courtesy of diplomatic immunity.

He is to be freed from custody immediately."

The signature was of the Special-Agent-in-Charge of the New York Office of the Federal Bureau of Investigation.

Needless to say, everyone in the room was stunned into silence, despite fierce anger boiling just beneath the surface.

"Thoughts or perhaps I should say, conclusions, anyone?" Porterfield asked.

Arty Swanson: "Rizzoli's dead, all right."

"Agreed."

"Vychon will be on his way to collect his son now, and from there, they'll be heading to the airport," Banta hypothesized.

"Agreed," Porterfield repeated. "Decker?"

"School's out, Chief. It's the perfect crime unless we find the anomaly that we're probably too tired to dig out now."

"Agreed again. I'm going to have the uniforms concentrate on the local airports and see who is getting on planes in the next few hours. We can still go and get some rest, because we can't stop the bastards.

"Kazakhstan? Can you believe that shit?"

"We have to believe it, Chief."

"Yeah. It's the law. See you all later, and let's damn well find whatever anomaly we can, if it is not too late already."

School truly was out, but at least I had a three-day vacation coming, as I wouldn't have to go back to the Hamlet P.D. today, and I had the coming weekend off. I wasn't sure I'd enjoy the time, as I'd have to face some form of wrath from the old Shit-fer-brains, but that was in the future, and I was too tired to worry about it.

Beyond that, the only thing I could think of at that moment, besides sleep, was to spend some time with my baseball cards. Maybe the anomaly would jump out at me.

If not, at least I was still alive and I still had my cards.

Rizzoli could not say—or brag about—either of those statements.

And he never would again.

# Epilogue

# The Anomaly

Luckily, my car had known the way home, because I was too tired to think, and I was afraid that if the ongoing events inclined me to pull out some of my baseball and football card collection, I'd wind up drooling on them.

That defines tired, and if I remembered to take the key out of the front door, it was the last thing I did before falling into a sound sleep.

The anomaly hit me while I was having a serenely pleasant dream about cute little gnomes who lived in thatched-roofed houses, with mushrooms out front that held itty-bitty little mailboxes. As the anomaly raced through that idyllic little setting, I awoke with a start and imagined I was hearing sirens.

Except I wasn't imagining them. I *was* hearing sirens. I peered at the clock that said 4:27 and, for a moment, I had not the foggiest idea if it was a.m. or p.m. *Maybe the gnomes knew.*

Suddenly, I faced the worst-case police dilemma: clearly, something was happening in the borough that paid my salary, but I was due back 'on assignment' as it were, in another town. It defined "ugly toss-up," but rather than lose my place on the Rizzoli case, I opted for Melrose. For all I knew, the local sirens were announcing the presence of a stray cat in the mayor's prized weeping willow tree and the fire department had been rousted for that horrific emergency.

I still had my uniform on, cream cheese smear and all, and I strongly suspected Porterfield wouldn't care what I was wearing when I got back to Melrose. Well, at least as long as I was wearing something.

But I quickly changed into a pair of jeans, grabbed a thermal shirt and a sweater, found some boots, regretting at that moment that I didn't own a bomber jacket. Another splash of water on my face, and I grabbed an apple and a banana on the odd chance that Porterfield did not have the catering truck handy.

As I was heading north, to Melrose, I had to stop at two intersections in Hamlet for pedestrian vehicles that were flashing lights and sirens. That meant "Fire Department," and I exorcised my mind of the theory that the mayor had, in fact, had called out the ladders and hoses because a cat had taken up residence on his property.

Something *was* burning, but at that moment, it wasn't my problem; although as a Hamlet cop, the sense of hometown responsibility was welling up in me.

Or at least I thought it wasn't my problem.

Arriving at Melrose, I found at least a dozen prowlers parked helter-skelter in the lot, as if they'd all arrived Code 3 and didn't bother with parking lanes. Cops can be like that sometimes.

Because I wasn't wearing the uniform, I had to introduce myself to the afternoon shift desk sergeant, and I showed my Hamlet badge, not that it carried any weight whatsoever. I might have been better off with the "Get out of Jail Free" card from Monopoly.

I hastened to the conference room, which was still set as if waiting for food to be delivered, with table cloth, plates and plastic flatware, but there was no food in sight. My stomach was telling me I should not have left the banana in the car, but who walks into a police station with a banana?

I was too tired to ponder if I would have made it through the banana detector.

Porterfield saw me and gave a gentle nod of his head and then pointed to another officer who was about to report on his observations at JFK International Airport. I didn't understand immediately, but apparently Porterfield had ordered all available officers to Newark Airport and to JFK, to the International Terminals, to see if anything could be learned about departures.

In each case, it meant roughly six men at each airport, with two on the outside looking for the ominous black vehicles, possibly with diplomatic plates, and four spread out at gates that would involve flights that either went to, or would connect to, Kazakhstan.

A tiny voice told me that there was no direct flight to that wonderful paradise, but I reminded myself that the Melrose officers could probably have figured that out. *If they knew where Kazakhstan was, as let's face it, not every one does.*

As I listened to the reports being given, I tried to focus on my hypothetical anomaly, and run it from start to finish to see if it made as much sense in a police department conference room as it did in the middle of a sleepy, bucolic village full of gnomes.

The reports, for the moment, took precedence, and in looking around the room, I caught sight of Swanson, Banta, Caldwell, and Lester, meaning although I'd been the first to arrive twelve hours earlier, now I was the last.

An officer totally unknown to me was speaking. "We took up positions at Newark Airport, as directed by Chief Porterfield, and after checking the plates against those reported in Hamlet, we verified that they were the same as one of the vehicles seen leaving the Russian's property this morning.

"Two adult males, well-dressed, one adult female, also well-dressed, and one juvenile, age approximately fifteen, very casually dressed, emerged from the vehicle and went directly into the terminal.

"A second vehicle, also bearing diplomatic license plates, arrived immediately behind the first, but the only person inside was the driver. He was dressed as a livery driver, and was an African-American, so there is the strong possibility he was not Russian. He walked to the skycaps, produced a sizable wad of currency, which he generously distributed, and the skycaps unloaded luggage from the front seat and the trunk, and a number of cartons from the back seat. The luggage gave every indication of being expensive, but the boxes were simple cardboard, and had labels saying "Donruss" and "Fleer" on the sides. A complete listing of all items sighted, as well as descriptions of the individuals will be in our final report, but a check at the gate confirmed that the individuals believed to be Vychon and his son were two of the four people described. The woman was tentatively identified as Mrs. Tatiana Nikolayevna Vychon, and the fourth individual displayed a passport showing him to be Boris Petrov."

My brain was screaming to say what I suspected, but the room was rather crowded.

The report concluded, "The four individuals boarded a Swiss Air Flight bound for Frankfurt, Germany, and we were able to ascertain that connecting flights from there were available to several locations in Russia. The plane was scheduled to depart just a few minutes ago, at 4:30, but it was wheels up after those individuals arrived. Swiss Air will have to roll out another plane for the 4:30 run, but that does not relate to this investigation."

Porterfield asked the reporting officer directly, "Did you ascertain from the skycaps where the luggage and boxes were headed?"

"We asked, but they said they could not say. It would be a guess, but I think the wad of money bought their silence."

Porterfield scowled. "Did you try to outbid the so-called 'wad of money' that had purchased the temporary silence?" Porterfield would have done exactly that. Men in blue uniforms didn't stand a chance.

Another officer spoke up: "What you are describing could also be going on another flight in the so-called 'diplomatic pouch.'"

Porterfield quietly stated the obvious: "We'll never know on that one. Okay, who was at JFK?"

Before anyone could speak, the officer—whose name I learned was Charles Bradshaw, a local legend in bowling—who had been at Newark jumped in with one final urgency: "I didn't mention this, Chief. We ran the diplomatic license plates, and, well, they don't exist. Sorry I forgot that."

"How could they not exist?"

My anomaly would explain that, but nobody else could, so they moved on to events at JFK Airport. That task might have been slightly easier, because the airport was so spread out that one smallish area was reserved for flights to the far north of Europe, Russia included. The report itself was basically the same story, two black cars, one with passengers, the second with luggage and cartons. The airline of choice was Finn Air, to Helsinki, and from there, nobody could know for certain, but reasonable guesses could be made, if for no other reason than Helsinki, Finland, was the entrepot of choice for trips to places that had once been the Soviet Union.

The reporting officer continued, "Those license plates were run, and they came back to an exclusive company that rented luxury vehicles. According to the company's records, they were rented to a 'Mr. Smith' and a 'Mr. Jones,' and the officers intended to impound those vehicles, since they had no diplomatic cover.

"It turned out not to be a problem, because everyone in both vehicles got on planes, leaving the vehicles behind. All that could be done was have a forensic team strip them down—really only for traces of Rizzoli, as the Russkies were not returning, and then have the rental company could come and get them."

My anomaly was like an overcooked egg, incinerating itself to get out of my head, but it still wasn't my turn, even though I think Porterfield knew I had something on my mind. He had no choice at the moment but to defer to his own men, and that did make sense.

Someone who had a decent view out the window announced that the catering truck had arrived, and I made a mental note to return the banana and the apple to the tray of otherwise wax fruit on the dining room table.

That news bought about thirty seconds of quiet, although I suspected that teams of cops who'd spent all day at airports were getting hungry, but that would have to wait.

The desk sergeant came in, wearing an expression about as happy as if Pee Wee Herman had asked him for a date. Porterfield knew something was up.

"Hamlet Fire Department just called to fill us in on that earlier event, Chief. Seems with the security detail having departed from the Russian's house, someone showed up there with a Molotov cocktail."

"Good Jesus, what next?" Porterfield asked, in the manner of a rhetorical question.

"What's next is that the house was rigged to blow. Hamlet sent a crew out there this morning, but there was a note on the door saying that deliveries would be resumed tomorrow, so they left without making entry, possibly saving their lives in the process. Hamlet's Fire Chief suspects that Vychon, or someone in the household, left the gas on, and when the Molotov cocktail went, so did the house—all of it. The driver of the vehicle who drove onto the circular drive on the property and then threw the gas bomb was incinerated by the blast, but that was the extent of the damage—one dead, the car driver, and nothing left of the house. The car looked to have been a new model red Mustang. Hamlet's asking the county for forensic help."

"Thanks, even if it's more bad news," Porterfield said. Then, to anyone still not entranced by that bit of news, "Could Rizzoli have been in that house?"

Caldwell spoke up: "If he was, he isn't any more…."

The door opened to admit the group bringing the food, and everyone waited about two or three minutes while chafing dishes were set up, with sterno placed underneath to heat penne, an alcoholic pot roast of sorts, and veal Marsala. *What the hell did Porterfield eat at home?*

When the caterers were all out the door, the lined formed for the food, but Porterfield asked everyone to wait, and then he asked me if I had something to add.

I said that I did, and I apologized for interrupting dinner, but I thought it was important.

Porterfield had everyone sit while the alcohol burned off the pot roast.

"To answer the question whether or not Rizzoli was in the house, I'm going to say I doubt it, because we are overlooking something. Five cars left Vychon's house this morning, and only four were accounted for by your officers, meaning that one of them did not take a passenger to an airport."

"And?"

"And I'd wager heavily that the fifth car, which now has about a nine-hour head start, is headed for some distant—and very large—airport, maybe O'Hare, Dallas, Fort Worth, or LA, and the car will be parked in long-term parking and remain there until the millennium, when someone gets curious as to why an expensive car is there, with no remaining license plates, and tires that are going flat. At that point, Rizzoli's body will be found in the trunk, but because by that time he's been dead a good while and he'll be a rotting version of something that was far from beautiful to begin with, it will be quietly covered up, so that airport security doesn't look bad."

"Yeah, given everything else, that would play," Porterfield said. "Anything else?"

The group was hoping my answer would be 'no' so they could eat, but I had to disappoint them. "I think I found the anomaly, Chief."

Everyone pushed their chairs back from the table and turned to look at me.

"The document you read to us this morning, discussing diplomatic immunity, was sent to Hamlet, and here, *by the FBI.* It's their job to run the prints, but it's the job of the Department of State to declare who does and who does not have diplomatic immunity. The FBI does not have jurisdiction to do so unless they are in actual possession of a diplomatic passport—and only then."

"Son of a bitch, of course," Porterfield said, slamming his hand on the desk. "But then, why was the FBI conning us?"

I slowly let out my breath. "I think our Mr. Vychon was given free rein to do anything he wanted in the United States—inside and outside of his porno ring—because he was reporting on Soviet bloc nations' activities *to the FBI.* He was their spy on the inside. His price for doing what he did was Rizzoli's fortune in collectibles, so he cost the feds absolutely nothing. And today, the Bureau covered his ass, and his son's ass and his friends' asses, and they've left town for good. They may not be going to Kazakhstan; they could take connecting flights from—I think it was Frankfurt and Helsinki, and wind up in some country where they cannot be extradited, and even if they could, who'd make the request? Not the feds. And the State Department probably gained a lot of diplomatic intelligence from this operation, so they, in turn will cover the Bureau's ass. At this hour on a Friday, you're not going to reach anyone at the State Department except night clerks, and they don't reopen until Monday morning. By then, Vychon and his goons will be hunkered down somewhere, and making contacts with one or two other "persons known to the FBI" to fence Rizzoli's millions in baseball cards."

I was praying I was right. When I said my piece, everyone in the room stood, and Porterfield began a brief spurt of applause.

"It was the perfect crime, and the United States Federal Bureau of Investigation orchestrated it," Porterfield said, "the perfect crime...except for Pete Rizzoli."

"And Edwina Griffin," I added.

At the mention of her name, one of the Melrose cops grabbed an empty plate and put some cash on it, and then passed it around. When it reached Porterfield, I can tell you that he was generous. Eventually, the money was put in a basket that had held sliced bread. Hey, bread is bread, right?

The money was brought to me, as the beginning of a fund to offset hospice care for people in situations like Edwina's. Over the next few months, the "Edwina Fund" would amount to several million dollars and make news all over the United States.

An elegant lady had not died for nothing. To do their part, the Hamlet Borough Council winked at the town engineer, and he created a document saying that because of remaining hazards, the Vychon property could never be used for anything of a structural nature. That left a beautiful piece of land where townsfolk built a beautiful park—not all that unlike my gnome village—and erected a plaque in Edwina's memory.

The yellow Camaro was eventually sold off to some distant state and those funds enhanced the Edwina Fund.

Porterfield used all his clout to give the FBI a black eye, and while there were limitations on what could be done, there were several key retirements announced well before their expected retirement dates.

Porterfield had the onerous task of visiting Mrs. Rizzoli and telling her that her husband would be kept on the "Missing" list until he was found, alive or otherwise, or until seven years had passed and he could legally be declared dead. She had already been through much of her grieving, so she took the news reasonably well. He had, however, made it clear that Melrose had no 'solid evidence' that Rizzoli had been murdered, but from a circumstantial point of view, that seemed to be the undeniable conclusion.

Apparently, even in her grief, she recalled the reward that had been offered, and she asked who was responsible for getting as close to the truth as the investigation had gotten, and Porterfield told her that two of her husband's friends, Arty Swanson and Chris Decker, had known her husband, remembered him fondly, and had done a lot of baseball card business with him. It was because of that that they had worked around the clock.

Accordingly, she wrote two checks, each for $125,000, to Arty and me. We each signed them and endorsed them.

To the Edwina Griffin Fund.